EXTREME WEATHER

LARGE PRINT EDITION

MYSTERY, CRIME, AND MAYHEM
ISSUE 20

LEAH R CUTTER JASON A. ADAMS ANNIE REED
DIANA DEVERELL CHRIS CHAN JOSLYN CHASE
CATE MARTIN KARI KILGORE MARIE SUTRO

KNOTTED ROAD PRESS

Extreme Weather
Mystery, Crime, and Mayhem: Issue 20

Published 2024 by Knotted Road Press
www.KnottedRoadPress.com

Cover art:
ID 170012837 © Denys Ved | Dreamstime.com

CONTENTS

"YOU TAKE OUR HISTORY" – ARCHIVE THEFT AND THE NATIONAL ARCHIVES ARCHIVAL RECOVERY TEAM

CHRIS CHAN

INTRODUCTION

In 1985, the educational video game *Where in the World is Carmen Sandiego?* was released.* The premise of the game revolved around players taking the roles of globetrotting detectives, tracking down stolen items and following the thieves around the world, learning geography along the way. Over the coming years, the Carmen Sandiego franchise produced additional computer and board games, books, and television shows,

* Douglas Martin, "Raymond Portwood Jr., Computer Game Pioneer, Dies at 66," The New York Times, 30 July 2000, < http://www.nytimes.com/2000/07/30/us/raymond-portwood-jr-computer-game-pioneer-dies-at-66.html> (27 July 2015).

teaching the geography and history of specific regions, and later additional topics as well.

Countless children played the Carmen Sandiego games, and wondered what it would be like to work for the fictional ACME Detective Agency: the crime-fighting organization that recovered pilfered national treasures. It may come as a surprise to many people that a real-life equivalent of ACME does indeed exist, and its goal is to track down real-life Carmen Sandiegos. That organization is the National Archives Archival Recovery Team, and its members are dedicated to retrieving pilfered pieces of American history.

The purpose of organizations like the National Archives is to preserve important pieces of historical memorabilia and to make them available to the general public. Historians, researchers, and other interested parties need to have access to the content of the National Archives in order to find the information that they seek. The contents of these archives are often of more than just historical and evidentiary value. Many of these items are of substantial monetary worth as well. For various reasons, thieves are taking various items from the National Archives and similar institutions, and bits of America's past are vanishing into private collections.

The National Archives Archival Recovery Team seeks to identify the perpetrators and bring stolen historical documents and other memorabilia back where they belong. The purpose of this study is to explain what the National Archives Archival Recovery Team (NAART) is, how they perform their work, and how they go about recapturing misappropriated property. The work of the NAART will be profiled in a series of case studies, covering NAART success stories, including the career of a serial archival thief, a case of infiltration by a longtime National Archives employee, the targeted theft of a significant collection, the identification of altered documents inside the Archives, and an instance where civilian volunteers played a crucial role in retrieving stolen goods. By studying these cases, this essay will hopefully provide insight into how archives can identify items that are missing from their collections, the steps that they can take to recover stolen materials, and the means by which archival theft can be prevented.

WHAT IS THE NATIONAL ARCHIVES ARCHIVAL RECOVERY TEAM?

The NAART is a group formed to address a serious problem. The National Archives is home to billions of items, including documents, artwork, audiovisual files, memorabilia, and many other materials. The holdings of the National Archives are so vast that no comprehensive list of the stored items has ever been created.* Of the immense number of items that have been catalogued, many are nowhere to be found. In many cases, foul play is suspected.

---

* Lisa Rein, "National Archives Hunts for Missing Treasures with Recovery Team," The Washington Post, 23 February 2011, <http://www.washingtonpost.com/wp-dyn/content/article/2011/02/22/AR2011022206661.html> (13 July 2015).

Over the course of time, the employees of the National Archives noticed that many priceless and historically valuable items were missing. The absent items include assorted letters and other documents from presidents and other major figures such as John Adams, George Armstrong Custer, Jefferson Davis, Millard Fillmore, Ulysses S. Grant, Rutherford B. Hayes, Andrew Jackson, Andrew Johnson, Abraham Lincoln, James Madison, Franklin Pierce, James Polk, Zachary Taylor, John Tyler, and Martin Van Buren. Other missing items of memorabilia include a US Coast Guard Academy class ring presented to Lyndon B. Johnson, an official portrait of Franklin D. Roosevelt, ceremonial daggers and swords presented to Harry S. Truman, patents for the Wright brothers' flying machine and Eli Whitney's cotton gin, and target maps for Hiroshima and Nagasaki.*

It should be stressed that just because an item is *missing* that it does not necessarily prove that it is *stolen*. It is incredibly easy for items to be lost, especially in an institution as vast and well-stocked as the National Archives. The phenomenon collo-

---

* "Missing Historical Documents and Items," National Archives, <http://www.archives.gov/research/recover/missing-documents.html> (27 July 2015).

quially referred to as the "*Raiders of the Lost Ark* syndrome," referring to the final scene of the classic movie, where the title object is boxed and once again lost in a mammoth warehouse filled with identical crates, is very real. It is all too easy for a careless employee, or a nearsighted person dealing with poor light, to file a box away in the wrong place, making locating it again a tedious task. Items may be moved during the course of routine cleaning or reorganization, and then not replaced in the proper spot. Identification labels fall off due to desiccated glue. Archivists compiling lists of where each item is placed may make typos. All it takes is a slip of the finger on a keyboard when crafting a directory, and that list may mistakenly state that one collection box is located in aisle "12" of a storage room instead of aisle "1," and that means that a hapless archivist may someday be fruitlessly searching for a collection box yards away from where it is actually located, with no way of finding it aside from checking every box in the storage unit in turn. Comparably, a document may have been misfiled in the wrong folder, or pages may have been mixed up out of order. Hence, it is completely possible that many missing items are actually merely misplaced.

Despite the fact that many missing items may

conceivably be merely misplaced, there are many reasons why one might be reasonably certain that an item has been stolen. Sometimes, for example, potentially valuable signatures are cut from documents with a sharp blade, leaving a little rectangular hole where the autograph ought to be. Assorted items are missing from storage boxes, and documents may disappear suspiciously soon after being studied by a visitor for the first time in years. Many archival holdings may go untouched for years or even decades, and institutions like the National Archives are simply too gargantuan to do a proper tally of all of their collections on a regular basis. By the time an archivist realizes that something is missing, a lengthy period of time may have passed, thereby creating a long list of people with the potential opportunity to steal the item, and no precise idea as to when the crime occurred.

Stolen items generally face one of three fates. First, archive thieves may take something for their personal collections. Second, archive thieves may steal something not for its value, but for the information that it contains, and seek to hide or destroy it. In these first two situations, it is very difficult to recover the stolen item, since one needs solid proof for a search warrant for a private residence, and there is no saving a burnt or shredded document. If a thief does not advertise the fact that an archival treasure is now in a private collection, then the odds of tracking down the item are considerably lessened.

The third fate, where an item is sold on the antiquities market, provides the best chance for recovery. By introducing other parties into the equation—a seller for the item and a buyer, it provides more of a chance for publicity. An advertisement for the sale of a historical document might —and often does—catch the attention of an alert agent or concerned citizen.

Since it is challenging to figure out if something is missing from an archive, one strategy to locate stolen items is to search the potential venues for where historical memorabilia might be stored, and then look for items with a doubtful provenance. Archival materials are different from many other frequently stolen items. Cash can be used anywhere, and pawnshops take many household goods, but antiquities have a much more limited variety of potential sellers. A relative handful of merchants deal in historical documents, so unless an archive thief has a specific buyer in mind, then the filcher has a limited number of options for turning a stolen document or other item into cash. Members of the NAART often visit venues where antiquities are sold, introducing themselves to the sellers and the other people there. By building connections to history lovers and reputable dealers, the NAART is unofficially deputizing members of the public to look for suspicious sellers and potentially stolen goods.

An example of this outreach can be shown when the NAART came to visit Nashville for what was referred to as "the country's biggest Civil War show."* A 2011 *Washington Post* article describes the NAART's visit, explaining how NAART agents handed out brochures with questions like "Does that document belong in the National Archives?" emblazoned upon them.† Raising such a point is not meant to accuse antiquities dealers or customers of complicity or illegal actions. The brochures are not meant to accuse people of complicity in archive theft so much as they are to create new potential assistants and sources of information. The NAART does not have the staff or resources to keep checking all of the venues where stolen materials may be sold reg-

* Rein, "National Archives Hunts for Missing Treasures with Recovery Team."
† Ibid.

ularly. However, historical materials dealers and potential customers may notice missing materials and alert the authorities.

There is one other major selling venue for stolen archival materials: eBay. A surprising number of archive thieves turn to the online auction site for unloading their ill-gotten gains. As the following case studies will illustrate, online sellers are a prominent venue for selling historical memorabilia, but the open nature of online sellers also makes it easier for government agents and concerned members of the public to identify and search for stolen or suspicious materials.

The National Archives Archival Recovery Team was formed in order to serve as a response to the vulnerability of the National Archives. Reporter Travis McDade described how the National Archives realized just how poorly its holdings were protected, writing that:

"Ten years ago, responding to $200,000 worth of thefts by curator Shawn Aubitz, United States Archivist John Carlin said he had 'appointed a high-level management task force to review internal security measures' at the National Archives. 'A preliminary set of recommendations are under review and a number of new measures are already in place.' Four years later, an unpaid summer intern smuggled 160 documents out of the very same Archives branch. His only tool was a yellow legal pad.

In the decade since the Aubitz crime was meant to alert us to the flow of documents stolen from American archives, our nation's most important cultural heritage institutions have undergone something of a bloodletting. Pilfered, plundered, and looted by a series of men whose sole motivation was money, the institutions that were supposed to be locked down remained more akin to open air markets."*

Through the use of three case studies, the thefts of Barry Landau, Samuel L. Berger, and Leslie Waffen will illustrate the various threats to the nation's archives and how the NAART can retrieve stolen goods.

---

* Travis McDade, "Barry Landau and the Grim Decade of Archives Theft," Oxford University Press Blog, 29 June 2012, <http://blog.oup.com/2012/06/barry-landau-and-the-grim-decade-of-archives-theft/> (27 July 2015).

BARRY LANDAU: WHITE HOUSE EXPERT, CUPCAKE ENTHUSIAST, ARCHIVE THIEF

One of the most prolific and brazen archival thieves in recent memory had an exceptionally colorful career. Barry Landau crafted a name for himself as an expert in presidential history, and as a collector of presidential memorabilia. Landau was a consultant on the television series *The West Wing* and had published a book, *The President's Table: Two Hundred Years of Dining and Diplomacy* in 2007.* Landau was frequently inter-

* Edmund H. Mahony, "Stolen Letters from George Washington, Napoleon, Coming Back to Connecticut," The Hartford Courant, 13 November 2012, <http://articles.courant.com/2012-11-13/news/hc-rare-documents-1114-20121113_1_landau-s-manhattan-jason-savedoff-landau-and-savedoff> (27 July 2015).

viewed on television shows and documentaries, and was widely recognized as a leading authority on life in the White House. It was not until a sharp-eyed employee at the Maryland Historical Society caught Landau pilfering rare papers that his reputation shattered.

In a 2011 article, CNN referred to Landau as "one of the foremost collectors of presidential artifacts and memorabilia."* Soon after CNN made that pronouncement, Landau was arrested for stealing a small fortune in documents from the Maryland Historical Society (MHS). After a MHS employee saw Landau mix archival materials with his personal papers, and slip papers into his pockets (at the trial, the prosecutor noted that several articles of Landau's clothing were decorated with specially designed pockets in order to aid the concealment of documents), a police search of Landau's locker led to the discovery of stolen Abraham Lincoln autographs and invitations to inaugurations, among other materials. Landau's heist was dubbed "The Great Cupcake

---

* Adam Clark Estes, "Barry H. Landau: Cupcake Enthusiast, Alleged Paper Purloiner," The Wire, 13 July 2011, <http://www.thewire.com/national/2011/07/maryland-presidential-papers-theft-barry-landau/39910/> (14 July 2015).

Caper" because of one of his trademark actions. When visiting an archive, he would often present the staff with a copy of his book, and he would frequently give the archivists baked goods such as cookies or designer cupcakes.*

Shortly before he was caught, Landau began visiting archives with Jason Savedoff, a would-be model almost four decades his junior. Landau was a polished presence in the archives, while Savedoff rose suspicions by seeming distinctly uncomfortable in these settings, making the claims that Savedoff was Landau's research assistant seem distinctly unlikely. David Angerhofer, the MHS who caught Landau and Savedoff, declared that the pair "were too schmooze-y to be regular people." Angerhofer saw Savedoff swipe a paper from the files, and the pair were held at the MHS until the police could come and search them. Seventy-nine stolen items were found in their computer bag, most of which were taken from the MHS. The recovered items belonging to the MHS were appraised at a value of over eight hundred thousand dollars.†

---

* Ibid.

† Sarah Brumfield, "Barry Landau, Presidential Historian, Expected to Plead Guilty in Theft Case," Huffington Post, 7

Landau eventually pled guilty to many thefts, and admitted to stealing from archives across the Eastern United States, adding some items to his personal collection and selling others. Among his many crimes, Landau confessed to taking seven speeches out of the Franklin D. Roosevelt Presidential Library. If sold legitimately, the speeches could have been auctioned off at a combined total of well over seven hundred thousand dollars. However, stolen items can generally be sold at only a fraction of their true value. As a result, Landau received thirty-five thousand dollars for four of the stolen speeches, less than nine percent of their estimated worth.*

Early in 2012, Landau was convicted and sentenced to seven years in prison. Shortly after Landau's sentencing, David S. Ferriero, the Archivist of the United States, expressed approval of the punishment, declaring that:

"[The judge] recognized the seriousness of this crime and meted out an appropriate punishment that will serve as a warning to others who may contemplate stealing our nation's history...

February 2012, <http://www.huffingtonpost.com/2012/02/07/barry-landau-theft_n_1259462.html> (14 July 2015).

* Ibid.

There is a very special bond that forms between researchers and research institutions. It's kind of like an insider's club. We speak the same language, share the same interests, explore the same minute details of historical knowledge that will eventually fill in the fabric of our shared history as a nation.

When a researcher turns out to be a thief and steals the documents that are the very underpinnings of our democracy, our trust and respect for the community is shaken.

Barry Landau is just that thief. Dressed in the guise of a scholar, he ingratiated himself with our staff and stole priceless documents from the Franklin Roosevelt Library. In essence he robbed from all of us—our collective history. And he did far worse damage to numerous other research institutions around the country."*

What can the career of Barry Landau teach archivists who are trying to prevent archival theft?

---

* "Barry Landau Sentenced to 7 Years for Thefts From National Archives, Other Institutions," National Archives, 27 June 2012, <http://www.archives.gov/press/press-releases/2012/nr12-133.html> (28 July 2015).

First, Landau's brazen thievery emphasizes the importance of having an archival employee supervising all of the visitors performing research and handling valuable documents. Of course, archivists cannot spend all of their time watching patrons like hawks, and in any case, such constant supervision might prove to be a public relations disaster for honest patrons, who might object to being scrutinized. Nevertheless, the presence of an alert employee might help deter or catch thieves.

The awkward behavior of Landau's accomplice illustrates that archival employees need to be on the alert for suspicious behavior, though employees cannot always act upon their suspicions. After all, a patron acting uncomfortable is not necessarily cause for confrontation, and under certain circumstances patrons—both innocent and guilty—might become angered or even litigious by accusations or requests for searches.

The hidden pockets in Landau's clothing, used for concealing documents, are a reminder that it is a sound policy to require patrons to leave their coats in a cloakroom or closet, and to prevent patrons from leaving excessive bags, folders, and notepads on the table where they are working.

SAMUEL L. BERGER: FROM SECURITY ADVISOR TO SECURITY THREAT

The story of Samuel L. Berger shows that archival theft is not all about the desire for financial gain. Sometimes theft can occur due to a desire to gain control of information, or possibly out of absent-mindedness. Samuel L. Berger was President Clinton's Assistant to the President for National Security Affairs, colloquially referred to as the National Security Advisor, for the last four years of Clinton's tenure in office.* In 2003, Berger was asked to testify about his knowledge of attempted ter-

* Tom Davis, "Sandy Berger's Theft of Classified Documents: Unanswered Questions," (Staff Report– U.S. House of Representatives 110th Congress Committee on Oversight and Government Reform, 2007), 7.

rorist attacks and other national security measures for the 9/11 Commission. In preparation for his testimony, Berger sorted through copies of classified information documents. One evening, Berger walked out with several documents that could only be viewed by individuals with a high security clearance level. One archival employee believed that he had stuffed papers into his sock surreptitiously, but Berger's counsel would later deny this accusation, attributing this observation to Berger adjusting his loose socks. In any event, Berger's suspicious behavior led to the investigation that later revealed his actions. Berger left the National Archives, walked to a nearby construction site, and stuffed the papers under a trailer. A few hours later, he returned to the trailer, retrieved the documents, and took them to his office, where he cut some of them to pieces with scissors and disposed of them.* While it is likely that most of the documents that Berger took were copies, a staff report of the U.S. House of Representatives later determined that it was possible that original, un-

---

* Josh Gerstein, "How an Ex-Aide to President Clinton Stashed Classified Documents," The New York Sun, 21 December 2006, < http://www.nysun.com/national/how-an-ex-aide-to-president-clinton-stashed/45551/> (28 July 2015).

copied documents had been taken, too.[*] Berger entered into a plea agreement, and received a $50,000 fine and the revocation of his security clearance for three years. No jail time was imposed.[†]

The details of the case quickly became politicized, particularly because the investigation took place around the 2004 presidential election. Berger was working as an advisor for the candidate Senator John Kerry, and the accusations against Berger had the potential to derail Kerry's campaign. At the time, many prominent Democrats came to Berger's defense, and numerous Republicans expressed skepticism of Berger's defense and his lenient treatment in court.[‡]

The motives for Berger's actions remain controversial to this day. Berger frequently contended that when he took the documents, he did so ab-

---

* Davis, 3.

† Eric Lichtblau, "Ex-Clinton Official Draws Higher-Than-Expected Fine," The New York Times, 9 September 2005, <http://query.nytimes.com/gst/abstract.html?res=9804EEDE1331F93AA3575AC0A9639C8B63> (28 July 2015).

‡ "Sandy Berger, Harvard, and Mel Martinez," The Weekly Standard, 18 April 2005, <http://www.weeklystandard.com/print/Content/Protected/Articles/000/000/005/472qs lvb.asp> (14 July 2015).

sent-mindedly, desiring to study the documents elsewhere, and with no felonious intent. Some of Berger's defenders contended that Berger was mentally exhausted at the time, leading to poor– but not criminal– decision-making. At his sentencing, Berger implied that he had taken the documents out of pure "personal convenience."*

Berger's supporters painted the incident as an unfortunate lapse, one that came from overwork and stress. Not everybody shared this "it could have happened to anybody" attitude. Many people reminded the public that Berger had hidden some documents under a trailer for at least three hours (where someone else could have picked them up and returned them), and shredded a few of the documents he took with scissors. Numerous rumors and alternative theories were circulated. Though nothing else was ever proven conclusively, many people remain suspicious that the true story of the incident remains unknown to the general public.

Berger's story has many lessons for the proponent of archival security. As with Landau's case, a prominent person's act of thievery leads to the

---

* Eric Lichtblau, "Ex-Clinton Official Draws Higher-Than-Expected Fine."

blunt conclusion that no one is above suspicion. Prominent scholars and powerful officials can be archive thieves, and that is why there is no standard profile of an archive thief. It seems untrusting to say that all visitors to an archive must be viewed with equal suspicion, but the plain truth of the matter is that most visitors to archives are strangers to the employees. One would probably be unwilling to allow a total stranger into one's home and allow that person access to one's jewelry box and silverware, and a comparable attitude might apply to archival employees and the valuable documents in their care.

The fact that Berger took copies of documents connected to national security issues illustrates the point that all archival holdings might be threatened. Archivists are understandably worried about documents of great historical value, autographs of famous people, and valuable memorabilia. Nevertheless, archival holdings of no intrinsic value might fall victims to theft as well. Archive thieves might take items not because of their monetary value, but because of the information that the items contain. In Berger's case, the information in the stolen documents might have reflected badly upon his own reputation, but there are many other instances where someone might not want other people to have access to certain facts available in an archive.

Many corporate and business archives contain documents that might be considered crucial evidence in a lawsuit. An unscrupulous legal researcher or interested party might want to steal papers that might reflect badly upon their side. Alternatively, false evidence might be planted in a file and "discovered" later to help improve one's case. Academic researchers might steal documents for similar reasons. Dorothy L. Sayers's classic mystery novel *Gaudy Night* features a comparable situation at the heart of its plot. In Sayers's book, a young scholar is infatuated with his own historical theory, but a document in an archive proves that his thesis was wrong. Having no time or inclination to revise or abandon his work, the scholar steals the document in order to protect his work, but is later caught and humiliated.* It is certainly possible that in real life, a researcher might want to remove documents that reflect badly upon a historical personage being studied, or which might challenge scholarly work for various reasons.

---

* Dorothy L. Sayers, Gaudy Night (New York: HarperCollins, 2012), 380-383.

Comparably, patrons might steal documents from archives in order to prevent rivals from having access to them. It is an unpleasant fact of life in many academic departments that competition runs rife and that the more unscrupulous members sometimes threaten the work of their rivals in order to improve their own standing in the department and to improve their chances at competitive grants and job opportunities. In one classic trick, a graduate student might learn what a rival is researching, and then hurry to the library and gather up a lot of books that the rival might need for the research. In one particularly nasty version of this stunt, the relevant books are then stuffed into a coin locker at the library, or in some similarly hidden place. The rival is then unable to find the necessary materials, thereby hindering the rival's research, at least temporarily. The same principle might apply to archive theft—for example, if documents that a graduate student needed to complete a dissertation were stolen or hidden by an enemy, that dishonest scholar might profit from his rival's problems.

LESLIE WAFFEN: A FOX IN THE HENHOUSE

Archivists may be continually on the watch for untrustworthy visitors, but the fact remains that the individuals with the most opportunities to steal valuable items are the people who work in the archive. One of the most famous cases of an archivist abusing trust is the story of Leslie Waffen. Waffen was an employee at the National Archives for over four decades, specializing in the preservation of audio recordings. During the last quarter of his tenure at the National Archives, Waffen started taking audio files home with him. In his confession in court, Waffen claimed that his pilfering began when he started bringing recordings home for evaluation, but he then neglected to bring back those items. As the years passed, he took more and more items, keeping most for himself and selling others. The stolen items included clips of the 1948 World Series and coverage of the Hindenburg explosion. According to one count, approximately nine hundred fifty-five assorted audio recordings were stolen, at a total estimated value of $83,238, although other reports place the total number of thefts at between three and four thousand items.[*]

Waffen's downfall began thanks to the observations of an alert citizen. J. David Goldin, an audio historian and former radio engineer, had donated numerous audio files to the National Archives over the years. After visiting eBay one day, he saw a recording of a 1937 conversation with Babe Ruth for sale, and immediately recognized it, declaring, "holy smokes, that's my record!"[†] Goldin identified the item because it

---

* Erica W. Morrison, "Leslie Waffen, Ex-Archives Worker, Sentenced for Stealing, Selling Recordings," The Washington Post, 3 May 2012, <http://www.washingtonpost.com/local/crime/leslie-waffen-ex-archives-w...ced-for-stealing-selling-recordings/2012/05/03/gIQAX0f7zT_story.html> (28 July 2015).

† "Amateur Sleuth Helps Stop National Archives Thefts," CBS News, 3 May 2012, <http://www.cbsnews.com/news/amateur-sleuth-helps-stop-national-archives-thefts/> (28 July 2015).

was believed to be the only copy of the interview in existence, and the sale price was just over thirty-four dollars. Goldin explained that he then "wrote a letter to the National Archives that said, in effect, hey, guys, if you're giving away the records that I gave you, I'd like to have them back. And almost as soon as I have [sic] mailed the letter, the feds were on the phone, saying we don't give anything away from the National Archives."* Goldin's observation prompted the authorities to launch an investigation, tracking down the source of the eBay seller, and leading to the eventual identification of Waffen as the criminal.

The National Archives and Records Administration's Office of Inspector General, which oversees the NAART, obtained a warrant and searched Waffen's home.† Nearly a thousand assorted audio recordings in multiple formats were

---

* Robert Siegel, "Former Archivist Convicted in Recording Thefts," NPR, 3 May 2012, <http://www.npr.org/2012/05/03/151962985/former-archivist-convicted-in-recording-thefts> (14 July 2015).

† Elahe Izadi, "National Archives Agents Raid Home of Leslie Waffen, Former Archives Department Head," TBD, 28 October 2010, <http://www.tbd.com/articles/2010/10/national-archives-agents-raid-home-of-leslie-waffen-former-archives-department-head-26544.html> (28 July 2015).

found, as well as evidence connected to the sale of some stolen items.

Waffen eventually confessed and was sentenced to a year and a half in prison, followed by two years of probation, and was compelled to make restitution for items that had been sold. The search for the stolen items was slow and not wholly successful, but several of the buyers were located and compelled to return the materials. When sentenced, Waffen declared that, "I violated God's fourth commandment... In doing so I have scarred my soul."*

The Waffen case illustrates that sometimes the greatest danger to archives comes from within the institution. Archives need to make sure that their employees are honest, or otherwise their holdings may be looted by the people with the most opportunity to do so. The archival profession has many rewards, but the financial remuneration is often not particularly high. The temptation for supplementing one's income with a little five-finger bonus might prove irresistible to some archival

---

* Richard Jordan, "18 Months for Man Who Took From National Archives," NBC Washington, 3 May 2012, <http://www.nbcwashington.com/news/local/18-Months-for-Man-Who-Took-From-National-Archives-150102375.html> (14 July 2015).

employees. This is a problem with no perfect solution: because there is no way that an archive can be assured of the integrity of the people working there. Often, the only people in a position to catch an archivist stealing are other archivists, but atmospheres of suspicion make for unpleasant work environments.

Furthermore, the Waffen case illustrates the necessity for members of the public to participate in the search for potentially stolen items. As stated earlier, J. David Goldin discovered that a recording that he had donated was being sold on eBay. Had he failed to do so, it is possible that Waffen might never have been caught, or at least, his thefts would not have been detected until much later.*

One of the most important side consequences of the Waffen case is that it led to increased scrutiny of the National Archives' security procedures. Shortly after Waffen confessed and was sentenced, David S. Ferriero wrote in a public statement that,

"As I have stated since I became Archivist of the United States, the security of the holdings of the National Archives is my highest priority.

Our Holdings Protection Team has been

* Siegel.

working closely with archival units to improve training techniques, institute new policies and procedures, and purchase new equipment to ensure that our holdings are safer.

We have heightened security in our facilities nationwide and continue to strive towards creating a culture of increased vigilance among our staff. New procedures include exit screenings, in which security officers check all bags of visitors and staff alike—including mine—at both our Washington, DC, and College Park, Maryland, facilities. This routine practice will soon be extended to all 44 of our facilities nationwide.

The Holdings Protection Team is upgrading its centralized registry of individuals banned from Archives facilities to a secure directory that keeps track of the facilities they visit, and the documents they ask for."*

It is unfortunate that sometimes the horses have to be stolen before the barn doors are locked, but

* David S. Ferriero, "Statement by the Archivist of the United States," National Archives, 4 October 2011, <http://www.archives.gov/press/press-releases/2012/nr12-01.html> (14 July 2015).

good can come out of misfortune, and it took a betrayal of trust to bring about the necessary action.

CONCLUSION

Agatha Christie wrote a novel titled *Murder is Easy*. Unfortunately, much of the time, archival theft is even easier. Archives lack the funds to provide complete protection to their holdings, and there is no way to ensure that all archival employees and visitors will be honest. Since archives contain items of monetary and informational value, their contents will be always be threatened by the greedy and unscrupulous.

Archival theft imperils the reputation of the National Archives and similar organizations. Archives are meant to keep their contents both safe and available to the public, but the latter mission often puts the former goal at risk. No security system is infallible, which means that the National

Archives Archival Recovery Team's work is crucial for retrieving stolen merchandise. An official branch of law enforcement tasked with finding stolen goods is necessary, because archival employees lack legal authority and can find themselves in deep trouble if they try to confront thieves under certain conditions—lawsuits and physical altercations can occur. Archivists cannot search the homes or personal property of suspected thieves without legal reprisals, which is why it helps to have a legitimate law enforcement authority to take care of warrants and searches and arrests if needed.

It should be observed that in the case studies recounted here, the NAART initiated their investigations due to the observations of lay citizens. The investigations into Landau and Berger started only because archival employees witnessed them taking materials, and Leslie Waffen was caught because of a concerned citizen discovering that an item he had donated was being sold online. In these cases, the NAART and its partners in law enforcement were able to pursue their investigations thanks to receiving crucial information from outside sources. This illustrates the importance of training archival employees in spotting and reporting thefts, and the need to create a network of citizen volunteers who patrol antiquities sales and online sellers, looking for potentially stolen items up for sale. Indeed, the earlier reference to the *Where in the World is Carmen Sandiego?* franchise is relevant here, for in most of the computer games, the detectives are only able to catch criminals thanks to the help of a steady stream of information provided by concerned members of the public.

Educating the public may do a great deal to promote the retrieval of archival materials. One point that could be publicized in order to prevent archival theft is the fact that in most cases, the crime is not particularly financially remunerative. Historical documents are not a fungible commodity. Autographs and other historical materials are primarily of interest only to collectors and organizations specializing in their preservation. As stated earlier, stolen materials can only be sold for a fraction of the value that they could fetch legitimately. Often, the value that a crook can receive by selling stolen materials is only between one and ten percent of the true price, since sales must be made surreptitiously or conducted with the aid of an unscrupulous dealer.* Therefore, one potentially

* Robert K. Wittman and John Shiffman, Priceless– How I

helpful deterrent to archival theft is that the risk far outweighs the often-negligible reward. Of course, if a wealthy collector hires someone to steal an item, the selling price can be higher, and documents stolen for personal collections or for information issues do not have to worry about reselling or financial motives, which means that concerns about profits are not a factor, and that this deterrence tactic will not be wholly effective.

Taking preventive measures and raising public awareness of the problem will not completely solve the problem of archive theft, but potentially lead to the retrieval of stolen items and encourage the implementation of more effective security protocols. Where archivists may see the preservation of their nation's history, the greedy and larcenous see only opportunities to plunder and profit. At Leslie Waffen's sentencing, U.S. District Judge Peter J. Messitte declared that, "You take our history if you take the thing to sustain our history," dismissing the idea that the stolen items were safer in a private collection.* Archive theft has serious cultural ramifications, and the recovery of stolen

---

Went Undercover to Rescue the World's Stolen Treasures (New York: Broadway Paperbacks, 2010), 14-16.

* Morrison.

items requires both the official power of the law, as embodied by the NAART, and the dedicated participation of concerned citizens. There is no permanent solution to the problem, but there are numerous ways that the guardians of America's past can protect its history.

BIBLIOGRAPHY

"Amateur Sleuth Helps Stop National Archives Thefts." CBS News. 3 May 2012. <http://www.cbsnews.com/news/amateur-sleuth-helps-stop-national-archives-thefts/> (28 July 2015).

"Barry Landau Sentenced to 7 Years for Thefts From National Archives, Other Institutions." National Archives. 27 June 2012. <http://www.archives.gov/press/press-releases/2012/nr12-133.html> (28 July 2015).

Brumfield, Sarah. "Barry Landau, Presidential Historian, Expected to Plead Guilty in Theft Case." Huffington Post. 7 February 2012. <http://www.huffingtonpost.com/2012/02/07/barry-landau-theft_n_1259462.html> (14 July 2015).

Davis, Tom. "Sandy Berger's Theft of Classified Documents: Unanswered Questions," (Staff Report– U.S. House of Representatives 110th Congress Committee on Oversight and Government Reform, 2007), 7.

Estes, Adam Clark. "Barry H. Landau: Cupcake Enthusiast, Alleged Paper Purloiner." The Wire. 13 July 2011. <http://www.thewire.com/national/2011/07/maryland-presidential-papers-theft-barry-landau/39910/> (14 July 2015).

Ferriero, David S. "Statement by the Archivist of the United States." National Archives. 4 October 2011. <http://www.archives.gov/press/press-releases/2012/nr12-01.html> (14 July 2015).

Gamerman, Ellen. "The Case of the Disappearing Documents." The Wall Street Journal. 30 September 2011. <http://www.wsj.com/articles/

SB10001424052970204422404576596873383476078>(14 June 2015).

Gerstein, Josh. "How an Ex-Aide to President Clinton Stashed Classified Documents." The New York Sun. 21 December 2006, <http://www.nysun.com/national/how-an-ex-aide-to-president-clinton-stashed/45551/> (28 July 2015).

Izadi, Elahe, "National Archives Agents Raid Home of Leslie Waffen, Former Archives Department Head." TBD. 28 October 2010. <http://www.tbd.com/articles/2010/10/national-archives-agents-raid-home-of-leslie-waffen-former-archives-department-head-26544.html> (28 July 2015).

Jordan, Richard. "18 Months for Man Who Took From National Archives." NBC Washington. 3 May 2012. <http://www.nbcwashington.com/news/local/18-Months-for-Man-Who-Took-From-National-Archives-150102375.html> (14 July 2015).

Lichtblau, Eric. "Ex-Clinton Official Draws Higher-Than-Expected Fine." The New York Times. 9 September 2005. <http://query.nytimes.com/gst/abstract.html?res=9804EEDE1331F93AA3575AC0A9639C8B63> (28 July 2015).

Lichtblau, Eric. "Report Details Theft by Ex-Adviser." The New York Times. 21 December 2006. <http://www.nytimes.com/2006/12/21/washington/21berger.html?_r=0> (12 April 2015).

Mahony, Edmund H. "Stolen Letters from George Washington, Napoleon, Coming Back to Connecticut." The Hartford Courant. 13 November 2012, <http://articles.courant.com/2012-11-13/news/hc-rare-documents-1114-20121113_1_landau-s-manhattan-jason-savedoff-landau-and-savedoff > (27 July 2015).

Maltagliati, Kelly. "Impact and Prevention of Archival Theft" and "The National Archives Archival Recovery Team." C-

SPAN. 3 March 2011 and 21 August 2010. <http://www.c-span.org/person/?kellymaltagliati> (14 June 2015).

Martin, Douglas. "Raymond Portwood Jr., Computer Game Pioneer, Dies at 66." The New York Times. 30 July 2000. <http://www.nytimes.com/2000/07/30/us/raymond-portwood-jr-computer-game-pioneer-dies-at-66.html> (27 July 2015).

McClane, Brianna. "Guardian of America's Heirlooms." National Journal. 13 September 2012. <http://www.nationaljournal.com/daily/national-archives-investigator-tracks-down-stolen-treasures-20120913> (15 June 2015).

McDade, Travis. "Barry Landau and the Grim Decade of Archives Theft." Oxford University Press Blog. 29 June 2012. <http://blog.oup.com/2012/06/barry-landau-and-the-grim-decade-of-archives-theft/> (27 July 2015).

"Missing Historical Documents and Items." National Archives. <http://www.archives.gov/research/recover/missing-documents.html> (27 July 2015).

Morrison, Erica W. "Leslie Waffen, Ex-Archives Worker, Sentenced for Stealing, Selling Recordings." 3 May 2012. <http://www.washingtonpost.com/local/crime/leslie-waffen-ex-archives-worker-sentenced-for-stealing-selling-recordings/2012/05/03/gIQAX0f7zT_story.html> (15 June 2015).

Rein, Lisa. "National Archives Hunts for Missing Treasures with Recovery Team." The Washington Post. 23 February 2011. <http://www.washingtonpost.com/wp-dyn/content/article/2011/02/22/AR2011022206661.html> (13 July 2015).

"Sandy Berger, Harvard, and Mel Martinez." The Weekly Standard. 18 April 2005. <http://www.weeklystandard.com/print/Content/Protected/Articles/000/000/005/472qslvb.asp> (14 July 2015).

Sayers, Dorothy L. Gaudy Night. New York: HarperCollins, 2012.

Siegel, Robert. "Former Archivist Convicted in Recording Thefts." NPR. 3 May 2012. <http://www.npr.org/2012/05/03/151962985/former-archivist-convicted-in-recording-thefts> (14 July 2015).

Simon, Bob and Katherine Davis. "National Archives' Treasures Targeted by Thieves." 60 Minutes. 28 October 2015. <http://www.cbsnews.com/news/national-archives-treasures-targeted-by-thieves-28-10-2012/> (14 June 2015).

Smith, Craig. "Special Agents Hunt Down America's National Treasures." Pittsburgh Tribune. 3 July 2011. <http://triblive.com//x/pittsburghtrib/news/regional/s_745064.html#axzz3d7feaa4R> (14 June 2015).

Twomey, Steve. "To Catch a Thief." Smithsonian Magazine. April 2008. <http://www.smithsonianmag.com/making-a-difference/to-catch-a-thief-1-31735490/> (15 June 2015).

Wittman, Robert K. and John Shiffman. Priceless– How I Went Undercover to Rescue the World's Stolen Treasures. New York: Broadway Paperbacks, 2010.

COLD DANGER

JASON A. ADAMS

Some days a man should just stay in bed.

Especially days when the windows were frosted so heavily—on the *inside,* mind—that the room was about as bright as a black cat in a closet.

Ben Vanover, Senior Sales Representative for Goose Mountain Outdoor Products, North-Central Division, hated to leave the toasty sandwich of down comforters and memory foam mattress. But, maybe today was the day he could get out of this refrigerated deep-freeze and get back to Virginia.

Last he checked, the temperature back home was due to hit thirty-four today. T-shirt and shorts weather compared to South Branch, Michigan. Here, what with the wind and all, today might, just *might,* get up to a balmy twenty.

Below zero.

Might.

The invitingly burnt aroma of coffee blacker than the afore-mentioned cat finally got Ben moving. The power had never gone out, thank goodness, and his personal hero, Mr. Coffee, was right on time. Bless whoever had invented programmable coffee makers. And microwavable cheese Danishes.

Ben counted one...two...three. Throwing back the quilts and sheets, he dove for the insulated black snow pants and black woolen pea coat hanging near the Sauron's Eye of the satellite-dish-shaped antique space heater. The thermal longjohns and Merino wool socks he'd slept in could last another day before washing. He wasn't about to waste body heat on cold duds from his suitcase.

Another howling gust of polar vortex bliss hit the cabin, shaking the walls and rattling the hoar-frosted windows until Ben felt sure they'd shatter. But the thick triple panes held on, keeping most of the bitter Arctic blast outside.

The cabin, what the brochure called a "rustic and idyllic getaway amid majestic fir and spruce forests," and what Ben thought of as a "shoddy nineteen-fifties clapboard shack, perfect for retirees who weren't too picky," sat on the outskirts of the miniature township, set back in the trees.

He supposed it was meant to be a summer cabin. Sure didn't have the insulation for *this* nonsense. The thermostat was set on seventy-five, but Ben still puffed steam in the chilly room. At least the pipes hadn't frozen, although the steady drip-drip-drip from the sinks and tub were driving him batshit.

Having successfully managed to worm his way into his heavy winter clothes, Ben pulled a thick pair of red-striped hunting stockings over the socks already on his feet, and began the laborious job of forcing said feet into boots rendered too small by the extra foot warmers. Next, a good slather of lotion on his wind-chapped forehead, cheeks, and nose. Christ, he looked like someone had took sandpaper to a tomato.

All he needed after that was a whole pot of Charbucks Heretic Roast and a couple of Danishes, then he'd be ready to face the challenge of navigating the world in northwoods mittens.

Ben had come up here last week for what should have been a two-day sales trip, taking orders from the local adventure supply retailers (read: Yankee shysters who made a living gouging hikers and hunters) with the latest in spring and summer gear for those hardy souls with more dollars than sense.

What he hadn't planned on was this godawful storm. While the snowfall wasn't near as bad here as it had been farther north and west, the few inches which *had* fallen were still blowing back and forth in the near-hurricane winds. Yesterday, he'd had to climb out an upper window so he could kick away the four-foot drift piled against the front door. Fifteen minutes, tops, and he'd had to run hot water over his hands nearly as long before the feeling came all the way back.

Thus, mittens. Ben snorted a cloud of steam. Only sixty bucks from one of his local clients. Sixty for a pair that wholesaled for thirteen and change.

Coffee and pastry first, then he'd play Admiral Peary and hit the road. Hopefully in the opposite direction of Peary's North Pole.

Ben coiled the extension cord around his arm as his exposed face tried to break off in the bitter air. He only got a few loops at a time between trips back inside to thaw out a little.

Ten minutes. Maybe fifteen. That's how long he had out in the open before frostbite became a real possibility. A mountain boy oughtn't be afraid of nippy air, but this was *crazy*.

He waited for his second space heater to cool down and the car to warm up, trying to keep his balance as the gale whipped around him. His bulky clothes kept the wind off his body, but it cut right through the toboggan snugged uselessly down over his aching ears and forehead.

The space heater had spent the night under the engine block of the deep green Subaru Outback he'd rented back in Detroit for the drive from the airport. The pimply kid at the Hertz desk told him the coolant was rated to fifteen below, but Ben had more faith in the heater than the sprat.

Sunlight unhindered by clouds or even humidity stabbed through his eyeballs. The only sound was the wind, and the occasional distant rumble of tractor-trailers from the highway. The only smells in the desiccated air were the rubbery stink of new weatherproofing and the acrid exhaust from his idling car.

The car was the only green in sight. He was surrounded by evergreens, all coated with nature's freezer burn.

Tossing the stiff cord back through the cabin's door, Ben heard the clanking of chained tires coming down the drive. Wiping frozen tears from brittle eyelashes, he cupped a hand against the sun's glare and saw a glossy black Chevy Blazer with gold lettering and stripes along the doors. Didn't really need the big star to recognize a county prowler.

Probably nothing. Ben hadn't crossed a law except a few speed limits since he was a teenager.

Probably just the local fuzz checking out the un-local visitor.

The SUV came to a stop, the wind forcing even more emissions reek up Ben's cracked nostrils. A reflected blaze of light made the windshield invisible, but he didn't mind. Seen one deputy, you seen 'em all.

Boy, howdy. When Ben was wrong, he went wrong whole hog.

The door opened and a massive figure hopped out, easily six-three with shoulders that looked as wide as the hood of his Blazer. Puffy pants browner than good Dutch chocolate. A parka even puffier in the same color. Puffy brown cap with furry earflaps pulled down. Hands in brown mittens even bulkier than Ben's. Fuzzy scarf wrapped around mouth, nose, and forehead. Brown, naturally. Thick black boots with coiled ice cleats strapped on. Only two narrow eyes the hue of spring leaves peeked out of the rounded chocolaty mass.

Except for the badge pinned to the cap's front, his mystery visitor looked like a marshmallow that spent too long on the toasting fork. Or maybe a grizzly bear trying to avoid the shivers.

Chocolate and marshmallows? Apparently he

needed more than Danishes this morning. Must be the cold.

The marshmallow said something, but between the heavy scarf and the wind, Ben only shook his head.

"Sorry? Didn't catch that."

The brownie tugged off his right mitten, revealing thick fingers like chapped bratwursts, then pulled the bottom of the scarf down. Ben saw a heavy jaw under a crooked nose that had seen a brawl or two. The guy's exposed skin glistened, but no way was he sweating in this version of hell.

"I said, why ya want your head to freeze? Where's your muffler?"

His voice was hoarse and friendly, but with that no-nonsense tone Ben remembered from his wilder days. Definitely a cop talking.

"I meant to buy one," he said. "But I'm hoping to make it back to Detroit so I can catch a plane back south. Too cold up here for me." He tried to chuckle, but ended up coughing instead.

"I thought ya might," he replied. "Vickie down at the café said you were staying out here at the Lindeman place, and she figured you could use a talking to. I'm Carl Anderson, sheriff and all-around good Samaritan. You're not a rowdy teenager or a suspect, so you can call me Carl. Ya got chains?"

Ben thought about it, realized he had no idea.

"Dunno. Never checked," he said, rubbing a mittened hand over an increasingly sore face.

"That's about what I figured," he said. "Well, hop in. I'll get you down to the hardware, see if they have any left. But I gotta tell ya, you don't seem the type knows how to drive on metal and ice."

"You got me there. Where I'm from, I don't get out on the road when it snows more than a dusting. Too many mountains and not enough guardrails."

He leaned in the Subaru and killed the motor, then got in the sheriff's SUV, gratefully slamming the door against the now-rising wind. The vehicle's interior smelled strongly of coffee and breakfast. Ben's stomach rumbled and he told it to shush for now.

Sheriff Anderson, Carl, had beat him into the car, shedding scarf and mittens. He slowly backed the Blazer around before heading down the drive toward the two-lane that would take them into South Branch.

Ben leaned back against the headrest and sighed contentedly as the heat blasting from the truck's vents slowly worked its way into his aching body. Pulling off his mittens, he rubbed again at his face, wincing at the pain.

One hand on the tiller and the other on the huge gunmetal Stanley thermos in the console, Carl glanced over at him.

"Face hurting? Ya look a little raw," he shouted over the clanking wheels.

"You could say that," Ben shouted back, his smile making his cracked lips sing. "You could also say the ocean's wet. I think Jergens lost battle this time."

"Lotion? Geez, you southern folks." He leaned across Ben, not letting off the gas a bit as he popped the glove box, reached in, and pulled out a small blue tub Ben hadn't seen since his Granny passed twenty years ago.

"Here's what ya need," Carl said, dropping the Nivea cream in his lap. "Spackle up good with that on anything not covered any time you go outside. *Any* time. I don't care if you just put some on two minutes ago. It'll keep the wind out and the water in."

"I thank you kindly," he said. What the hell, when in Rome, listen to the locals. "I'm sure not used to cold like this. Or wind. Down home, anything over a few miles an hour is a hurricane, and it hardly ever gets in the teens, let alone this nonsense."

He scooped some of the thick cream from the jar and spread it over his face. And damn if the stinging didn't let right up! Ben might fall in love.

"Man, that sure feels good," he said, working the goop in deeper.

"Don't mention it," Carl said, grinning.

The drive to town was only about four miles, which took less than ten minutes.

Usually.

A friendly conversation about the relative merits of the Braves and the Tigers, laced with a few friendly cultural slurs and comments about profane versions of cornbread, was interrupted when Carl slowed the vehicle, leaning forward over the wheel and squinting at a dark shape on the roadside.

"Ah, shit."

With the ease of long practice, Carl eased on the brakes. The heavy Blazer barely slid on the icy road before coming to a stop.

"Wait here," he said, grabbing the Nivea and slathering white goo over his face before quickly winding his scarf back on and shoving his hands back in his mittens.

Just in case, Ben pulled on his own mittens and toboggan.

Carl jumped out, grabbing the door as his ice cleats slipped before digging in, and walked carefully toward the hump on the edge of the road, all but buried in snow on the windward side.

But sticking out from the leeward side of the drift was a back. An unclothed human back. Bluish-gray where it wasn't ice white.

Ben gulped as his stomach ran loops, all thoughts of chocolate and marshmallows gone.

He got out and slowly worked his way toward the sheriff and the corpse, barely noticing the wind knifing through him.

Carl was brushing snow carefully from the body, exposing the man's face. He looked to be on the far side of middle age, judging by the wrinkles and the mostly gray hair and beard.

The eyes and mouth were closed. The arms crossed and knees drawn up, almost fetal. The only mark on him was a four-inch-long number 1 tattooed on his shoulder in bright red ink.

"Where the hell are his clothes?" Ben whispered. His own voice startled him, his low whisper like a shout in the silent forest.

"Over there, by that spruce," Carl said, pointing to a pile of cloth nearly buried under the drifts. "Don't touch anything, okay?"

"Okay. But why isn't he wearing anything?" Ben started to shiver. Only partly from the cold.

"Hypothermia," Carl said, his face grim but all business. "Froze to death. Cold does strange things to a guy. They always seem to strip right before they go down for the count. Something to do with heat from capillary expansion *in extremis,* according to the medicos. You ask me, it's just because they go crazy when their brains freeze."

Carl pulled his scarf aside and barked into an old-fashioned hand-held radio, calling in the find and ordering up an ambulance.

"I don't care what's happening on the freeways!" he snapped. "I need a meat wagon and a photographer, toot-fucking-sweet!"

"God-damned lazybones," Carl grumped, shoving the radio back in its holster as he moved toward the pile of clothes. "You'd think they'd never been chilly befo—"

His words cut off as he began pulling the stiff cloth from the snow. A pair of jeans, a t-shirt...

And that was all. Ben's temperature dropped another couple of degrees.

"Ben, you see a vehicle anywhere? Snowmobile, dirt bike, anything?"

Both men turned in a slow circle, seeing nothing but snow, ice, and the sheriff's black and gold Blazer. Its were the only tire tracks in an otherwise unbroken blanket of glittering white.

"What are you thinking, Sheriff?"

"I'm thinking," Carl said, again drawing his radio, "that we just found a murder victim."

"So why do you think he was murdered?" Ben asked.

He and Carl were back in the safety of the Blazer, taking turns at coffee from Carl's mighty thermos. Two elderly crime scene techs in the same brown marshmallow suits as Carl had already arrived from the station house in town, and were by turns snapping pictures and running back to their car, doing what they could without joining the corpsicle they were examining. Only pictures, since there wasn't anything to bag up except the two items of clothing. No tracks or other markings remained to measure after however many hours of stiff wind and scouring ice crystals.

"Simple," Carl said. "There's nowhere he could have, or *would* have, walked from in this kind of weather. We're a couple of miles from town, but at hell-and-gone-below zero, that might as well be two states and a good-sized lake. So, he didn't come from town. He might've been heading toward it, but I don't think he could've made much more than a half mile given what he was wearing. Or what he wasn't."

The big man took another deep gulp of coffee, blew out a deep breath that fogged the windshield, then went on.

"My guess is somebody kicked him out of the car somewhere back toward the Lindeman place where you're staying, then drove off and left him to start walking. Wind chill last night was minus forty-three. With no coat, hat, gloves, and so forth, I'd say he got maybe a couple of hundred yards before the freeze started to set in. If it wasn't so damn nippy, the animals would already have him eaten and gone."

Hypothermia. Confusion, incoordination, lack of control... Ben knew what Carl meant. It might not get like this in Virginia, but every year some fool of a deer hunter would fall in a creek or drink too much beer or misjudge the weather, usually all three, and end up dying or close to it.

Most folks knew better, but then most folks didn't end up needing a medflight to try and get their stupid fixed.

One of the two techs who'd been going through the jeans pockets came hurrying toward them. He opened the back door on Ben's side and dove in, slamming it behind him.

"Geez, it's cold as Christmas out there!" the tech said through chattering teeth.

"Pretty sure Christmas was warmer than this at Santa's house," Carl said. "Find anything, Mike?"

"Yep," Mike said. "Still had his wallet. No cash or credit cards, but the DL is there. Stanley Chesnik, from down Battle Creek way. Only other thing in the pants was this."

He handed a crumpled white paper to the sheriff. Ben saw the not-quite-black ink of a thermal receipt printer (Epson ReadyPrint T20, available as part of Goose Mountain's point-of-sale Solution in a Box).

"This is from Harry's bait and tackle shop," Carl said, glancing at the logo. "Dated yesterday. Don't know what kind of fishing gear Chesnik would be buying this time of year. There's no ice fishing nearby."

Ben knew Harry Eberhardt pretty well. As

well as any client, anyway. He'd been in Harry's shop earlier this week, in fact. He was a twitchy little dude, but seemed harmless.

"What's on the receipt?" he asked, curious.

"Only one thing," Carl replied, pointing at the tiny type. "You know what this is, Ben?"

Ben took the slip and scrunched his eyes, wishing his readers weren't buried under all the winter duds. He saw only one sale listed. SHM-MOJ SPN RL $1500.

"This doesn't make a lick of sense," Ben said. "This is for a Shimano-Mojave spinner reel. It's a nice river reel, but they only retail for about eighty bucks. Ain't a fishing reel in the world that costs upwards of a grand, so far as I know. Besides, Harry doesn't have any Shimanos left in stock. He put in a big order with me for a case of the new Saharas."

"You don't say," Carl said. His eyes went hard, but he wasn't looking at Ben. Or at the tech in the back. He was staring down the road toward town. Behind the Blazer, an ambulance crawled toward them, lights flashing but siren silent.

"Mike, you go help the guys get the stiff loaded and transported. Tell 'em I want the coroner cutting as soon as the body thaws. Full screens, check for whatever he can think of. Get his prints on the wire as fast as you can."

Once Mike the tech joined his buddy and they were loading the corpse, still curled in a ball, Carl got the prowler moving down the road.

"Where we headed?" Ben asked.

"You'll see," Carl said. "But first, let me ask you a question. If I were to take you to the station, run your prints and make you piss in a cup, what would I find?"

Ben stared at him. His first reaction was to bless him out for even asking such a thing, but they'd just found a dead man, after all.

"You'd find caffeine, blood sugar a tad on the high side, cholesterol a tad on the low side, and a moldy old National Guard record from the dinosaur days. What else might you want to know?"

"Nothing personal," Carl said, eyes still straight ahead. "I had to ask. And now that I've asked, I'll answer. We're going to pay Harry a visit."

The main street was mostly deserted, and the chains' clanks echoed from the shuttered tourist shops and seasonal bars on either side of the road.

Harry's Bait & Tackle Emporium stood at the corner of Main and 2nd, right between Harry's ATV Rentals and Harry's Cottage Rentals.

Harry got around, but Ben noticed for the first time that the Lexus parked in the alley between the fishing and ATV shops was an awfully nice car for a man who did most of his business over the space of three months every year. A white plume of exhaust filled the narrow gap, and the sparkle of rock salt trailed from the front wheels to the street, which looked to be freshly scraped.

Carl parked the Blazer across the mouth of the alley.

"You stay here. And I mean it this time," Carl said, poking Ben's chest repeatedly.

"Why? Harry might or might not be involved, but he doesn't seem dangerous himself."

"Harry spent a few years in the sandbox with the Eighteenth Infantry back during the late oughts. As part of a forward recon team. He never talks about it, but he's not like he was in high school. Friendly, but in a too-friendly way. And he gets a whole lot of shipments for a guy who doesn't do a whole lot of selling outside tourist time."

"You know what he's up to?"

"I always had an idea, but never any proof. He

keeps quiet, and so do his off-season customers. At least here in the county." The big sheriff sighed. "I guess I should have looked harder, but he hasn't ever caused any problems. He *may* not have caused *this* problem. The iceman back there may have only been a customer, although I doubt it. That receipt seems like a laundry ticket for dirty money. The shoulder tattoo was The Big Red One. First Army Division. Of which the 18th Infantry is a part."

"I guess that's a lot of coincidence, ain't it?"

"Yeah, sounds like it. So anyway, stay put."

Carl left the prowler running, but locked his door as he got out and motioned for Ben to do the same. Ben turned in his seat and watched Carl walk back up the salted and sanded sidewalk, then through the shop's door.

Nothing happened for a couple of minutes.

Then a loud report, the crack of a mid-caliber semiauto or Ben weren't no hillbilly, and Harry Eberhardt came bolting through the shop's door, smoking pistol in hand.

Oh shit shit shit.

The Blazer blocked the sidewalk and alley, so Harry came around on the street side just as Carl exploded through the door behind him, fluff flying from a tear high on the left arm of his parka.

Carl had his own revolver in a two-hand grip but pointed down and away. Judging from the size of the cylinder, the sheriff was worried about shots going through whatever they hit, and then through whatever was past that.

Ben had no time to think, but mamma hadn't raised a dummy.

He swung the passenger door open just as Harry came alongside.

The small shopkeeper hit the door full tilt, his feet and then his body losing grip on the slick road and sliding under the door.

"Ben! Down!"

He didn't need telling twice.

Ben dove for the driver's seat as death roared from Carl's hand cannon.

He didn't see what the sheriff hit, but Harry didn't get up again.

~

"I hate to see you leave so soon, Ben." Carl said, shaking his hand.

They were back at the Lindeman place. Statements and such had kept Ben in town another day, but at least the weather was up on the positive side of the dial this afternoon. Should be an easy drive back to the big D, but just in case, a canvas bag filled with shiny new chains sat under the hatch and a fresh jar of Nivea sat in the passenger seat. Four hours in the air, and he'd be able to lose this damn snow suit and get by on flannel again.

"How much fuss will you have with the DEA?" Ben asked before opening the Subaru and settling in. The engine fired right up. Space heater under the block did the trick every time.

"Trouble?" Carl said, laughing. "Hell, after that forty kilos of heroin and sixty of hash? They're as happy as a prom queen the day the rabbit lived."

"How about Harry?"

"He probably won't be bowling any tournaments after a .357 hollowpoint in the shoulder, but he'll live. For a long time. At Fort Leavenworth or some other sunny destination."

"Leavenworth? Isn't Harry a civilian now?"

"Still in the inactive reserves. The Army's getting involved, since some of their transport was used. Somebody's about to get a hell of a deal on a couple of business opportunities, and summer'll be here before you know it."

"Yeah, I know," Ben said, rolling down the window before shutting the door. "After this storm and the other excitement, I'm behind on my sales calls. I reckon I better get on down the road. Might make it home in time for supper."

"You should come back up in a few months," Carl said, leaning down and resting his meaty arms on the door frame. "We can hit the river and do some fishing."

"Might could do," Ben said, grinning. "I can set you up with a brand-new Shimano spinner, cheap!"

Both men laughed. Ben pulled away, his left arm out the window in a long wave before he wound the glass back up. He drove toward the two-lane, which would take him to the four-lane, then to the highway, the airport, and back home to his own neck of the woods.

Where he wouldn't need any more snow suits or face cream.

MOTHER NATURE LENDS A HAND

DIANA DEVERELL

I spend Martin Luther King Day afternoon hiking through the petroglyph national monument, which is only a ten-minute-drive from my Albuquerque condo. Clouds clutter the pale blue sky and the air temperature around me is a crisply dry fifty degrees.

I grew up in the moist Pacific Northwest. I'm a half-Salvadoran female and I find the southwest's desert climate suits me better.

Back in my condo, I strip off my dark-blue parka, hiking shoes, and jeans. Thirsty, I grab a chilled IPA from the fridge and pop the cap. Crossing to my favorite overstuffed armchair, I settle in to rehydrate. I lift the cold beverage to my lips but before I can take a sip a woman's voice croons "*Estrellita dónde estás?*"

My ringtone is the Spanish version of "Twinkle, Twinkle, Little Star." Logical, as whoever is calling is looking for me, Estrella Stevens.

I set the bottle aside, bring up the screen on my phone, and see that Joseph Conrad Stevens, my seventy-five-old American father, is on the line. I greet him with "Hi, Dad."

"Star," he says, using the English shorthand for my given name. "I need you to help me solve a big problem. How fast can you get yourself to Eugene?"

Dad's thirty years older than I am and stubbornly self-reliant. He proudly solves his own problems. His urgent summons tells me whatever's bothering him is serious and time-sensitive.

Luckily, I'm a self-employed freelance fraud investigator and I can travel at the drop of a hat.

"Soon as I hang up," I say. "I'll book a flight and send you the details."

"Getting to Eugene may be tricky," Dad says. "We got hit by an ice storm this weekend and we're still dealing with aftermath."

"I'm on it," I reply. "Hope to see you soon."

I manage to find a Tuesday morning flight to Seattle with a connection to Eugene and I send the Eugene ETA to him.

By the time I land at SEA-TAC, the January ice storm has closed Eugene's regional airport. The airline rebooks me on a flight to Portland the next morning and I buy a train ticket from Portland to Eugene for that afternoon.

I phone Dad to report the delay. Given the iffy travel situation, I tell him I'll call next when I'm on the ground in Eugene. I spend Tuesday night in a Seattle hotel watching weather reports and travel advisories. I go to sleep hoping my plan holds up.

Next morning, I'm at the airport waiting to

board when the airline cancels the Portland flight due to mechanical problems. By the time I reach the head of the line of disgruntled passengers at customer service, Eugene has managed to clear their main runway. I get a seat on the next flight and cancel my Amtrak reservation.

I land in Eugene at six-thirty Wednesday evening. Dad hates to drive after dark. Instead of phoning him, I head for the taxi stand. I wear waterproof boots, jeans, and my dark-blue parka over a sky-blue cotton sweater. I grip my combo laptop and carryon bag in one hand. Despite the not-yet-melted ice on the pavement, I feel warm and well-protected in this outfit.

The first cab in line is a recent model SUV. I knock at the driver's window. The tinted glass powers down to show me a young woman wearing a tan ballcap, her sable ponytail snugged through the opening at the back.

"I'm going to the Whit," I tell her and add the street address in the Whiteaker neighborhood.

"Lot of trees are down in that area," she says. "Not all the streets are clear yet. We may have to make some detours but I'll get you as close as I can. Worst comes to worst, I have a chainsaw in the luggage compartment."

"Great," I reply, opening the rear door to the back seat.

I inhale deeply as I climb in, enjoying her SUV's confidence-inspiring new-car scent.

She pulls slowly onto the airport access road. The power must be out because the streetlights don't shine. She flicks her headlights to high beam, piercing the darkness. Her tires crunch over thick patches of ice.

Glancing out my window, I see that tree limbs made heavy by the coating of ice have broken loose, dangling dangerously over the shoulders. Larger branches and whole trees have crashed to the pavement. Sawn-up trunks, huge limbs, and leafy debris line the roadside.

I was born in El Salvador and Mom and Dad moved to the US when I was three. I experienced four or five ice storms while growing up in Eugene. But those memories pale in the face of this devastation.

The cabbie turns onto US Highway 99 and heads downtown. She's got both hands on the wheel, concentrating on the hazards ahead.

Twenty minutes later, we're in the northwest end of downtown, on the wrong side of both the railroad tracks and the butte named for town founder Eugene Skinner.

The cab pulls up in front of the modest one-story house my parents bought in the late 1980s. Broken limbs are scattered across the patch of front lawn. An older Buick is parked in the graveled driveway. Beside it, someone's cleared the narrow cement walk leading to the front porch.

The driver positions the cab so that the rear door on the passenger side opens directly to the walkway.

"Looks like that route's been salted," the driver says. "Safer than this icy street. Best you slide over and exit onto the walk. You might make it to the house without falling."

I pay the driver and add a ten-buck tip. "I appreciate your coming to work tonight," I say.

"I figured we pros should turn out in force," she replies.

"Your passenger applauds your dedication," I say. "I may need your services again while I'm in town."

"Any time." She gives me her business card.

I glance at her name, Autumn Chase, before I tuck the card into my pocket. Grabbing my bag, I move across the back seat.

With a quick goodbye to Autumn, I climb out and shut the door. I step carefully to the porch and edge up the three concrete steps.

Dad must have heard the taxi motor. By the time I face the front door, he's swinging it open.

He's only five inches taller than my five-foot-four. His baggy jeans fit comfortably around his large belly. His ponytail is all-white, but his full beard is a curly mixture of gray and reddish blond hairs against his faded blue-plaid flannel shirt.

He pulls me indoors and into a welcoming hug. I breathe in his scent, a faint hint of Mom's favorite English Leather cologne, the lingering odor of pot smoke, and lemony hand soap.

The living room embraces me with the homey smell and sound of a crackling fire in the wood-stove. The warm rectangular room is brightly lit by three lamps. I feel as though the familiar, comfy furniture arranged in the open space is greeting me with open arms.

Dad waves me into the battered leather arm chair closest to the stove. He sinks into the matching chair across from me. "You coming from the Amtrak station?" he asks.

"Nope," I say. "Airport reopened and I flew in. A cab was waiting, so I grabbed it."

"Good move," he said. "Storm made a mess of things."

"Sure did," I agree. "I saw more fallen trees than I could count, blocking streets and driveways. One had crashed on a carport roof and crushed the vehicle under it."

"Probably too dark for you to see the broken branch sticking out of our roof." Dad sighed. "No leak so far, but this is the first day the temps have gotten above freezing. Could be a while before we thaw out."

"I was stunned by what I saw," I say. "Looks like this ice storm was on steroids. Hugely muscular and extremely angry with Oregonians. I was happy to be riding in a newer SUV with studded tires, four-wheel-drive, and an eagle-eyed cabbie accustomed to driving after dark."

My forehead wrinkles again. "Mom's Honda isn't in its usual parking spot. Don't tell me she's driving around in this?"

"No, Luz is staying with her former co-worker Juanita Gomez. Few days ago, Juanita fell on the ice and sprained her ankle."

"She's making sure Juanita takes no more risks," I note. Mom, aka Luz de Maria Stevens, retired last year from her job as director of the local Centro LatinoAmericano. She's been helping others all her life. Retirement hasn't changed her.

"Safer for your mom, too," Dad adds. "Falling branches and trees continue to sever utility lines in our part of town. Power's on at the moment, but it's been off for hours five times since Saturday. Juanita's condo is in a neighborhood with buried electric lines and her power stayed on. I'm glad your mother has reliable heat and light."

"Why didn't you go with Mom?" I ask.

He shrugs. "Juanita's condo is too small. I can manage on my own. And if this place looks occupied, I'm less likely to have my generator and firewood stolen. These conditions don't bring out the best in everyone."

I lift one shoulder in my own shrug. "Maybe the thieves don't see any other way to keep their loved ones safe."

"I help anyone who asks me for help," he says. "Nobody needs to rob me."

I wave a dismissive hand. "I know that. Maybe they don't. Is that why you asked me to come? Because Mom can't help with your problem?"

He grunts a negative. "The two of us don't have the right skill set. You're the only person I know who does."

My eyebrows go up in disbelief. Dad is no capitalist wheeler-dealer. "*You* need a trained financial fraud investigator?"

"Bingo." Dad gets to his feet. "Let me get us each a bowl of chili. I'll fill you in while we eat."

Five minutes later, I'm tucking into a steaming bowl of rich, thick chili con carne topped with grated cheddar and sour cream. The meat is shredded round steak, not hamburger. The tomatoes are from Mom's backyard garden, sun-ripened and canned by her. Dad himself soaked the kidney, pinto, and black beans to lovely plumpness.

I taste chili powder but the strongest flavor for me in Dad's signature dish is love. Despite relocating physically to the southwest, wherever Mom and Dad are located will always be my heart's home.

Dad brings in two uncapped beers and a basket of warm, handmade tortillas fresh from the vendor.

My insides soon feel as comfortable as the rest of my body. I'm ready to reward Dad for this luscious meal.

I rest my spoon in the bowl. "Okay, what's your financial fraud problem?"

Dad sniffs. "This concerns Rocky's finances, not mine."

Rocky is Oscar Quarry. Dad and Rocky have been friends off and on since the cradle. Rocky no longer owns the thriving titty bar that made him a wealthy businessman, but he still sees himself as one.

Dad's frequent clashes with Rocky tend to be around Dad's conviction that capitalism has been replaced by what his favorite pundit calls a "technologically advanced form of feudalism."

Dad adds, "Rocky thinks he's making a great real estate deal. I think he's being scammed."

I sniff. "Rocky's been buying and selling property as long as I've been alive. He won't fall for a scam."

Dad puffs out air, a snort of derision. "When I voiced my concerns, Rocky used those same words to shut me up. He's as cocky as ever. But I think he's a likely sucker for someone who knows how to push his buttons."

"You think some scammer's taking advantage of him?" I ask.

"I'm afraid that's what's happening," Dad replies. "Two days ago, Rocky was crowing over this deal. But the scheme he describes sounds to me more like a disaster waiting to happen."

"Tell me what Rocky told you," I say.

"First," Dad replies, "he's going to use a government program to convert the equity in his current home to cash."

"A reverse mortgage arrangement?" I guess.

Dad nods. "Rocky used those words. Says the

plan is government-backed and absolutely risk-free."

I narrow my eyes and lean toward Dad. "Does Rocky understand that in a reverse mortgage he borrows that amount of money?"

"Sure, but he says he'll still own his home and he'll pay no interest on the loan. Only property taxes and insurance and maintenance so long as he lives in it. When he or his estate sells the property, the proceeds will pay off the loan. If the housing market goes bad and the house sells for less than he owes, FHA insurance covers the difference."

I hold out my hands palm up, showing I see nothing wrong. "This sounds reasonable so far. Although details can vary, you're describing the basic structure of a government-insured home-equity-conversion mortgage."

"And you think Rocky qualifies for one of those?" Dad asks.

I shrug. "Rocky's over age sixty-two and his current property is his primary residence, which makes him eligible to apply. If the HUD-required financial assessment shows he has enough equity to cover his other payments on the house, he should be able to get a lump-sum payout of the equity."

Dad grunts. "Okay, I'm fine with that end of

his deal. The rest of it still concerns me. Rocky said a realtor came to him pushing a not-yet-listed property available to the right buyer at a below-market price. The realtor recommended the reverse mortgage payout be used to purchase the property. He assures Rocky he'll make a profit when he sells it."

"Wow," I say, "That scenario sends up a lot of red flags for me. If Rocky were one of my Albuquerque clients, I'd have a lot of questions for the realtor."

Dad brushed a hand across his forehead. "I said as much to Rocky. But he won't listen to me. I'm hoping he'll take your professional opinion more seriously."

"I need to start by talking with Rocky," I say. "Why don't you phone him?"

Dad yanks his phone from his shirt pocket. "What do you want me to say?"

"Tell him I'm in town and you and I would like to see the house he wants to buy."

Dad puts the phone on speaker and places the call. Rocky picks up right away and they say their hellos.

Dad says, "Star's paying me a surprise visit and she'd love to see you. I have the phone on speaker so she can chime in while we work out a meet."

"Hi, Star," Rocky interjects.

"Hi, Rocky," I reply.

"I was telling Star you plan to buy a house as an investment," Dad says. "How you suggested I might want to make a similar deal. She and I would love to take a look at that property you say you're interested in buying. To get a feel for what your realtor has to offer."

"Of course, I don't have a key for it yet," Rocky says. "Though I'd love to show it to you from the outside. Unfortunately, I won't feel safe driving myself until the streets are in better shape."

"No problem," I interject. "The cabbie who brought me in from the airport has the perfect vehicle for these conditions. She's willing to drive me around and her SUV is big enough for all three of us. Are you free tomorrow morning?"

"Free as a bird and always happy for a chance to catch up with you, Star. Pick me up at 9:30."

"I've got the address," Dad says, and ends the call.

I phone Autumn Chase and book her services for the next day. Dad and I spend another couple of hours chatting before heading for bed.

We're waiting out front at nine-twenty on Thursday morning when Autumn arrives in her

SUV. Dad claims the front seat beside her while I take the seat behind. Ten minutes later we reach Rocky's house and he joins me in the back.

Rocky's once-black hair is silver, shaved to quarter-inch bristles that show off his nicely-shaped head and bronze skin. The shade matches my own skin tone. I'm sure Rocky has a Latinx ancestor.

Rocky wears a heavy Navy peacoat over a close-fitting cranberry turtleneck and neatly-pressed heather Dockers. He was fit and slender in his sixties when he and Dad and I worked together on a movie being filmed in Eugene. I doubt he's gained any weight since.

With his thick steel-rimmed spectacles, Rocky's a fine-looking older man and when he leans in to give me a hug, his citrus cologne blends nicely with the new-car smell.

Up front, Dad spends most of our drive interrogating Autumn. From the little I overhear, he's found she has no connection to the Eugene family who managed a large greenhouse operation in the area for a hundred years.

And though Autumn lives in a community several miles west of the airport, she is not involved in the three-day counterculture country fair sited in that area which he's been attending for more than fifty years.

Rocky's busy interviewing me. "So, Star, how'd you end up in New Mexico?"

"Totally by chance," I say. "I was exploring the southwest with a friend and fell in love with Albuquerque. The friend moved on, I stayed."

"How'd you end up as a fraud investigator?" he asks.

"I was volunteering at a local charity, helping walk-in low-income clients with various problems. Was surprised to discover how many were victims of various internet scams. I thought scammers only targeted people with big bucks."

"People with any bucks," Rocky corrected.

"True. I took some college courses in fraud investigation. I learned that fraudsters and con artists tend to go after older adults because they believe that population has plenty of money in the bank. But they don't target only wealthy older Americans. Older adults with low income are also at risk. And they're the majority of my clients."

"Since you became a trained fraud investigator," Rocky clarifies.

"I work free-lance and most of my work comes via referrals from the charity where I volunteered. The charity pays my fees from grant funds and the defrauded client keeps any money I'm able to recover."

Rocky gives me a warm smile. "I know your dad's worried that I'm being scammed but I'm on top of things."

"Dad tells me an out-of-town realtor approached you regarding this house we're going to see."

"Right," Rocky replies. "The guy came to me, not the other way around."

I laugh. "As you can probably guess, that fact alone sets off a tiny alarm in my brain. My clients aren't big investors. They rarely initiate the interactions that lead to them being defrauded."

"Glad you can see I'm different," Rocky says. "The realtor told me he'd asked his local contacts to identify people actively buying and selling property and my name came up. I told him I was doing that more than ten years ago when I owned multiple properties and was nimble enough to leverage the financing. Told him I no longer have the financial flexibility to do that."

"I take it the realtor didn't give up," I say.

"No, he said that from what he'd heard, I'd recognize a great deal when I saw it and he had one to show me. His seller, the owner of an attractive three-bedroom house in the South Hills neighborhood, is in a bind. Needs to find a buyer quickly, one who doesn't need to make the purchase conditional on selling his current home."

Another alarm bell dings in my brain when I hear the pressure for a fast sale. I keep my mouth shut and let Rocky finish his story.

"To get the quick action he wants, the seller lowers his price below market. And because the realtor is handling both ends of this unlisted sale, the realtor lowers his commission. Win-win all around, is how the realtor puts it. He suggests I apply for a home equity conversion loan to raise the purchase money."

Another ding in the brain. "You didn't come up with that option on your own?" I ask.

"I had no idea I was eligible. I checked out the house. Decided I could easily re-sell it for more than the seller is asking." Rocky smiled. "Irresistible opportunity."

"You're saying the seller is willing to wait for your loan to be approved?" I ask.

Rocky makes a *who-knows* gesture with his hands. "I guess he has a little wiggle room for the right buyer. But not much. I'm trying to make things go as quickly and smoothly as possible. The realtor gave me a certified appraisal of the property and a copy of the most recent home inspection. No question I'm getting the place for half what it's worth."

No question for Rocky, lots of questions for me.

"Another hundred yards and we'll be at the property," Rocky continues. "You'll see what I mean."

I watch from the back seat as Autumn maneuvers her vehicle slowly up the steep road, wending her way between the smaller pieces of debris littering the pavement.

She stops at the bottom of a driveway leading up to a two-story wood-and-glass-house. A tall uprooted Douglas fir tree lies across the drive, blocking entry.

"I can't get any closer," Autumn says. "You'll need more than my chainsaw to clear the driveway."

"No problem," Rocky says. "We'll walk in. If you'd like to have the tour, feel free to join us."

He shakes his head. "I'm surprised my realtor hasn't sent a crew to deal with this."

I'm not. I'm guessing the realtor prefers no one get close enough to the house to see any defects exposed by the storm damage.

"The walk looks too treacherous for me," Autumn says. "I'll stay with the vehicle."

Rocky, Dad, and I exit the SUV. "We'll be careful," Rocky tells Autumn before turning to lead us single-file up to the fallen tree. Luckily, the lower branches had been trimmed. We easily clamber over the trunk near the root end of the tree. Tendrils of roots shoot skyward and the ground is torn open.

I spot the gleam of metal at the edge of the muddy root ball. Moving closer, I realize I'm seeing a cylindrical storage tank.

I point it out to Dad. "Does that look like an old oil tank to you?"

"Probably installed as part of the original construction," Dad says. "Later, the heating system was converted the heating system to natural gas. Should've been removed and the soil checked for leakage."

Rocky crowds closer to peer in. "The inspection report the realtor gave me doesn't mention the tank is still in place."

"You'll have to remove it before you re-sell this house." I shake my head. "The next buyer won't be able to get bank financing till it's gone. I recommend that before you close this deal, you get another inspection by someone you trust."

"Might do that," Rocky mutters.

The ice is patchy on the driveway and we

make our way to the two overhead doors fronting the garage without anyone falling.

The garage structure itself is pristine, the roof intact and debris-free. "This end of the house looks okay," Rocky says, and leads us up a concrete stairway to the left of the garage.

The steps are slippery and I keep my right arm looped over the narrow concrete wall paralleling the steps. They lead to a wooden deck on the uphill side of the house. Entry to the deck is blocked by a huge fallen limb. The tip has penetrated the house roof and the heaviest part of the branch has smashed the covered hot tub and several slats in the deck floor.

Rocky waves a hand at an opening in the railing beyond the tree limb. Wooden steps lead down to the forest floor. "I thought we'd be able to continue around the house by following the path at the bottom of those steps. Guess we better return to the driveway and see if we can get through that way."

Ten minutes later, we abandon the tour, our path again blocked by debris.

Standing at the top of the driveway beside the garage doors, I pat Rocky on the shoulder. "What are you thinking?" I ask.

"That I'm not buying this house until the owner repairs all the storm damage," Rocky says.

"I recommend you also get a new appraisal."

"What's the purpose?" he retorts.

"To rule out the possibility that the realtor you're working with is running what is known as a House Flipping Scam. I ran into this with one of my New Mexico clients. A scammer posing as a realtor convinced a pair of senior homeowners to get a reverse mortgage on their existing home and use the proceeds to buy another property."

"As my realtor advised me to do," Rocky says slowly.

"Yes, same scenario so far. My New Mexico clients diligently applied for the mortgage and dealt with all the bank-required paperwork for that end of the deal. In the process, they didn't realize no bank, government institution, or other third party was overseeing their purchase of the new property. They relied completely on the man posing as a professional realtor."

Rocky sighed. "I know how this goes. The phony realtor took advantage of the situation to steal their money."

"I'm afraid so," I say. "Turns out that the scammer owned the New Mexico property my clients were buying. The scammer got it for a low price and made enough cosmetic improvements to make it appear more valuable."

"I thought this house looked pretty solid," Rocky said.

"And maybe it is," I retort. "However, in my case, the scammer provided a fraudulent appraisal and a sloppy inspection report which my clients accepted without question. Only after the deal closed and the scammer pocketed his profits did the new homeowners discover the house had undisclosed defects like that buried oil tank we saw. Defects that made it likely they'd lose money on a sale."

"Well, damn," Rocky said. "I hear you, Star. I'm accustomed to buying and selling undeveloped land and I haven't done that for ten years. My current home is the only residential real estate I've purchased and that was in the eighties. I'm not familiar with all the current hazards. I imagine wiring, zoning, flooding, and other issues may be relevant."

"Very relevant," I say. "I guess you'll have some questions for your realtor when he gets back to you."

Rocky laughs sourly. "I doubt I'll hear from that realtor again. Most likely, he fled the scene as soon as he heard the timber falling on that house.

I don't see him coming back to fix it up again. And I bet a new inspection will show more problems with this house than that oil tank. Thanks for looking out for me."

He turned and grinned at the sky. "And thanks, Mother Nature, for showing me the light."

Dad snorted. "You can find something to celebrate in the most god-awful situations."

"But that's why you love me," Rocky said.

I grin. "What a trio we make. I love hanging with you two old farts."

"Old farts?" Dad repeats. Turning to Rocky, he says, "You sure you want a buy a drink for a woman who insults us?"

"Insults us?" Rocky says. "I heard only truth —we are old farts. And she loves us. We gotta love her back."

"I guess we do," Dad mumbles.

"Never mind your awful weather," I say. "You make me happy I'm home."

FASTPITCH

JOSLYN CHASE

Cold rain pelted down like gunfire, peppering the concrete landing beneath Jake Parkin's feet and sending him into a skid as he rushed around the corner toward the staircase. The pounding barrage blotted out the sounds he was used to hearing—the plaintive cries of hovering seagulls, the whir and crank of traffic on the avenue running alongside the high-rise apartment building where he worked as head of security.

A low ominous boom of thunder, like a cannon in the distance, rose above the rainsound as Jake gripped the glass door leading into the staircase vestibule, fighting the wind to get it open. He had fifteen floors to patrol and rarely used the elevator. The stairs helped keep him fit. Maybe not as toned as he'd been before retiring from the Virginia Beach Police Department, but reasonably ready to roll with whatever punches fell his way.

This afternoon, he had a more immediate reason for shunning the elevator.

Hurricane Pablo.

The tropical monster was sweeping toward the coast with a voracious hunger, heralded by a lash of wicked thunderstorms. The city's power grid was holding, but the juice could stop flowing at any moment and the last thing he wanted was to be trapped between floors in a heavy, metal box.

Many of the building's residents had followed the recommendation to evacuate but by Jake's reckoning, thirty-two people remained. Harvey Browning, the building's owner, had offered to let him off the hook.

"It's going to be a bad one, Jake. People have been warned. The smart ones are long gone."

Jake coughed into his hand. "Some of those still here are staying out of necessity," he said, thinking about Anna and her bed-ridden grandmother on the second floor. He watched his employer's ginger-colored eyebrows waggle up and down like boats on a choppy sea and knew the man was worried.

"I can't force you to stay under these circumstances. Get yourself clear, Jake. Stay safe. Then haul your butt back here and help me clean up the mess."

A moment passed, punctuated by the wind howling at the window. "I'll stay, sir," Jake said quietly. "I wouldn't feel right leaving my post at a time like this."

Browning nodded. "I figured that's how you'd feel about it. As for me, I'm grabbing the wife and high tailing it out of here. I wish you the best."

Now, six hours after he'd made that choice, Jake wondered if it was the right one.

He'd spent the intervening time checking and re-checking the security system and storm protection measures, reassuring nervous residents about the approaching hurricane. The building housed eight apartments on each level, with a luxury penthouse occupying the entire fifteenth floor.

The couple leasing the penthouse were currently basking on the French Riviera, so at least they were safely out of it, though damage to the apartment could potentially destroy a lot of expensive furnishings.

Or worse—breach the security system, putting the Franzen treasures at risk.

Jake had seen a copy of their insurance policy. He knew they kept jewels on the premises, rare and valuable coins, bullion. He'd be willing to bet they had a hefty stash of emergency cash, as well.

Testing every door, every junction box and connection, Jake walked his beat. Each apartment's entrance opened onto a common landing in the center of the building, open to the sky and circling the two elevators and sets of stairs.

He'd made his rounds, floor by floor, to the top of the building and back down again, getting soaked by the wind-blown pellets of rain. He stopped now at Apartment 203 and pressed the doorbell.

Anna's face as she peered out was wan and creased with worry. "Jake, you're sopping wet! Come in. I'll get you a towel."

Jake waved off the suggestion. "I'm okay. How are you and Juanita holding up?"

"I'm hanging in there, and grandma's in good spirits. Dr. Caldwell—he's the new therapist she's been seeing—prepared her for this eventuality. She's feeling strong."

"Glad to hear it. How are you feeling?"

She laughed. "Some of the good doctor's healing has rubbed off on me, I guess. I attend all grandma's sessions with her and..." She stopped, a rosy blush coming up on her cheeks. "He's been kind enough to give me some free counsel, as well."

Not a bit surprising. Anna, with her sweet, earnest face and obvious devotion to her grandmother, would elicit kindness in an eel. Jake touched her gently on the arm.

"Do you have enough flashlights and fresh batteries?" he asked. "What about bottled water?"

"We've got all that," Anna told him, a small smile easing the tension behind her eyes. "We'll fare better here on the second floor than those in the apartments above."

"Yes, count yourselves lucky," Jake said, packing some cheer into his voice. He refrained from pointing out the flaw in her reasoning, because she was right.

Unless the storm surge led to extensive flooding.

Originally from Puerto Rico, Anna Torres moved last year to Virginia Beach to be with her grandmother and help care for the ailing woman. The 28-year-old paramedic was known and loved among the residents for her warm and open spirit, bravery, and dedication to helping others.

Sentiments heartily shared by Jake.

With almost twenty years between their ages, Jake tried to squelch anything else he might feel for her. But it was becoming increasingly difficult to tamp down the admiration that grew as they spent time together on their local fastpitch softball league where she covered second base while he manned the pitcher's mound.

The after-game pizza dinners. The good-natured joking around while waiting in the dugout. The euphoric group hugs after a victorious game.

"Don't worry, Anna," he said, giving her hand a quick squeeze. "This'll blow over before you know it. In the meantime, I'll do all I can to keep everyone safe."

"I know you will."

Her words rang in his ears as she shut the door, leaving behind a bitter and mocking resonance. She believed him, trusting that he would do all he could to keep everyone safe.

But she didn't know about the man lying dead after the last disaster Jake had managed.

She didn't know about David.

Maxwell Kane braced his palms on the sill as he stared out the window, his back to the three-man crew waiting silently behind him. Two of them, Joiner and Conrad, didn't want to be here, had voiced their opinions on the violence of the storm and their desire to join the residents fleeing the city.

Lutz, the remaining member of the team, had impressed upon them the necessity of staying. Impressed it very firmly upon them, backing his argument with a description of what had happened to the fourth crewman as he'd attempted to run.

They would stay.

The rain continued, flung sideways by the

turbulent winds and carrying the taste of salt from the Atlantic, just two blocks to the east. It spat against the window glass with monotonous severity. Kane turned, jaw set, and surveyed his men.

"There is no security on this earth; there is only opportunity," he said, quoting his favorite role model, General Douglas MacArthur. "This, gentlemen, is ours."

"Tailor-made, in fact," Lutz added. "With the Franzens out of the country and the building's security force pared down to one man, the pickings ought to be easy."

Kane felt a grim stab of satisfaction as he thought of that lone man standing between them and the Franzen treasure house. He wouldn't be standing for long.

"Let's not get ahead of ourselves," he cautioned. "Easy may not be the best word applied to our situation. But possible. Yes, gloriously possible."

He lifted his bottle of beer from the table, gone warm in the sullen humidity brought by the storm. "To Pablo," he said, tapping the amber glass against Lutz's own.

"To Pablo," the crewmen echoed, raising their bottles.

~

Back at his security post, Jake reviewed the emergency protocols for the building as he chewed on a roast beef sandwich that stuck dry in his throat. He considered tossing the whole thing in the trash but knew he'd need the energy to get through this storm. Instead, he washed it down with half a glass of gingerale and ignored the burn rising in his gut.

The TV screen mounted high on the wall to his left cast a blue glaze over the desk, tinting the spreadsheets and loosely organized stacks of paperwork scattered over its surface. A change in the shifting colors caught Jake's attention and he peered up at the screen, pointing the remote to raise the volume.

"...now classed as a Category 5 hurricane and predicted to strike land along the North Carolina and southern Virginia coastline sometime during the next hour."

Jake watched the news reporter's expensively-styled glossy dark hair pull away from its moorings and flap around her head like a flock of desperate bats. With the palm trees blowing sideways in the background, it made for dramatic television viewing.

"Despite orders to evacuate," the woman continued, shouting to be heard over the shriek of the gale, "some residents are opting to ride out the storm, stocking up on bottled water and non-perishable snacks, boarding up windows and sandbagging against the flood."

Something that looked like a barn door blew past behind her head and the camera angle shifted violently for a second or two before static claimed the screen. Jake switched it off.

Outside, the whiny pitch of the wind rose to a maniacal roar, shaking the building and sending a shiver along the fine hairs at the back of Jake's neck.

Pablo had arrived.

Maxwell Kane steered the white panel truck down the deserted avenue, tightly gripping the wheel as a long series of vicious gusts threatened to take control. There was virtually no traffic to deal with, but flotsam thrown by the storm littered the road, some of it stationary, requiring him to dodge around it.

And some of it still moving in jerky, unpredictable snatches. It gave Kane the willies, making him feel like prey stalked by a pack of moonstruck wolves.

He tightened his jaw and kept his eyes fastened on the rain-lashed street ahead. The apartment building's underground garage was blocked by a wall of sandbags in an attempt to keep the storm surge from flooding in.

Pulling the van to the curb, he set the brake and glared out the windshield. He'd planned this operation and waited for a big storm, counting on it to provide the cover and confusion he'd need to pull it off. But, capricious and volatile, the hurricane could work against him, as well.

A lot would depend on luck.

"The best luck of all is the luck you make for yourself," he growled under his breath, reaching once again for the wisdom of MacArthur. Kane had spent the last year grinding out the details, making his own luck. Things would fall his way.

He shifted his gaze to the rearview mirror, locking eyes first with Joiner and then with Conrad in the back. Turning to Lutz, he nodded.

"Let's move out."

As they'd been drilled to do, his crew grabbed their equipment and deployed, moving into position. Kane, Lutz, and Joiner slipped quickly inside the building, melting into the shadows, while

Conrad made ready in the van parked far below the penthouse balcony.

Uniformed as maintenance workers carrying toolboxes and wheeling large protective packing crates, each had a vital function to perform in a short amount of time. Seventeen and a half minutes later, Kane joined Lutz in the foyer outside the penthouse apartment. He watched his lieutenant wipe a bead of sweat from his forehead.

"It's done," Lutz announced. "The entire alarm system is ours."

"And the elevators?" Kane asked.

"Locked down tight. No one is going anywhere."

Kane ran a diagnostic to confirm he had control of the building's security system. As the green light flashed on his tablet's screen, he heard the clang of metal on metal and looked up to see Joiner snap the padlock on the last looped chain blocking off all doors to the stairwells.

"Building is secure, sir," Conrad said, standing at attention.

"Excellent." Kane slipped the tablet into his pocket and turned to Lutz. "Time to advance. Get us in there," he commanded.

~

Jake watched in horrified frustration as the malfunctioning security network beeped and wailed. He'd cast in his two cents when Browning asked his opinion on the building's new protection system. He thought it relied too much on internet connections and not enough on old school redundancies.

The hurricane was wreaking havoc on it and the surveillance monitors had been the first to go. Jake felt like a blind man as, one by one, the screens winked out, going black. He fiddled with the control panel to no avail and tried rebooting the system without success.

Something was wrong.

Jake checked his weapon and holster. Zipping into a charcoal gray windbreaker, he raised the hood and exited the security office. Buffeted by frenzied gusts, he pushed his way toward the staircase vestibule and froze. The chill that feathered down his spine had nothing to do with the cold rain slapping against his bowed head.

A heavy chain snaked through the door handles, secured by a sturdy padlock.

Jake yanked the cell phone from his pocket, almost dropping it, and dialed 9-1-1. The call didn't go through.

He wasn't surprised. He knew cell towers were

likely overburdened or knocked out of commission by the storm. Jake also knew exactly what the chain and lock signified.

Burglars in the penthouse.

He thought about the Franzen's hefty insurance policy. Though it cut against the grain, he reasoned that maybe his best move was to hunker down in the office and let it happen. He had no way of knowing how many intruders were involved and it appeared as if they'd planned well. It was only material goods, after all. Property that the insurance company would pay to replace.

But what if it wasn't?

What if someone else tried to intervene, got in the way? What if the burglars decided shaking down one rich plum at the top of the tree wasn't enough?

Jake had pledged to protect everyone in the building. He could not just sit on his hands and hope no one got hurt. He knew, by wretched experience, how it felt to carry the guilt of a death he should have prevented, and he didn't want to add a single ounce to that burden.

Rubbing a hand across his forehead, he flicked rainwater off his face and gnashed his teeth, squinting up through the building's open central column at the fifteen stories rising above him.

He was going up.

~

Jake let himself into the maintenance room and surveyed the shelves, hoping something helpful would jump out at him. The air felt heavy on his skin—ominous, smothering, and briny. It cast over Jake the sensation of drowning and he gulped down a breath, savoring the swell of oxygen in his lungs.

He found a length of nylon rope and a box of large metal hooks the manager used for suspending heavy potted plants in the building's exterior walkways. Using three of the hooks along with a couple feet of sturdy flexi-wire and a bottle of no-nail super tack adhesive, Jake fashioned a grappling hook and fastened it to the rope. He knotted the rope at four-foot intervals.

The storm, as he stepped back outside, sounded like a hell-bound freight train full of shrieking passengers. He shuddered to think of the devastation it was leaving in its wake. Here, down low and inside the protected column of the well-built high-rise, the raging effects were mitigated. But each floor he ascended would bring him closer to the monster outside.

And the demons within.

The rain had slackened but still dripped down, bringing occasional debris with it, plucked from the littered sky. Jake gathered some essential items into a backpack and slung it over his shoulders, glad now that he'd forced down that roast beef sandwich. Something told him he'd be calling on all his energy reserves before the storm blew over.

Standing in the central courtyard, Jake swung the rope, propelling his makeshift grappling hook up and over the railing of the second floor. It caught and he tested it with his weight before using it to help him climb up and slip over the balustrade.

Releasing the hook, he took his contraption with him as he hurried to Anna's apartment and quickly explained the situation.

"Stay hidden," he warned her, "and keep your grandmother safe."

"But Jake, I should go with you. I'm a paramedic. There's no telling what you'll encounter up there. You may need me."

He gave her a quick smile. "I appreciate that, Anna, but Juanita needs you more. You have to be here for her."

A crease rose on Anna's forehead. Jake wanted

to reach out and smooth it away. "You know I'm right," he said instead. "I have to go. Stay safe."

Hearing the door of her apartment snap shut behind him, Jake felt utterly alone. He was probably stupid for pushing ahead on his half-formed plan to defend and protect, yet he knew he couldn't do anything else.

Doubt pressed heavily on him as he leaned out over the second floor railing and tossed the hook up to the third floor landing. He was remembering the last time his plans had gone all wrong, forcing his retirement from the job he loved.

What if something like that happened again?

Despite the dark and violent frenzy happening outside the thick plate glass windows, the interior of the Franzen apartment looked like the layout of a glossy magazine. Kane felt a jab of malicious glee that went beyond the satisfaction of riches within his grasp. Such a perfectly put-together life deserved to be disrupted. Begged for it.

He was happy to oblige.

The three polyethylene packing crates lay open on the living room floor, ready to receive.

Lutz had found the wall safe and was working his magic on the dials. Joiner began filling a crate with silver from the dining room, wrapping pieces of priceless Sevres porcelain and Capodimonte figurines. The place was like a museum filled with treasures.

Kane couldn't wait to see what the safe contained. Geoffrey Franzen collected coins and was quoted in *Forbes* as a big believer in stocking up on precious metals. His wife adored extravagant jewelry and Geoffrey was known as an indulgent husband.

Licking his lips, Kane peered over Lutz's shoulder, gauging his progress. He was about to urge him on when a voice sounded from the front hall.

"Geoffrey? I saw your door was open...Hope it's okay if I come in."

A high-pitched male voice. Finicky-sounding. "I thought you were still enjoying the sunshine in southern France. What a day you picked to come home!"

Joiner looked up from his wrapping, a question on his face. Kane shook his head. "I'll go," he mouthed. Drawing his pistol, he stalked into the penthouse apartment's entrance hall.

"Back out, the way you came," he commanded, holding the gun steady, aimed at the guy's head.

Geoffrey's neighbor stammered, his sweaty moon face going pale, mouth opening and closing soundlessly, like a fish. Raising his hands, he stepped backward on the marble tiles. Kane motioned with the gun for him to continue out the door.

Following, he backed the hapless neighbor up to the railing and sensed the guy was about to find his voice in a nasty scream. Before that could happen, Kane stepped forward and rapped him hard with the butt of his gun. The man crumpled.

"Joiner!" Kane called. "Help me out."

Together, they lifted the unconscious man.

"He got a good look at your face," Joiner said, scowling.

"True," Kane agreed. "But anything could happen in a storm like this."

Joiner met his eye. Nodded. "Yeah, anything."

Both of them grunting under the man's considerable weight, they heaved him over the rail.

From the corner of his eye, Jake saw something flash past, falling from above. It thudded onto the pavement below with a sound that sent an icy weight sinking in Jake's gut. He was nine stories up now, climbing the slippery rails floor by floor with his rope and homemade grappler, fighting the squall that threatened his every move.

Peering down into the courtyard below, he saw a dark human-shaped heap on the pavement and knew that some malevolent force—storm or otherwise—had claimed a victim. Despite his best efforts.

It was clear there was nothing he could do for the man on the ground, and there were others at risk, vulnerable and unaware of hazards beyond the storm. Jake pressed onward and upward.

The lights outside each apartment flickered and went out, casting a dark shadow over the courtyard and the tiers rising above it. Power to the building had failed.

Or been deliberately cut.

As Jake flung his leg over the rail of the tenth floor, he heard a long, drawn-out scream. The roar of the hurricane rose to an unbearable pitch, drowning out the rest of it. Jake leapt from the rail as a nearby apartment door burst open, almost blowing off its hinges.

A man and woman rushed out, clinging to each other, their faces etched with terror. Behind them, the interior of the apartment seemed to swirl and buckle, one entire wall blasted away by the ferocious gale.

Jake shoved the door closed, managing to latch it shut. Another couple erupted from the apartment next door, shouting something Jake couldn't hear over the howling storm. Wordlessly, he shepherded the Crowleys and Goodmans to the leeward side of the building and dug in his pocket for the master key, using it to open a vacant apartment.

Once inside the gloom-shrouded space with the door closed, he was able to make himself heard. "Stay in here," he told the foursome, "and keep the door locked."

"Shouldn't we go down to a lower level?" Gene Crowley asked. "Hurricane could blow the whole top off the building."

"I'm afraid we're dealing with more than just Pablo," Jake said.

Jill Goodman stared at him, her eyes wide and rimmed with smeared mascara. "What do you mean?"

Jake didn't want to scare them more than they already were. "Just stay in here together and lock the door."

"Jake's right," Crowley said. Giving his wife

and the others a nudge toward the kitchen, he drew Jake aside. "I saw the rope hanging from the railing. What's going on, Jake? Why don't you want us going down?"

"The stairs are blocked, elevators useless. I'm using the rope to make my way to the penthouse."

"Blocked how? What are you talking about?"

"The building is under seige, Gene, and the hurricane's knocked out all communications. I'm sure the Franzens are the target. I'm hoping the intruders will limit their activities to the fifteenth floor."

"But you're going up there? To what end, Jake? To try stopping it?"

Jake shifted, impatient to get going. "That's not my primary objective. I'm concerned with the safety of the tenants. We've already—"

He broke off, but Gene Crowley picked it up. "We've already...what?"

"We've already lost one," Jake admitted. "There's a sight on the courtyard floor you won't want the ladies to see. Just stay here and keep your group safe."

Crowley's face was gray in the shadows, his eyes like sunken pools of darkness. "Okay, Jake. I see your point. I'll man the fort."

"Thank you."

Without another word, Jake left the apartment and hurried back to his grappling hook, half afraid the storm might have stolen it. But the hook and rope waited for him, and Jake used them to gain the eleventh floor and then the twelfth, checking each before proceeding.

Hurricane Pablo showed no sign of weakening or departing. It continued to rage and Jake felt the savagery of its bite more and more with each level he rose. Poised on his slender rope, high off the ground as the tempest buffeted him like a kite on a string, Jake fought his way from the twelfth floor to the thirteenth and then to the fourteenth.

His stomach knotted tighter than the rope as he threw his leg over the rail of the penthouse level, pulled himself up, and reached for his gun. With the stairway doors secured and the elevators out of commission, Jake figured the burglars would not be expecting him or anyone else.

He was wrong.

"Hello, Jake."

Shock rammed the breath from his lungs and Jake gasped, working to get it back. Squinting in the dark, he stared at the man in front of him and felt the fine hairs at the back of his neck rise to attention.

Maxwell Kane stood before him.

David's brother.

~

Kane allowed himself a smile, gratified at the look of stupid amazement stamped over Jake Parkin's features. Maybe the man had been trying hard to forget him, to forget how things went down that day.

Trying to forget how David had died from the bullet meant, instead, for him.

Maybe the man before him, panting like a dog, had put all his efforts into forgetting. But Kane had spent every day since that awful event remembering.

And anticipating.

Kane pointed his pistol at Jake, motioning for him to drop his own gun. After a moment's hesitation loaded with a dirty look, he did.

"Kick it over the side."

Another pause while Jake glared. Then, almost casually, the man nudged the gun under the railing with his boot. It disappeared into the gloom.

"Why don't we go inside," Kane suggested, pitching his voice like a thoughtful host inviting his guest in for lemonade. Once past the threshold, he shouted for Joiner who brought a dining chair into the living room and placed it beside the three crates, now nearly full and ready to be closed.

"Have a seat, Jake. We're just finishing up." He nodded to Joiner and watched him fasten Jake's wrists and ankles to the chair's appendages with sturdy cable ties.

"You may be wondering why I don't just shoot you now," he said.

Jake said nothing.

"Or maybe it's occurred to you that I could simply bludgeon you over the head with any number of handy instruments and blame it on Pablo."

Jake said nothing.

"Or shove you over the side like I did with your fat former resident."

Kane waited, but the man in the chair remained silent.

"I do none of these things, Jake, because any one of them would be too quick. Too painless. I want you to live with the torture of guilt for a good long while. I want you to suffer, as I have, for eternity."

Kane moved to the crate now filled with the contents of the wall safe. It had met, and exceeded, his expectations. Opening a velvet case, he lifted an exquisite emerald necklace and let the silken jewels slide across his fingers.

"Have you noticed the howl of the storm letting up? The eye of the hurricane is upon us. In this lull, we will lower these crates to the van below and make our escape. I do not think anyone will stop us."

Jake's silence and expressionless face fanned the flame burning in Kane's gut, fueling his desire to stab at the man, get beneath his skin.

"Oh, but there's one stop I have to make before I leave here," he said, squatting to put himself on Jake's level, not wanting to miss one scintilla of the pain and fear he meant to instill.

Reaching beneath the collar of his shirt, he pulled forth a lanyard with a laminated ID card attached. He showed it to Jake, reveling in the look of distressed alarm crossing the hated man's face.

"Dr. Caldwell needs to make a house call," he said.

Jake stared at the ID card dangling before him,

recognizing the name. Understanding its significance.

Kane had been watching him, planning this moment with meticulous cunning. Somehow, the vindictive man had been masquerading as the therapist treating Juanita Torres and worming his way into the confidence of her unsuspecting granddaughter.

Preparing to betray them all.

Kane smirked, malicious and gloating with delight. "And here's the kicker, Jake. You'll enjoy hearing this—Anna imagines herself in love with you."

The words hit like a sucker punch to the gut—lightning fast, unexpected, releasing a blast of pain. Jake gritted his teeth, determined not to show how hard the blow had landed, and glared at the man in front of him.

Kane's eyes, cold and calculating, held his gaze. The corner of his mouth flickered in contempt. "I thought you should know that before I kill her. You can live with the agony of how things could have been, stew in the misery of losing the one who loved you."

A wave of anguish shimmered through Jake as he thought of Anna in the hands of this monster. But it was David's face that flashed in his memory, the look crossing his features as he'd fallen, struggling to speak and unable to utter anything beyond a burbling groan.

Whether David had deliberately shielded Jake or stepped inadvertently into the trajectory of the bullet fired from Kane's gun no one would ever know. But there was something Jake knew about David that his brother didn't.

Jake had believed he was being merciful and discreet by not divulging it, by sparing Kane the sting of knowing. If he'd let the whole story come out, would any of this be happening now?

Or would the rage and malice riveted on Jake be exponentially greater if Kane knew? If he'd understood that David was the confidential informant working with police to foil the meticulously mapped-out bank job?

Despite the fact that he had been the one to pull the trigger, Kane held Jake solely responsible for the death of the big brother he idolized. If Jake cracked that veneer, revealed David's betrayal, what would happen then?

He thought it could be the straw that would break Kane, stripping away the leash holding his fury in check, turning it loose.

It could be the last thing he ever said, but it would focus Kane's killing intent on Jake.

Away from Anna.

And once Jake was dead, Kane's reason for harming Anna would be too. His sense of self-preservation would kick in and he'd vanish along with his stolen riches.

Would it happen that way?

Jake thought it would. He opened his mouth to speak.

And the world went black.

It was the smell that woke him.

Jake swam up into consciousness, the strong odors of ozone and sea brine acting like smelling salts, pulling him to the surface. The roar and swirl of the storm hit him like an ocean wave and his eyes snapped open, staring about him in the dimness of the Franzen apartment.

Still strapped to the chair, Jake tugged at his bonds but they held tight. Kane and his crew were gone. The crates were gone. The balcony slider gaped wide open, letting in gusts of wind as the eye of the hurricane passed and the storm's violence began to rise again.

Rocking and scooting the chair, Jake inched toward the apartment's stone fireplace, hoping to find a projection within reach and jagged enough to saw through the cable tie holding his left wrist.

He had no luck there, but found an artsy brass-rimmed table nearby that offered a semi-sharp edge. Jake's efforts caused the tough plastic of the zip tie to tear into his flesh and the honed brass left its bite, as well.

Accompanied by the ghostly shrieks and wails of the strengthening gale, his forearm now slick with blood, Jake continued to work the tie back and forth, leaning into it, until at last the cable popped, falling away.

He flexed his wrist, feeling the pins and needles of returning circulation. With frantic haste, he hobbled the chair into the kitchen, grabbing a knife from the butcher block with his freed left hand.

The roar like a freight train in the distance grew louder as Jake cut through the remaining ties. He ran to the balcony and ventured to the rail, peering out into the gathering darkness. On the street below, he saw a white van and one of the crates. Presumably, the other two had already been loaded.

Debris fluttered and flitted along the road, but Jake saw no human movement. He went inside and closed the door.

He hoped to heaven he wasn't too late.

Grabbing a heavy Remington sculpture from the brass-rimmed table, Jake ran from the apartment to the chained stairwell door. He used the Remington to smash open the padlock and raced down the stairs, pausing on the second floor. The chain and lock disabling the door were on the outside, out of reach.

Agonizingly torn, Jake weighed the option of going down to the courtyard to search for his gun against the need to reach Anna and her grandmother as rapidly as possible.

He raised the Remington and heaved it against the glass of the door.

It bounced off, leaving only a small crack. Jake retrieved the sculpture and threw it again. And again.

Desperate with fear, unable to keep visions of what Kane might be doing to Anna and Juanita from flooding across his brain, Jake picked up the heavy bronze horse and hurled it with all his strength.

A spiderweb of cracks appeared and Jake kicked at it with his boot, clearing away enough of the glass for him to crabwalk through the gap. He sprinted to Anna's apartment. The door was locked, and he used the master key to let himself in, hands trembling, mind fizzing with urgency.

As he entered, he heard Juanita's voice but couldn't distinguish her words. The tone was fretful and bewildered, rather than frightened. It was Anna's voice, as she comforted her grandmother, that held fear and awareness. She understood they were in danger.

Thank heaven they were both still alive.

Jake drew a shaky breath and moved stealthily toward the hall closet door. The noise of the storm provided cover as he opened it and grasped the softball bat Anna kept there. He'd seen her stow it after their Saturday morning league games. After a second's hesitation, he grabbed the ball, as well.

The short entryway ended in a ninety-degree-angle turn into the dining room and the living room beyond that. Jake stood, his back against the wall as the sound of Pablo outside spiked intermittently, wiping out most of the tense exchange taking place. Risking a peek around the corner, Jake saw the women seated on the sofa with Maxwell Kane standing six feet in front of them, holding a gun.

He wasn't aiming the gun at Anna or Juanita.

Just holding it casually at his side, knowing the threat of it would be enough for his purpose.

Which was what, exactly?

Jake fully believed Kane's announcement that he intended to kill Anna. Why hadn't he done it immediately?

Because he meant to do it in such a way to cause maximum pain to Jake. Which translated to maximum pain for Anna.

He meant to do something unbearable to her first.

The clamor of the storm washed over Jake, sounding like a crowd gone wild at a close-run ballgame. Biting his lip, he stepped around the corner and blasted the softball at Kane's gun hand as if the league championship—and something far more important—depended on that single pitch.

The ball struck Kane on the wrist and he dropped the gun, stepping back in surprise.

Jake rushed him, switching to the football tactics he hadn't used since college. They landed together in a heap on the floor, knocking over the coffee table.

"Take Juanita and get out of here," Jake shouted to Anna. He couldn't spare a glance to see if she'd heard and was complying. All his attention was on the man straining beneath him, trying to reach the gun three feet from his groping fingers.

Outside, Pablo was roaring and the seas were rising at his command. From the corner of his eye, Jake saw foamy waves licking against the window glass of the second-floor balcony.

Kane had given up on reaching the gun, instead aiming his clawed fingers at Jake's eyes. Jake grabbed his hand and twisted hard, feeling something snap as Kane growled and writhed beneath him.

They wrestled. Sweat dripped into Jake's eyes, stinging. He felt himself tiring and as he struggled to find his second wind, the floor suddenly sagged beneath them, dipping so they both slid along its surface toward the hole opening in the dissolving wall of the apartment.

Kane got a foot planted and levered himself over, flipping out from under Jake and ending up on top as they rolled along the slanting floor. He slammed a fist in Jake's face, smashing into the cheek bone. A gray haze crept into the corners of Jake's vision and Kane's hands went to his throat, squeezing.

But whatever Jake had done to his fingers made the stranglehold impossible to sustain. With a curse, Kane let go and Jake gasped in a breath as a piece of the apartment wall disappeared, sucked into the maw of the storm.

"Know this, Jake!" Kane shouted. "I'll find that girl and kill her. Like you killed David. No one in this world cared about me as much as he did."

Face twisted with fury and malice, Kane stared down, locking eyes with Jake. "You took him from me!"

Jake bucked, trying to shake Kane off him. "I'm sure you're right. David probably did care about you more than anyone else."

Grunting in rage, Kane dug an elbow into Jake's gut. Jake knocked it aside and huffed, "Maybe that's why he came to me and filled me in on all the little details of your heist. He wanted to stop you from doing something stupid."

Kane's eyes flew wide, and he grabbed Jake's face with his good hand, gouging in with the fingers. "You're lying! David would never!"

Jake bit at the hand and Kane pulled it away. "David did. How else would we have known all about your plans."

"You lying sack—"

The floor beneath them collapsed. The wall opened wide, a hungry mouth, sucking greedily. Salt spray slapped, cold and shocking the breath from Jake's lungs. He scrambled to grab hold of something solid and got a hand around a pipe as Kane slid off him and tumbled into the watery void, disappearing, his scream cut off like a butcher's cleaver coming down.

"Jake!"

Getting both hands on the pipe, Jake clawed his way up to firmer ground as turbulent salty water sloshed over him. Anna stood in the entryway of the apartment, her face chiseled thin by fear.

Fear for him.

"Get back, Anna."

Instead, she grabbed the softball bat he'd dropped and edged into the living room. Another piece of the floor fell away, almost knocking Jake from his clinging perch.

"Anna—it's not safe. Will you please get back?" he pleaded, scrabbling for a better hold.

For answer, she stretched herself flat on the floor and extended the bat, both hands wrapped tightly around it.

A million thoughts raced through Jake's mind. Things he wanted to do if he made it out of this alive. Things that might be possible which—before Pablo—had seemed impossible. The thrill tracing through his chest wasn't all due to the floor crumbling beneath him.

He grabbed the bat.

Harvey Browning, the building's owner, followed up on his promise to make Jake help him clean up the mess.

It took five and a half months to get it done.

Jake didn't mind. He liked the work, liked putting things right with his hands, liked the industrious feeling of seeing builders repairing, painters painting, and decorators laying carpet.

He liked the promise of something new and better coming to life.

And if he was honest, it felt just as good to know the life of Maxwell G. Kane was over. His body had washed up six miles down the coast after Pablo blew town. He wouldn't be coming after Anna.

Ever.

One chapter over. Another beginning.

Jake found himself humming contentedly as he walked into the newly refurbished two-bedroom apartment he shared with Anna and her grandmother. He kicked off his work shoes, leaving them on the entryway mat, and grabbed a soda from the fridge as he went to join the two of them on the balcony patio.

Passing through the living room, he stopped at the fireplace to admire the handsome stonework and polished mantelpiece. They were nice, but what really held his gaze was the two items lying, in pride of place, atop the shiny mantel.

A well-used softball and the scuffed-up bat that went with it.

He smiled and stepped into the sunshine.

NOT THE NORTH POLE

MARIE SUTRO

The Norse god of thunder swayed back and forth as if picking his way home to Valhalla after a weekend bender. Hanging from the rearview mirror on a braided leather cord, the three-inch figurine's toothy plastic grin taunted Bailey as she struggled to keep the rented SUV on the road.

"Are you sure we should be driving in this?" Amber whined from the passenger seat.

Keeping her grip loose enough to correct for the constant slipping and sliding in the ever-deepening snowpack, Bailey peered over the steering wheel. Beyond the windshield, what little was visible of the Icelandic countryside was rioting in white.

Raising her voice to be heard over the scream of the oncoming blizzard, she replied, "Of course. We're fine."

Amber stole another glance at the dashboard. "You're only going like...ugh, I don't know what kilometers per hour even means..."

Not risking to take her eyes off what she believed to be the road, Bailey took a deep breath. A highly acidic scent resembling heated cat urine tore through her nasal passages. Amber's high-priced perfume was another in an unending string of purchases that prized name brands above inherent desirability.

"You don't want me to risk us ending up like that truck we saw back there?" Bailey managed around the threat of a sneeze.

Forty kilometers back they had happened upon a black vehicle lying belly-up alongside the elevated coastal highway. It had been quickly disappearing beneath a blanket of white. Bailey had insisted on checking to see if the occupants needed help, but the vehicle had been abandoned.

Rubbing her thighs, Amber relented with a pout. "No, but do you really think we'll make it to the next place? I mean, it's freezing in here."

Bailey's best friend still looked incredible despite her recent foray into the dangerous weather. Amber's makeup remained camera-ready, and her wavy blonde curls were no worse for the brief stint inside the hood of her pink puffer jacket. "Does this stupid heater even work?" she asked, stabbing at the buttons on the dashboard.

"I told you we had to leave earlier to get ahead of the storm but you wanted to re-do your makeup. It would have helped if you'd worn the waterproof pants I bought you. And the knee-high snow boots."

"But ankle-high is way cuter." One-half of the pair of footwear in question thudded against the dashboard. When the display failed to draw Bailey's attention from the road, Amber's limb dropped back to the floor. "And, no offense, 'cuz I know you lost a lot of weight when you were sick, but those pants make you look like a total whale! Even if you want to let yourself go, you should at least care what Matt thinks. Maybe some collagen treatments for your skin...and you totally need to come back to my spin class."

Before her illness, Bailey had dutifully attended Amber's spin classes at the last four gyms where she'd been an instructor. Unfortunately, Amber's eye for a handsome face, especially those that were already spoken for, combined with her lack of tact, made it hard for employers to keep her on staff for very long.

Tone turning as icy as the weather outside, Bailey replied, "I do care what my husband thinks. But I wouldn't freeze my rear end off for him or any guy..." Her words trailed off as the car suddenly veered to the right. Catching the wheel, she eased it back to the center of the road.

Amber crossed her arms over her chest. "I still can't believe you dragged me through a snowdrift in the middle of a blizzard for nothing."

"The blizzard hasn't caught us yet, and there was no way of knowing if someone was in that car until we got down to it. And if there were, I couldn't have hauled them back up to the road in the middle of the storm by myself."

"I went, didn't I? Anyway, it's not that I'm ungrateful, 'cuz I know you spent a lot on this trip to celebrate your recovery, and it was super cute how you bought this little guy to reveal the surprise..." she swatted at the grinning god, "...but this whole thing sucks. Did you hear what that guy at the rental car place said? If we don't park at the right angle and hold on to the doors when we open 'em, the winds can freakin' rip 'em off! That's insane!" She slumped deeper into her seat. "I told you, we shoulda' gone to Greece, not some island at the north pole!"

"Iceland is not at the north pole. And tourism in the Greek islands shuts down after October—there would've been nothing to do there."

Amber thrust a hand toward the windshield. "What's there to do here besides die a miserable death?"

Bailey allowed the hidden side of her mouth to quirk upward. Amber was right. Dying a miserable death in Iceland was definitely on the agenda. The only question was which of the two friends would leave the island alive.

~

Gym-sculpted buttocks bounced against Bailey's shoulder as she brought the SUV to a stop about fifteen feet from the front door of the concrete-walled farmhouse.

"Don't turn off the engine yet!" Amber called over her shoulder as she plunged headlong into the back seat.

"What're you doing?" Bailey demanded.

"Getting my stuff. I'm not walking around to the trunk in this insanity!"

Shifting the engine into park, Bailey watched in the rearview mirror as Amber hefted her monogrammed carry-on over the back seat.

Her gaze slipped back to the structure illuminated in the headlights. In the time it had taken them to traverse the winding road up from the highway, the blizzard had arrived in full force.

She could barely make out the details before her. Roof bearing the weight of a few feet of snow, glow from the windows all but iced over, with drifts piling up all around, the farmhouse appeared to be sinking in a sea of white. Bailey could relate.

Zipping up her parka, she pulled her neck gaiter over her nose and secured her hood. Steeling muscles she had worked hard to gain back, Bailey unlocked the car door and placed both hands against it.

The door almost tore from her grasp as if a frost giant from the sagas had grabbed the other side. The high stakes tug-of-war chilled her bones deeper than the frigid air blasting into the vehicle.

"Holy shit!" Amber screamed. "Do you want me to die of hypothermia? Close the damn door!"

It took some doing, but Bailey complied. Slumping back against her seat, she gave voice to the inevitable. "It's crazy out there."

"Told you so!" Bailey's simple, gray canvas duffel joined Amber's on the back seat with a thump. "Since it was your dumb idea to come here, you can go check us in."

Bailey shot a bewildered look over her shoulder. "Are you serious?"

"Hell, yes! What if they don't answer the door right away? I'm not gonna stand out in this deep freeze for one more second than I have to!"

"The owner's email said they'd leave the front door unlocked for us."

Amber's movie star features turned to granite. Bailey knew the expression all too well. There would be nothing she could say or do to change Amber's mind. Instead, she took another deep breath of feline wastewater.

"Fine." Bailey reached back and dragged the duffel between the front seats. Slipping the strap diagonally over her head, she grabbed the door handle, leaned her left shoulder into it, and pushed.

"Hurry on, it's freezing!" Amber whined.

"I'm trying," Bailey grunted through clenched teeth. Where she was pushing in one moment, in the next she was holding on for dear life as the door suddenly threatened to blow out of her hands.

She waited until the wind slammed the door back against her shoulder. Another push and she dropped down into a cushion of fresh snow. Her calves disappeared in deep powder.

It took some doing before she could manage to slam the door shut behind her. She plodded toward the house with the jerky movements of an old stop-motion character.

Wind screeched against either side of her hood like a scorned banshee. In one second it flattened the fabric tight against her head, then it promised to tear it off completely.

The time for fun and flirtation had passed. Nature had come to collect its due for the bounties bequeathed in the preceding three seasons. Clenching her teeth, Bailey concentrated on the idea that Amber's long overdue tab was about to join the collection effort.

A sudden gust from behind sent her reeling face-first. She got her hands out just in time to avoid calamity. Righting herself, she pushed through the last several feet to the front door.

She reached for the handle and prayed to the Norse gods.

~

Bailey entered the living room of the farmhouse accompanied by a blast of icy white air. After a brief, but pitched, battle she managed to shut the door.

"Gott kvöld," a feminine voice called out behind her.

Pulling down her gaiter, Bailey spun around to find a sixty-something blonde woman studying her. A neat gray braid rested over the stranger's left shoulder framing a kindly face. Wearing charcoal leggings with an oversized sweater, she stood at least a head taller than Bailey.

"Gott kvöld, Hildur." Bailey repeated the greeting tacking on the name she'd seen on the confirmation email.

"Would you prefer English?"

"Please. My Icelandic is not very good."

Gentle hands took hold of Bailey's parka."I hope you made it here without too much trouble from the storm."

"Yes, thank you."

"And your companion? You are registered for two travelers, correct?" She hung the heavy coat on a peg by the door with quiet efficiency.

"My friend is in the car. She asked me to come in first while she gets her things."

"Okay. You can leave your boots on the mat by the door."

Bailey cast her gaze about the room as she set to work. Simple Scandinavian touches throughout the open plan made for an enchanting oasis.

A beige sofa with a coffee table sat along the left wall. To the right, an oak dining table with four chairs stood near a massive wooden island in the middle of the open kitchen. Indirect light shone from under the upper cabinets. The walls and ceiling were alive with the golden glow from candles of various shapes and sizes sprinkled throughout the living space.

Boots stowed, Bailey made her way toward the couch in her wool socks. Her shoulders, which had been near her ears since they had first ventured out on the road, eased back down as she moved.

"Your home is absolutely lovely," Bailey breathed.

"Tak," Hildur shook her head. "Sorry, I mean thank you."

"Thank you for opening up your home to travelers."

"It's my pleasure. It was so lonely here after my husband died. This farm has been in my family for generations. I needed a way to keep it going and this has done the trick. Besides the money, it helps to have guests around."

"I'm very sorry for your loss."

"I've grown used to it. Are you married?"

"Yes." Bailey forced a smile. "That reminds me, I'd better let my husband know I made it here." She pulled out her phone.

Hi Babe! Made it to the rental safe and sound. Weather's crazier than expected and the drive was really sketchy. But we made it. Call you when we're settled!

The message to her husband of the last six years dripped with lies. What it lacked in truth, it made up for in utility. Seeking to sweeten the pot, she added a few kiss emojis.

The warm scent of baked apples and sugar

enveloped Bailey as she hit send. Her nose instinctively turned toward the kitchen.

Hildur explained. "I always make dessert for our guests. Meals are up to you."

Nodding, Bailey walked to the nearby window and pulled back the drape. Amber was a few feet from the front door dragging her carry-on through the snow. The blonde shook violently, fumbling with her burden while being plummeted by the taciturn winds.

"Is your friend on her way?"

Bailey dropped the window covering. "She is."

"Good. I'm going to catch up on email. I'll be just down the hall. Call out when your friend arrives and I'll show you to your rooms."

Bailey watched the woman disappear into the hallway before turning back to the window. Lifting the drape, she retrieved the keys from her pocket and held the fob an inch from the window. The SUV's headlights blinked a couple of times before all light from the vehicle was extinguished.

The car was locked. Amber had no way back. Dropping the drape again, Bailey's eyes drifted to the brass deadbolt mounted above the front door's handle.

Without thinking, she drifted closer and closer until her index finger made contact with the cold metal. Bailey traced the outline of the lock with her fingertip. *It would be so easy...*

Someone who was already poorly dressed and suffering from their earlier foray into the elements would not last long outside. Not if they couldn't get into the car...

Amber had mentioned hypothermia. It had almost been an invitation...

She threw the bolt into place just as the door handle began to move. One step back, and then another. Each punctuated by a high metal whine as the door handle shifted manically from left to right.

The corner of the couch stopped Bailey just as thunder broke out on the other side of the door. The sound was laden with desperation—a violent knocking that set the door bouncing in its frame.

A voice screamed out in her head, *what about Hildur?* Sprinting back to the entrance, Bailey threw back the bolt and pulled the door open.

Whirling snow formed a corona around Amber who stood with all the imperious fury of a wrathful ice witch. "Why did you lock the freakin' door?" she railed as she dragged the luggage behind her across the threshold.

Letting the frosty air quell inner rage, Bailey

feigned innocence, "I didn't. The latch must have stuck."

"That can happen. Old things don't always work as well as new ones. I can tell you from experience." Hildur emerged from the hallway. She set about offering her new guest the same hospitality she'd shown to Bailey.

An hour later, Amber sat on the couch sullenly scrolling through her social media feeds. In the kitchen, Bailey helped Hildur put away the last of the dishes.

"Thank you again for making dinner for us. I know it's not included in our stay."

Hildur nodded. "That storm didn't give you many options. I'm just glad I had enough for all three of us. And thank you for helping with the clean up."

She cast a pointed look over at Amber, who had retired to the couch after pushing her food around on her plate without bothering to taste what had been offered. Bailey watched as Hildur's gaze dropped to Amber's stripe-socked feet crossed atop the coffee table.

"I'm sorry," Bailey offered before hanging her hand towel over the oven handle and scurrying over to her friend's side.

Bailey could see Amber's texting app was

open, but her friend dropped the device to her chest before she could make out with whom Amber had been corresponding.

"Really Amber?"

Moody blue eyes rolled laconically in her direction. "Really what?"

"Your feet? Hildur lives here, you know."

"I'm on vacation. This is what I'd do at a hotel. Staying at someone's house is ridiculous. There's not even a damn TV here."

Bailey gently lifted the striped socks and swung them under the table. "Hildur has a beautiful home, and she's allowing us to live like Icelanders. No hotel could offer us all this."

"Whatever." Amber groused, turning back to her screen.

Bailey opened her mouth to reply but Hildur cut her off. "Iceland is not for everyone. My ancestors fought hard to make this land habitable when they first sailed to these shores."

Tucking the last plate into the cabinet, she turned back to stand at the island. Light from a short candelabra danced across her fair features. "They took to this land, learning its ways and growing from their relationship with it. Over time it has come to accept us. Perhaps that's because we accept it for what it is."

She looked wistful. “Here we find more value in books than television. Weather like this...” the dull howl of the storm grew louder as she paused, “...is perfect for reading. It is a solitary pursuit that does not let you hide away from who you are. This island is like that, and this weather is a part of it. They have a way of revealing who we are. Sometimes that is not so easy to see. Art helps us to see the truth about ourselves and the world around us.”

Shaking her head, she turned to Bailey. “Did you hear back from your husband yet?”

Pulling her phone out, Bailey found confirmation of what she had already guessed. “No. He’s a lawyer and it’s the middle of his workday back home. I probably won’t hear from him until he has a break.”

Amber’s lips drew into a dark smile, but she remained silent, other than the frantic tapping of her thumbs on the phone screen.

“But he knew about the storm, yes?” Hildur pressed.

Bailey’s eyes narrowed for a split second. “Yes.”

“Ah, well I’m sure you’re right. How about some dessert?”

Amber grunted something resembling a negative while Bailey joined Hildur back in the kitchen. The two women spent the next few hours chatting amiably at the dining table about how Hildur's mother had knitted the lopapesa she wore, how Icelanders give books at Christmas and local lore about the mountain behind the farmhouse.

Bailey's gaze had often drifted to Amber, specifically to her phone. Other than a few failed entreaties to join them at the table, she hadn't bothered to directly engage with her friend.

As unmovable as Amber had been, Bailey found Hildur a much harder nut to crack. By the time she headed to bed, she still had no idea whether the older woman had seen her try to lock Amber out earlier.

Bailey awoke with a start. Light from the electric candle on the nightstand eased the transition from the dream world. The blizzard was still busy having its say outside, but it wasn't as loud as it had been earlier.

Laying on her right side, facing the heavily draped window, she recalled what had awakened her. A floorboard creaking from somewhere behind her—the exact sound she heard in her dream.

Hazarding a look over her shoulder, she caught the outline of a figure standing over the bed. Before she knew what she was doing, she opened her mouth and screamed.

"What is going on here?" Hildur demanded turning on the overhead light.

Her expression shifted in the faux candlelight. It happened so fast, that Bailey had no idea what she had actually seen.

Hopping out of bed, Bailey turned to find Amber standing on the other side of it. She watched her friend jam something into the pocket of her fleece pajama bottoms and take a step back.

"Well?" Hildur looked from one of her guests to the other.

Face scrubbed clean of makeup, Amber raked a hand through her hair. "I dunno. She was calling out in her sleep. I came in to help her settle down, but she woke up all of a sudden and started screaming."

Hildur looked to Bailey whose gaze was fixed on the lump in Amber's pocket. "Was it a nightmare?"

Bailey met her eye. "I'm sorry, Hildur, I think

so. I guess waking up suddenly to find someone else in the room freaked me out a bit."

"Want me to fix you a warm drink?"

"That's very sweet of you, but I'll be fine." Bailey climbed back under the sheets.

"You sure you'll be alright tonight?" the older woman asked.

"I will, thank you. I'm very sorry I woke you." Her gaze drifted to Amber. "Both of you."

Amber murmured something unintelligible and slinked past their host. Once Hildur was gone, Bailey crept from her bed and locked the door. For good measure, she shoved her duffle against it.

Otherworldly icebergs floated across the lake beneath heavily leaden skies. Water lapped gently against the shore of Jökulsárlón, delivering a bounty of tiny turquoise gems at Bailey's feet. Across the lake, Vatnajökull glacier lay sprawled between the mountains, watching over its wayward progeny like a drunken giant who'd fallen and had no reason to get up.

A few feet down the shore, Amber was busy mugging for the camera. Looking no worse for wear after last night's storm, she posed for selfies, alternating between coquettish smiles and open-mouthed invitations.

Scores of other tourists milled about. Except for Amber, all were clad in serious winter gear. The blonde bombshell had drawn questioning gazes from the other tourists for her white cable knit mini dress paired with a white puffer jacket. Below inches of exposed skin, her thigh-high stockings sought to offer some semblance of warmth before disappearing into knee-high boots. Almond-colored fur lining unified the outfit—at the hem of her dress, around her hood, and at the tops of her boots.

Lowering her camera, Amber bounded over to Bailey. "Got what I needed. Let's get the hell out of here! I'm freakin' freezing!"

Bailey turned her gaze back on the serene landscape.

"Don't just stand there, let's go!" Amber demanded.

"Are you sure you want to?"

Amber rolled her eyes. "You promised the next spot is the best spot for pics." Tucking her phone in her pocket, she zipped up her jacket and grabbed hold of Bailey's arm. "Come on!"

Bailey leveled her friend with a thousand-yard gaze. "Okay."

Less than ten minutes later, Bailey was pulling back off the highway and into another parking lot.

"Diamond Beach?" Amber asked, reading a large sign.

"A river runs from the lake and empties here into the North Atlantic." Bailey pulled into a spot and turned off the engine.

"Forget it!"

"Why?"

"We're on a damn island. If you've seen one beach you've seen them all. I mean, it's not like beaches in Bora Bora."

"Bora Bora has nothing like this..."

"I can't do any more stupid countryside crap. Let's go back to Reykjavik. At least they had decent shopping there."

"No!"

The vehemence in Bailey's tone caught Amber's response in her throat.

Noting the blonde eyebrows tightening with uncharacteristic worry, Bailey took a deep breath and slumped back against the seat. "I'm sorry," she murmured. "It's just that we...

"We've been through a lot over the years, Amber. And we are fundamentally different people. I guess..." A flood of memories came back, chasing away the anger that had burned in Bailey since she began to recover.

The earliest memory of discovering the pinup beauty she'd seen in Chem class trying to wrestle a plastic bag off the head of a stray cat on the north side of campus. In the end, both girls had been covered in scratches and the cat had hightailed it for some nearby shrubs.

It was followed by the time Amber dumped a guy who had questioned why a beauty like Amber hung out with a nobody like Bailey. And then there was what had been the memory that had been the worst of any in Bailey's life.

The night Bailey's mom had lain dying in the hospital after a car crash. She had been raised by an adoring single mother with an open, giving nature, who had taught her to always see the good in people.

Amber had stayed up with her all night. Pacing with her through the hours when there was hope. And holding her as she sobbed through the moment when the doctors announced there was no more hope to be had. Amber had been a daily fixture in Bailey's life for the next three months, teaching her to sail on waters for which she no longer had an anchor. Of course, she'd also moved into Bailey's place and had been living rent-free for the entire time she'd been "helping" her get over the painful loss.

Bailey closed her eyes.

"You guess...?" Amber prodded quietly.

Brown eyes slowly reappeared. "I guess I've lost sight of things lately."

Amber squeezed the white puffer tighter across her thighs and stared awkwardly out the front window. "No, you didn't. You never do." She turned and looked out the right-side window. "You're a really good person, B. One of the best. You never make mistakes, but you're always there to clean up everyone else's."

When she turned back to Bailey, tears sparkled from the corners of her eyes. "It's hard to live up to your standards. I'm not as good as you, B. I never will be. I don't deserve you." Her lips trembled. "I'm just so glad we didn't lose you. I still don't know how those doctors cured you, but I'm so grateful they did."

Bailey unlocked her seatbelt and shot across the front seat. "Maybe we deserve each other," she choked as she wrapped her arms around her friend.

More recent memories flooded back. Wasting away in the hospital bed that had been set up in the guest room. Drifting between consciousness and sleep. The horrible trial required for doctor visits. So many questions with no answers. And the worst part of all—feeling she had lost the fight and was read to surrender to a world without pain.

When the answers came, the pain increased beyond her wildest imaginings. Nothing her body had felt could compare with the sensation of having her heart chewed up by reality.

It had happened in the wee hours of a summer night. She'd first believed the snippets of conversation from the hallway were fragments of a dream. The vile truths whispered between her husband and best friend had been too impossible to comprehend.

Believing Bailey was still asleep, they had rehashed the lurid details of what had transpired during the alleged business trip to Colorado fourteen months before. The hits kept coming with the name of the strange-sounding drug, Bailey's sizable inheritance, and Amber's annoyance that she had not yet succumbed to the poison in her nightly tea.

Matt had been too dumb to notice that the palm near her nightstand started to die about the same time Bailey started to recover. His betrayal had been bad enough. But Amber had been a sister to her. A sister for whom Bailey had sacrificed so much, including crucial time from her marriage.

It hadn't been enough for Amber to take her money and her time over the years. She had to take the very last thing that she had promised she never would—Bailey's husband and worse than that—her life.

The longer they embraced, the more the light in and around the SUV brightened. Warmth blossomed across Bailey's face.

She opened her eyes to find the sun hanging low over the horizon. Pulling away, she pointed out the window over Amber's shoulder. "Sun's coming out!" she crowed. "This is going to be perfect!"

Bailey reached into the center console and pulled out a package of tissues. "Now fix your face. Your Instagram fans are about to be blown away!"

Amber accepted the proffer. "We could always go back to Reykjavik…"

"Do you trust me?"

Amber smiled. "Always have."

"Good. I brought you halfway around the world, let's go find out why!"

"All right then." Amber yanked her bag from the back seat and set about touching up her makeup.

Minutes later, Amber stowed her beauty tools and announced, "Let's do it!"

No sooner had Bailey closed the car door behind her, than Amber struck her from behind, wrapping her in a bear hug. They duck-walked toward the shore teasing each other about some of the worst guys they had dated in college.

Bailey didn't bother to interrupt the shared good humor by stopping to read any of the signs posted about. Eventually, the hard-packed earth gave way to loose ebony-colored sand as they headed down a small embankment.

Face pelted by the viciously wild wind blowing in off the North Atlantic, Bailey threw her arms wide. "Welcome to Diamond Beach!"

Fur whipping around her face, Amber stood transfixed by the reflection of what appeared to be diamonds littering the shore. Some were as impossibly large as boulders, others so small they might fit on a ring.

Sunlight illuminated them from within, transforming each block of ice into a chunk of mind-boggling beauty. Strewn out across the expanse of black sand, they looked like the proud display of a world-class jeweler's most precious collection.

Bailey grabbed her hand. "What do you think?"

Amber turned, scanning one side of the beach and then the other. The unusual formations continued as far as the eye could see in both directions. "Wha...what is this place?"

"Remember the river?"

"Yeah."

"It carries icebergs down from the lake to the ocean,tide polishes them before depositing them back onto the black sand. At the lake, they looked blue because the sky was overcast, but in the sunlight they look like diamonds."

The last word was punctuated by a short cry from Amber. "OMG! Look at the waves crash around them!"

The two women waited in silence until foamy white froth erupted again between the polished glass.

"These are gonna be the best pics ever!" Amber exclaimed as she ran toward the water.

Bailey hurried along after her. About thirty yards away, a couple cast smiling glances in their direction before turning their attention back to the stars of the shore. The rest of the tourists littering the beach paid them little attention, all equally lost in the magic.

Reaching the line of mini icebergs, Amber scrambled back and forth like a child freshly arrived through Main Street at Disneyland, unsure which world to lose themself in first. She settled on a massive one that stretched lengthwise, its proportions as perfect as a marble chaise carved by Michelangelo.

Her voice dropped five octaves. "Imagine me laying on this when a wave breaks around me! Serious little mermaid, slash snow princess, slash sexy-chic!"

Bailey didn't bother to ask for a translation. Instead, she grinned at her friend's childish enthusiasm and pulled out her phone. "Let me know when you're ready for me to start taking pics!"

Amber took her time considering the berg from every angle. Finally, she dropped down on her haunches to the left of the icy bench and bellowed triumphantly, "This is perfect!"

"I'm on it," Bailey announced gamely as she trotted to the indicated location.

She took a knee on the sand, steadying herself against another berg as she lowered herself down.

As she descended, the shape of a smaller bit of ice caught her eye. Wedged just below Amber's targeted backdrop, it reminded Bailey of the ring Matt had given her.

The one that squeezed uncomfortably into her left glove. The one that represented everything that had gone wrong.

In the next moment, her ring finger seemed to burn with the strength of a thousand suns. The heat extended through her body, searing her with shame, humiliation, and betrayal.

She watched as Amber clambered onto the icy chaise, the wind plastering her jacket to her body, blue veins standing out against the milky white skin on her thighs.

Bailey felt her lips parting to call out a warning—a reminder of the warnings posted all around the beach. The ones Amber hadn't bothered to read. Warnings of the unforgiving North Atlantic tides that too often claimed the lives of tourists caught unawares. The same North Atlantic that could deliver Bailey of the pain Amber had caused her by destroying her marriage to the one man she had ever loved. The warning froze in her throat.

Amber rose to her knees. Grabbing the hem

of her miniskirt, she tucked her chin and parted her lips.

Bailey watched as a dark blue menace rose behind her best friend, gathering its strength from the undertow as it prepared a violent assault on the island.

"Take it!" Amber called out playfully, waiting for Bailey to raise the camera.

She did as instructed, watching the screen as the seething giant rose above Amber. Tapping the screen, Bailey whispered, "Take her, please."

Nature's neat efficiency stole her next breath away. In one heartbeat, Amber was alone posing for the camera. In the next heartbeat, a wall of water smashed over the icebergs, rushing up the beach and flooding around Bailey's ankles.

Despite all the planning, Bailey screamed in horror as Amber was dragged out with the surf. Her blood-curdling cry rose over the pounding crash of the sea to startle the nearby couple.

Her high-pitched screeching continued long after Amber's fur-lined hood disappeared. The couple reached her just as she crumpled to the sand. By the time the emergency responders had come and gone, Bailey was numb and Amber was dead.

Thanks to the island's great wi-fi, Amber had

achieved the level of fame she'd always wanted. The couple had been live streaming for their YouTube travel channel. Thousands had watched Amber's final moments on Earth.

Alone on the beach, Bailey reached into her pocket and removed the little figure she'd pulled from the rearview mirror when they'd left the SUV. Staring down at the god's toothy grin, she recalled how calculating she'd been when she bought it to surprise Amber with news of the trip. Yet another way to assure her friend everything was as it had always been between them.

Her fingers tightened around the bit of plastic as a single tear slipped down her cheek. Gritting her teeth, she hurled the figure as far past the breakers as she could.

A police vehicle was parked in front of the farmhouse. Bailey coaxed her SUV alongside it and killed the engine.

She stalked toward the entrance, careful to trade her relieved expression for one of grief. Inside, the officer who had questioned her at the beach sat alongside Hildur at the dining room table. About ten years older than Bailey, his deeply lined face was impossible to read. A plate littered with crumbs from last night's apple pastry sat before him.

He and Hildur had steaming cups in their hands. Both raised their eyes in Bailey's direction as she began stripping off her parka and boots.

"Halló again, Ms. Ryder." His voice was as inscrutable as his expression.

"Halló."

"Officer Jacobsson came to complete his paperwork on your friend," Hildur explained, standing and fetching another mug from the cabinet. "I helped him find her passport."

"Thank you. I'm not sure I could face going through her things..." Doing her best imitation of the quivering lower lip Amber had used to get herself out of more than one parking ticket, Bailey, raised her fist to her mouth to stifle a sob.

"Here," Hildur swept over, gently pressing a cup of aromatic tea into Bailey's hands. Sympathy swam in her eyes. "Some days are far harder than others. Go to your room. I'll check on you soon."

Grateful to be out of the line of fire, Bailey nodded to the officer and headed down the hall.

Leaving her door open, Bailey perched at the edge of her bed. Hushed Icelandic voices tickled her ears. She hadn't done anything she reminded herself.

It was the beauty of the plan. She hadn't actually killed Amber. In fact, she had never even told her to go anywhere near the water.

The irony of it all was that Matt, Amber's stupid accomplice, had given her the idea. One night in bed, instead of keeping his cheating mouth shut so she could sleep, he'd mumbled to her about a brief he was preparing on a case—something called an attractive nuisance case. He explained that certain things were so attractive to people that they often put themselves in harm's way just to get to them.

After he had fallen asleep, it hadn't taken long to settle on Diamond Beach on the internet. Travel blogs and internet sites were as cautionary about the dangerous tides at the beach as the signs erected around it. The fact that multiple tourists had been swept out to sea there sealed the deal.

The bet had paid off. The beach's incredible beauty had made it impossible for Amber to resist pushing the boundaries for the perfect shot. Bailey hadn't had to do a single thing, other than take her there, and there was no crime in visiting a tourist attraction.

A few moments later, chair legs scraped

against the hardwood floor in the other room. Footsteps. More Icelandic. The front door opened and closed. Bailey exhaled.

It didn't take Hildur long. She came to lean against the door frame, sage blue eyes taking inventory. "I'm sorry you lost your friend."

"Thank you."

"They say when one door closes another door opens."

Bailey nodded, taking a sip of tea.

Hildur continued. "Sometimes those we love are a burden too great to bear."

Fighting to swallow the scorching liquid, Bailey cast a wary eye over her host.

"My husband was such a burden. But he was taken away from me, just as your friend has been taken from you."

Frowning Bailey lowered her mug to her lap. "What do you mean?

"I mean the lock on the front door doesn't stick." She turned on her heel without waiting for a response.

Smiling to herself, Bailey pulled out her phone. Matt still hadn't responded to last night's email. It was a safe bet he'd been messaging with Amber. That wouldn't happen anymore. Her phone, along with its owner, was on a permanent trip around the Atlantic Ocean.

Opening the internet, Bailey started searching for the perfect spot to take Matt on vacation. Two victims of attractive nuisances in a short period of time would be a problem. That was fine. Bailey could wait.

After all, Matt had just lost the woman for whom he'd been willing to kill. Bailey couldn't imagine anyone she'd enjoy watching suffer as much as her husband. Actually, there was one, but she was already dead.

WHITEOUT

ANNIE REED

Nobody ever expects to get caught in a blizzard. Especially not driving alone at night on a two-lane highway in the middle of the Nevada desert.

Bad enough, you think, but you're a good driver. Slow down, concentrate on the center line. On the taillights of the only other car on the road with you. You're following those taillights like they're a pilot car leading you out of the wilderness, and you pray those lights don't lead you off a cliff. You tell yourself you'll be fine even though the heavy snow blowing right at your windshield is blinding white in your headlights, and it's given you the mother of all tension headaches.

You keep thinking you'll be okay right up to the moment something slams into you and you find yourself spinning out of control on a road that's as slick as an ice rink.

Until you realize the truck hit you on purpose because it's coming at you again, and you find yourself wondering if you're going to survive long enough to unwrap the present your girlfriend left for you beneath the dinky little Christmas tree in the apartment you share with three of your buddies.

Christmas Eve had started out pretty good for Kit Chalmers. In fact, since he'd started it off in bed with his girlfriend—the first time they'd spent the entire night together—it was pretty much the best Christmas Eve he'd had in his nineteen years.

Sure, she had to leave to drive home to Reno to spend Christmas Day with her parents. But she'd promised to come back as soon as she could get away so they could spend the rest of winter break together before the next semester started at UNLV. And she'd left him a little present with strict instructions not to open it until Christmas morning.

"I'll know if you open it early," she'd said.

His buddies had given him all sorts of shit about it.

She's going to find a hunk back home. Transfer up to UNR, and that'll be that.

He probably deserved it. Andrea was a stone-cold fox and smart to boot. Kit? He wasn't. Tall and gangly and not what anyone in their right mind would call handsome—he certainly wouldn't—he'd been into computer games and all sorts of trading card games when he'd been in high school. At least, when he could afford to buy the stuff, which wasn't often.

When it came to girls, his high school life had been pretty pathetic. He'd only had a handful of dates. Except for one less-than-memorable fumbling in the back seat of a buddy's car after a party, he would have graduated still a virgin. Mostly he'd gone out in groups with his buddies and their girlfriends, a perpetual third-wheel.

He had no idea what Andrea saw in him, but he wasn't about to question his good luck. Sure, he wished the two of them could spend Christmas Day together, and he would have been a little worried she might find somebody better back home even if his buddies weren't razzing him about it. But there was that present under his tree. That had to mean something, right?

He'd been about to settle in for a marathon computer game one of his roommates had bought himself as an early Christmas present when Andrea called. She sounded totally freaked out. Her car had broken down right outside of Tonopah.

"It's after four on Christmas Eve," she said. "There's no place open around here where I can get it fixed. I was lucky this guy stopped to help me push it off the road."

Kit had been in Tonopah a couple of times when his family went to Reno on vacation. It wasn't exactly what you'd call a city. It wasn't even much of a town.

"Can you come get me?" she asked. "If you leave now, we could make it to Reno by midnight or one. Please?"

He didn't want to think about the logistics, but he couldn't help it. He was in school on a couple of little scholarships and a part-time busboy job at a local restaurant. He didn't have enough money to rent a motel room, even a cheap motel room. If there was even a room available on Christmas Eve.

She lowered her voice on the phone. "Please, Kit? I don't like it here. They've been nice to me, but they know I'm all by myself, and you know what it's like out here." Her voice got even quieter. "I don't feel safe, and this place gives me the creeps."

The middle of the state was full of right-wingers. Easy to tell from the election billboards he'd seen on the drive up to Reno. That had been a couple of years ago, and he doubted things had gotten better since then. According to his PolySci professor, the whole country was going to hell in a handbasket. He'd gotten a weird vibe from the locals when his parents had stopped for gas, like they were sizing him up and finding him barely worth their contempt. He'd never been more glad when his parents had ordered their fast-food meals to-go. That had been during the middle of summer when it was all light and bright in the

Nevada desert. Not at the end of December when it was all dark and cold.

He told Andrea to hold on a minute while he brought up the weather app on his phone and looked up Tonopah. Light snow showers, it said. Then he brought up his map app and asked it how long it would take him to get to Tonopah. Two hours and forty minutes. He figured he could shave at least twenty minutes off that if he drove a bit over the speed limit.

Where he'd stay once he got to Reno would work itself out. His girlfriend was asking him to come rescue her. Not her parents. Not any of her Reno friends. (Okay, the drive from Reno to Tonopah was a lot longer, but still.) No, she'd asked him. What kind of a boyfriend would he be if he said no?

A jerk, that's who.

He told her he'd be there in two and a half hours, give or take.

Then he'd asked her where he was supposed to meet her, expecting it would be the same big combination mini-mart/gas station/fast food place in Tonopah where his parents had stopped to gas up and grab burgers.

Only it wasn't.

If he wasn't sure he was halfway in love—

maybe all the way in love—he might have called the whole thing off.

She was waiting for him at the damn Clown Motel

~

Kit had been okay with clowns until he spent the summer with his cousins when he was eight years old.

That had been the year his mom got sick. Even now, Kit was a little vague on the details. Most of what he remembered was that she'd had to go to the doctor a lot and felt pretty rotten when she was home. His dad tried to take up the slack, which meant Kit got a lot of extra chores added to his list. Like taking out the garbage, cleaning the downstairs bathroom, and mowing the lawn. He'd still been pretty small then and pushing the mower hadn't been easy, and he had to hold the handle just right or the motor would shut off. But he did it.

Right up until his aunt and uncle had offered to let Kit stay with them the entire month of July.

Which meant Kit had to sleep in his cousins' room.

His cousins were three and four years older

than Kit and way bigger. They were also into sports and riding their bikes and wrestling with each other, which they called practice because his older cousin wanted to make the wrestling team. They didn't like getting saddled with Kit whenever they went out to play or just hang out at a neighborhood convenience store with their friends.

Kit didn't like having to tag along with them either. He would have rather stayed inside, reading a book or playing a game on the tablet his parents had given him the year before at Christmas.

The Christmas before his mom got sick.

But his uncle was adamant. Boys should play outside, not stay inside and read. Only sissy boys kept their heads in books when they could be outside.

The one time Kit had been in Tonopah with his parents—he'd been older then, and his mom had long since recovered from whatever had made her so sick that summer—he thought his uncle would have been right at home in a town like that.

So Kit's cousins hated him, and he wasn't all that thrilled with them. But he hung in there and tried to stay out of their way. And one day he let it slip that he thought clowns were creepy. Not scary. Just creepy. All that white face makeup made them look like they were dead.

That's all he'd said.

Two nights later, he woke up in the middle of the night to find a clown face inches from his own.

He slept on an air mattress on the floor of his cousins' bedroom. He was supposed to sleep in his younger cousin's bed, according to his aunt, but the cousins had made it clear they weren't giving up their beds for a pest like him, so it was the air mattress or nothing. Kit told himself he didn't mind the mattress —he was the smallest anyway, and he didn't have to make his bed in the morning, just fold up the sheet.

He would have screamed when he woke from a sound sleep to see that clown face, but the clown had his beefy hand clamped down over Kit's mouth.

"Scared of clowns now, you little shit?" the clown asked.

Its leering grin didn't change, and Kit realized the clown face was a mask. Instead of eyes, it had deep black holes that seemed to glitter with evil intent in the dark of his cousins' room.

Kit couldn't answer with his mouth covered up. He tried to shake his head, but he couldn't move. The clown was straddling him, his heavy body pressing Kit into the mattress.

"Clowns aren't just creepy," the clown said. Its voice was rough and raspy and distorted by the mask. "Clowns are out to eat you. Bite your pecker right off."

Kit had heard his uncle call penises peckers, so he knew what the clown meant. It made his own penis shrivel up inside his pajama pants.

"Or maybe we'll just do this."

With that, the clown used its free hand to hit him.

And it wasn't just one clown. A second clown mask swam into view through tears that had gathered in Kit's eyes. This clown didn't hold him, it just punched him. Its punches weren't as hard but they hurt just the same.

Kit tried to fight back, but he wasn't very good at it. He tried to roll into a ball, but he couldn't do that either.

The clowns seemed to hit him forever, but they finally stopped. The one straddling him leaned in closer. "If you tell anyone about this, we'll come back and do it again. You don't want that, do you?"

Kit had managed to shake his head no.

"Shut your eyes, little boy," the clown said, and Kit did.

When he opened them again, the clowns were gone.

It wasn't until the last day he spent at his cousins' house, when he went to get his suitcase out of the basement so he could pack up all his clothes, that he found two clown costumes inside a half-open cardboard box. Halloween costumes.

He'd been so scared that night, he'd never considered that his cousins had deliberately put on old Halloween costumes just so they could beat him up. They'd never teased him about it, never said a thing, and he'd been too frightened and too embarrassed to tell anyone what had happened. If it wasn't for the bruises, he might have thought it was all a horrible nightmare.

Even though he knew real clowns hadn't beat him up, it didn't matter. Kit couldn't stand clowns. He'd had to close his eyes when his parents drove past the Clown Motel with its huge-ass clown right next to the highway on the way out of Tonopah. Even at nineteen, he was still deep down terrified of clowns.

And now he had to go pick up Andrea at the Clown Motel.

Childhood trauma was a bitch.

The snow started to really come down when Kit passed through Goldfield, a blink-and-you'd-miss-it town about a half hour to the south of Tonopah. One fat, wet snowflake after another, splatting on his windshield.

Scattered snow showers? Really?

Kit shivered. The temperature outside must really be dropping. He should have thrown his sweatshirt on the passenger seat in case he needed to put it on under his jacket, but he'd stuffed the sweatshirt in his duffel along with his laptop and a couple of changes of clothes, and he'd put all that in the trunk. He'd figured he wouldn't need to layer up until he got to Reno. So much for that idea.

He'd inherited his car from his parents. It had been old when they bought it, and the heater wasn't the best. He turned it up anyway. He didn't need to turn on the heat much in Vegas, just like he didn't need snow tires. For the first time he wondered if he should have called his parents and asked to borrow their car. They had a four-wheel drive, which would have done marginally better in the snow.

At least the road, or what he could see of it, still looked wet, not frozen.

A couple of minutes later he switched from heater to defroster when his windshield started to fog up. He had to really concentrate to see the taillights in front of him through the heavy snow. There was next to no traffic on the two-lane highway north out of Las Vegas. In fact, he couldn't remember the last time he'd seen any headlights coming toward him heading south.

Maybe people just weren't out driving this late because it was Christmas Eve and most people were already where they wanted to go. Like Andrea would have been if he hadn't kept her late at his apartment with their own celebration. Like she'd be if her car hadn't broken down.

The thicker the snow got, the harder it was to tell where the road was. He concentrated more on following the taillights in front of him than trying to see a center line that had gone practically invisible.

At least the car ahead of him had slowed down when the snow really started coming down. When the speed limit went back up right after Goldfield, the car had passed him like he was standing still. He'd gotten a brief look at a slick-looking sedan with the driver illuminated by the dashboard lights, then the car had streaked past. Now Kit had a good chance of following the car, although he had to drive faster than he really wanted to in these conditions.

His windshield wipers were starting to build up a berm of snow at the base of his windshield. If the snow kept up like this, he was going to have to stop to scrape the snow away, only then he'd be lost without his pilot car. He'd have to drive even slower, creep along to make sure he didn't drive off the road.

He'd read about glow-in-the-dark lines on roadways in some European country. Why couldn't they have things like that out here in the middle of nowhere where you really, really needed to see the lines on the damn road? Come to think of it, why was this highway only two lanes wide? Did that make sense when it was the major road between Vegas and Reno, the state's biggest cities?

Kit grumbled to himself. He couldn't even call Andrea and tell her he'd be late picking her up. His cell phone had zero bars out here, and he'd shoved it back in his pocket in disgust.

He had to be close to Tonopah by now, didn't he? He'd forgotten to look at the odometer when he'd hit Goldfield. If he had, he could have done the math and figured out how many more miles he'd have to go before he got to the Clown Motel. At least there he could safely pull off the road until the storm died down.

A sudden gust of wind buffeted the side of his car. It blew snow against the driver's window that sounded more like icy pellets than thick wet snowflakes. Another gust of wind hit the side of his car harder, and the rear end started to fishtail. Great, add hydroplaning to everything else going wrong this Christmas Eve. Or was the highway icing up too?

And the day had started out so great!

Kit tried to loosen his white-knuckle grip on the steering wheel. The best way to get through something like this was to think of it as a game. To rescue the princess, he just had to get through a series of increasingly difficult obstacles. Okay, so he hadn't equipped his character (himself) with the best tools for the job, but he was resourceful. And patient. Even if he had to crawl along the highway with his head out the window so he could see the road with his car slip-sliding all over the place, he'd make it. Because Andrea was definitely worth it. He'd even told her why his parents had named him Kit, and she'd never once made fun of him.

Up ahead, red taillights flared through the snow as the driver hit his brakes.

Kit let up off the gas. If the guy had hit a cow or a coyote, he didn't want to have to slam on the brakes to avoid doing the same thing. Then his car really would go into a spin.

Then the guy's taillights disappeared.

Not driven off the road. Just flat out disappeared.

"What the..."

Before Kit could get the rest of the thought out, something came out of nowhere and hit the back of his car. Hard.

The impact threw Kit against his seatbelt. Pain flared in his left shoulder even as his car jerked forward and the rear end started to slide around toward his left.

A memory rose to the surface. His dad had told him how to get control of the car if he hydroplaned. Vegas was known for flash floods. The occasional torrential downpour. Kit's dad wanted him to know what to do if he hydroplaned while he was driving on the freeway, since Vegas had a lot of freeway traffic these days.

Only that relied on the car's anti-lock braking system. The little ABS light on the dash hadn't come on. Had the impact screwed up the system?

Kit let off the gas even more, hoping that the car would slow down enough to let the tires grab onto something. His car was almost sliding sideways on the highway, still going forward, but the back of the car had to be in the middle of the southbound lane by now.

Headlights flared to life on the passenger side of his car, harshly bright in the snowy night. The headlights belonged to a truck, one of those ugly-ass monster trucks that guzzled gas like nobody's business.

The truck roared right at him.

Kit turned the wheel, but his tires hadn't caught yet. He stepped on the gas, but all that did was spin his tires.

He threw up an arm in a vain attempt to ward off the truck right before it slammed into the passenger side of his car.

Kit's world turned into an icy cacophony of sound. Screeching metal. Squealing tires. The roaring sound of the truck's growling engine as it pushed his car off the side of the road, and then Kit was thrown against his seatbelt again as his car rolled down an embankment, the world rotating around him again and again.

The last things Kit was aware of before he blacked out was the sound of wind shrieking around him and the icy cold of snow blowing in through the broken windows of his car.

Game over, he thought.

Game over.

~

Kit became aware of voices coming from somewhere outside.

At least he thought there were voices. His head was throbbing, his shoulder felt like it was one big bruise, and he was pretty sure something had cut his scalp because it felt and smelled like he had blood running down the center of his forehead and dripping off his nose.

His car had landed right side up, of all things, but it was a mess. The headlights were still on, but the windshield was totally gone. Beyond the headlights, the snow had turned clumps of sagebrush into mounds of snowy beasts, ready to tear him to pieces.

If the crash hadn't done that already.

His entire body hurt, just like it had after his cousins beat the crap out of him that summer. They hadn't broken any bones though. They'd been careful about that. All that wrestling training and all.

Was anything broken now?

Kit started testing for broken bones with his legs, small movements while he braced himself against any sudden sharp pain. When that didn't come, he moved on to his fingers. His hands. It wasn't until he got to his left arm that he hissed in a sharp breath as the world went red.

Something in his left arm between his wrist and his elbow was broken, or if it wasn't broken, it hurt like it was broken. His left shoulder still hurt from the seatbelt, but it was a manageable pain. His left arm? The pain there made him sick to his stomach, and he squeezed his eyes shut, trying to control the urge to puke.

The second impact must have slammed him against the car door. At least he hadn't broken both wrists when the airbag exploded. He'd heard that happened sometimes, but he'd gotten lucky.

Lucky.

That was a laugh.

The wind was still whistling outside, but the embankment was actually shielding his car from the worst of it. Otherwise, he'd be a frozen popsicle. His jacket wasn't exactly cut out for Arctic weather.

He heard voices again, this time he was sure of

it. Men, shouting at each other. Two at least. Maybe three.

He opened his eyes. There were lights above him, up on the road. Headlights, yes, but also flashlights trying to cut through the blowing snow.

Snow that didn't seem quite as heavy as it had right before the crash. The storm must be blowing itself out. That happened with rainstorms in Vegas. If you were in the right place, up high enough with a view of the valley, you could watch a rain squall move across the valley. His mom worked in a tall office building, and he'd visited her once during a rainstorm.

Focus. He needed to focus, even though his mind didn't seem to want to.

He was in some serious trouble here. He'd been run off the road. He hadn't seen the first impact coming, which meant the truck that hit him didn't have its headlights on. Headlights as icy bright as the ones on the truck, he would have seen those coming half a mile away even through the snow.

The second impact, the one that shoved his car over the side of the road, that had been deliberate. The truck had accelerated into him. The asshole probably had snow tires or even... what did one of his buddies call them? Studdy tires? Studded tires? Something like that. Chris had grown up in Montana and knew all about things like that. Kit was a Vegas boy. He didn't. Nobody needed studded—that was it, studded—tires in Vegas.

Concentrate!

The guys with the flashlights weren't looking for him to help him out. Whatever they were after, it couldn't be good.

He couldn't just sit here and wait for them to do whatever they planned to do. His princess was waiting for him to come rescue her from the evil Clown Motel. What would he do if he was playing a video game? Roll over and die?

Not on your life. He might be a gangly nerd in real life, but he was one brave-ass warrior in game space. He'd even been on his way to beating Chris at that new game when Andrea called.

There had to be a way out of this.

He couldn't run. The passenger door was smashed in and the driver's door was facing the embankment. Even if he could get the door open, the guys with the flashlights were above him on that side of the car. They'd see him open the door. If they had guns—he had to assume they had guns; this was the middle of right-wing central

Nevada and everybody out here had guns—he'd make himself a perfect target. His jacket was red because UNLV's school colors were scarlet and gray. Nothing like standing out in a world gone white. If he left the jacket behind, he'd freeze to death.

So he couldn't crawl out any of the broken windows either.

That left the inside of the car. There wasn't anywhere to hide in here.

Not even in the footwell of the back seat. This wasn't a horror movie where the killer hides in the back seat, just waiting for the victim to get in her car without checking out the back seat first.

He couldn't even hide in the truck. Even assuming he could get the trunk open—the first impact had been hard enough to shove his car forward—he'd have to go outside to get inside.

So, he'd have to fight. Except the only thing he had in the car that could conceivably be a weapon was a little emergency flashlight in the glove box. He didn't even have a pocket knife. In this age of metal detectors everywhere, he'd quit carrying one.

He was screwed. He was totally screwed. His left arm was next to useless, he had no weapons to defend himself, and at least two badasses were slipping down the snow-covered embankment ready to do whatever they planned to do to him. He was as helpless to get himself out of this mess as a baby stuck in a car seat with a stinky diaper and an oblivious parent.

Car seat.

Think!

Something about a car seat and the back seat of this car.

A fresh gust of wind blew icy pellets against his face. It was like getting hit with a bucket of ice water.

And just like getting a faceful of ice water, the snow jumpstarted his brain.

He unlatched his seatbelt.

Maybe he wasn't so helpless after all.

Kit's parents had bought the car he currently drove (and would probably never drive again) used from a couple down the street who'd just had a baby.

"We don't trust the back seat," the couple said. "Not with the car seat, but your son's older and..."

Kit hadn't needed a car seat in over ten years,

which he didn't point out since his parents would accuse him of talking back. He'd been along with his parents when they'd gone to look at the car because, as his dad said, it might someday become his car. If he took care of it. Which he did, because what thirteen-year-old boy didn't dream of driving instead of being driven around?

His dad taught him to change the oil and check the tires. Check all the fluid levels. How to change a flat tire with the scissor jack, and how the spare tire was just a baby spare and only good enough to get him someplace where he could get the flat checked out, or more likely, buy a new tire.

When he'd asked why the couple didn't trust the back seat, his dad had showed him a little strap off to the side of one of the back seats.

"Pull on it," his dad had said, "but pull hard."

Kit pulled, and for a second he thought he'd broken the seat because the back folded down, revealing the inside of one side of the trunk.

"For hauling long stuff," his dad had said. "The seat's built to fold down. They could put the car seat on the other side, but..." He'd shrugged. "Their loss, our gain."

His dad had never hauled anything that required him to fold the seat down, and Kit had long since forgotten that feature even existed.

Until now.

He pulled himself over the center console and into the back seat. His left arm screamed at him, but the pain didn't seem quite so bad. Maybe the cold wind blowing in through the broken windows had acted like an ice pack, or maybe his whole body was numbing up. Kit didn't care. He'd never been so glad that he was a skinny guy, although he had to fold up his legs nearly to his chest before he could turn around enough in the back seat to even look for that little strap.

He found it mostly by feel. The fingers of his right hand weren't quite numb, but it still took him several tries before he got the seat back to budge.

When he finally got it to fold down, he looked at the opening in dismay.

It was tiny.

Yes, he was skinny, but was he *that* skinny? Especially with his coat on? He couldn't afford to get stuck halfway through. He had a sudden image of getting shot in the ass, and he couldn't imagine a more painful or humiliating way to die.

Andrea. Think about Andrea. She was still waiting for him.

He took his coat off as quickly and as carefully as he could. He shoved it into the trunk through the opening. By now he was almost getting used to the pain every time he moved his left arm.

He started to hold his breath as he began to climb through after his coat, then thought that might expand his chest too much. So he forced all the air out of his lungs, stretched his arms through the opening, and pushed himself through with his legs.

His left arm was screaming at him so much by the time he got into the trunk he thought he might pass out. But he wasn't done yet.

He had to pull the seat back up to fill in the hole, otherwise the guys with the flashlights would know where he went. They might figure it out anyway, but he didn't want to give them what would amount to a flashing arrow with the words "he went in here" written in neon above the hole.

The seat back had no strap on this side.

Of course not. No one was supposed to climb *into* the trunk from the back seat. That wasn't how these things were supposed to work.

He got the seat back up most of the way with one hand. Then he worked his fingertips into the narrow ridge between the plastic back of the seat and the padding he'd sat against countless times when he'd been a kid and relegated to the back seat while his parents drove.

He couldn't get it closed all the way, not without shutting the seat on his fingers. He still scraped his knuckles pretty badly before he gave up. He hoped the bad guys would just think the back seat had been damaged in the crash.

The trunk was actually pretty good sized. Good enough to hold a couple of bodies, one of his buddies had told him once. Even after the crash, the trunk hadn't crumpled in on itself. Right now it was still big enough to hold Kit and roomy enough that he could get his coat back on.

It was also black as night.

He'd taken the flashlight he always kept in the glove compartment with him, but he didn't want to chance turning it on. There was a cold breeze coming in from somewhere—he could feel it against his face—and he didn't want to risk the bad guys seeing a light coming from inside the trunk.

He thought about trying to get to the tire iron, but the spare and the tire iron, along with the jack, was covered with a board beneath the trunk's carpet. Easy to lift up if you were standing behind the car. Impossible to lift up when you were hiding in the trunk.

When it came right down to it, he only had one weapon.

His laptop.

It was an older model and pretty damn heavy compared to all the thin tablets and laptops most of his friends used. The laptop used to belong to his dad. It was good enough for Kit to use for his homework. It sucked for video gaming, and maybe that had been his dad's idea when he'd given Kit the laptop in the first place.

He could hear people walking around outside now. They were arguing about where he'd gone, that there were no tracks. Had he been thrown through the windshield? Was he out on the highway somewhere? Neither one of them wanted to go look.

Kit unzipped his duffel as quietly as he could. He didn't use a carrying case for the laptop since he never took it to class—that would have been embarrassing. Now he was happy he didn't. One less thing to unzip.

The laptop's metal case was as cold as ice, but even after the duffel had been thrown around inside the trunk, it still looked like it was in one piece. Maybe it was a good thing he'd thrown his sweatshirt in the duffel along with the laptop. Sweatshirts make good cushions in a crash. He'd have to remember that.

Damn. His mind was doing strange things again. Shock setting in? Probably.

He gripped the laptop with his right hand. Swinging it two-handed was out of the question.

Now all he had to do was wait.

And not pass out.

Not passing out was the important part.

If he did, he'd wake up dead.

As it turned out, he didn't have long to wait.

The bad guys, as he'd come to think of them, rifled through his car. He heard them open the glove box. Open the center console. Looking for cash? For drugs? Who knew? All he could tell was that they were angry they hadn't found anything.

The trunk would be next. It was the only place they hadn't looked.

He steeled himself.

Laptop clutched in his right hand. Flashlight in his left. He'd practiced turning on the flashlight with his left hand, aiming the beam directly at his chest.

He could do it. It hurt like hell, but he could do it.

He hadn't thought to take the keys out of the

ignition. The car had a key fob with a button that opened the trunk. If the trunk still popped open like it should.

He held his breath as he heard one of the men walk past the driver's side of the car toward the trunk. The other one shouted something about going back to look at the highway now that the snow was letting up.

He was going to look for Kit's body. Probably to see if he had any cash or drugs on him.

Modern-day highwaymen. Lovely.

His keys jangled as the guy got close to the back of the car. Kit had two different keychains attached together. One held the fob. The other keychain had a metal UNLV logo that Andrea had given him on their one-month anniversary. "To prove you're a real student," she'd said with a grin.

The fact that one of the bad guys was touching that keychain made Kit angry. He'd been scared before—frightened out of his wits, in horrible pain and sure he was going to die—but now he was just angry.

Strangers had run him off the road, and for what? A few dollars and maybe some drugs? What in the actual hell was wrong with this picture?

He'd been a wimp all his life, only brave in

video games. Well, this wasn't a game. This was real life, and he was about to be real dead real soon unless he fought back.

The trunk unlocked with a clunk. The hydraulics on the lid had long since died, and the heavy lid had to be opened manually. He heard the bad guy curse as he lifted the lid.

That's when Kit turned the flashlight on, aimed right in the guy's eyes.

Whether it was the flashlight or just the shock of finding someone in the trunk, the guy hesitated. His own flashlight was in the hand he'd used to open the trunk. He had a gun in the other hand, but before he could use it, Kit hit that hand with his laptop.

The gun flew off into the night, but somehow Kit managed to hold on to the laptop. He unfolded himself and got up on his knees, and swung the laptop again with all the strength he could muster.

This time he hit the bad guy square on the chin.

The guy went down.

He was a little guy, shorter than Kit and just about as skinny. He dropped his flashlight as he fell in the fresh snow.

Kit clambered out of the trunk. His feet were

numb, his left arm an agony of molten fire, but he didn't stop. He still had the laptop, and he used it to hammer the little guy's head. He had a knitted ski mask on, white with dark circles around the eyes.

Kit didn't see a ski mask. In his mind's eye, he saw that hateful clown mask his cousin had worn while he'd beaten the shit out of Kit.

"How do you like it now?" Kit hissed between teeth clenched against the pain. "Asshole! Tell me, how do *you* like it?"

He didn't stop hitting the little guy until blood had soaked through the mask.

He was breathing hard now. The laptop slipped from his fingers, the metal case dented and streaked with blood. He guessed he'd have to get a new one now. Maybe his dad would give him one the next time he upgraded.

Kit almost forgot the other bad guy until he heard someone shouting a name that wasn't his.

Crap.

He grabbed the little guy's flashlight. It was more powerful than his own. He aimed it around the back of what was left of his car, searching in the snow for the gun the bad guy had dropped.

He found it a split second before a shot rang out. The bullet missed him, but not by much. It slammed into the trunk, uncomfortably close to the gas cap.

Kit had never used a gun before in real life, but he'd used a lot of weapons in the video games he played.

The other bad guy was next to the road, still holding his flashlight. He made a perfect target, and the bad guys had been right. The storm had blown itself out. It was barely snowing now and the wind had died down.

Kit held the gun in his right hand. His shoulder didn't like it, but he ignored it. He had a princess to rescue.

The bad guy's next shot hit the ground next to where Kit stood.

Kit didn't hesitate.

He fired back, and he kept firing until the bad guy went down.

Tonopah didn't have a hospital. The regional medical center had closed almost a decade earlier, and the nearest hospital was nearly a hundred miles away.

Or so the trucker Kit had flagged down on the highway told him.

The guy had taken one look at Kit and the wreck off the side of the road, then bundled Kit into the truck. "We're only about fifteen miles outside town," he said. "I know a local doc. He'll open up if I ask him."

Even on Christmas Eve. Imagine that.

The trucker had radioed ahead, alerting law enforcement as well as his doctor friend. Kit asked the man if he could call the front desk at the Clown Motel so he could tell his girlfriend he'd be a little late.

"A little late?" The trucker had snorted. "Son, you're gonna be a whole lot late. Hope you don't have plans for Christmas. You're gonna have to cancel 'em."

He supposed he would. He'd shot one man, beaten another with a laptop, after they'd run him off the road and planned to kill him.

He'd found the truck off to the side of the road, motor still running. The other car, the one whose taillights he'd been following, had pulled off to the side of the road. No one had been inside. Kit had looked before he'd flagged down the trucker.

They'd set him up. The lead car had driven past him, probably saw the UNLV sticker on his bumper. Figured him for a college student who maybe had some drugs on him. The snowstorm had given them perfect cover, and when they saw his car fishtail on the highway, they took their shot. They probably figured he'd been badly injured in the crash since his car had rolled over more than once. He'd be easy pickings and they could just leave him to die. Or beat him over the head enough to kill him outright.

Only he'd turned the tables on them.

The trucker managed to get the Clown Motel on his radio. He passed the handset over to Kit. He'd never been so glad to hear Andrea's voice in his life.

After he'd told her what had happened, after she'd stopped crying, he told her they'd probably have to spend the night in Tonopah.

"I'm sorry about Christmas with your parents," he said. "I guess you can call them to come get you."

"Or we can spend the night here," she said. "What's left of it. They have a room available here. I checked. The other motel's booked solid thanks to the storm."

A room at the Clown Motel?

Could he do that? Childhood trauma was a bitch.

But you know what? He'd just fought back

against a guy in a sort-of clown mask. Against two guys.

He'd fought back.

Suddenly the idea of spending the night in the Clown Motel wasn't so scary. He could deal with clowns. He *had* dealt with clowns, and he'd beaten them.

Besides, he'd be waking up on Christmas Day with Andrea next to him.

"Book the room," he said.

He had a long night ahead of him. He'd have to explain himself to law enforcement, and that was after the doctor got done with him. He might even end up in a cast.

But he had a princess waiting for him, clown room or no clown room.

Take that, childhood trauma.

Everything considered, this was turning out to be a pretty good Christmas after all.

I SPIT ON YOUR HAPPINESS

CHRIS CHAN

"I spit on your happiness! I spit on your idea of life--that life that must go on, come what may. You are all like dogs that lick everything they smell. You with your promise of a humdrum happiness--provided a person doesn't ask much of life. I want everything of life, I do; and I want it now! I want it total, complete: otherwise I reject it! I will not be moderate. I will not be satisfied with the bit of cake you offer me if I promise to be a good little girl. I want to be sure of everything this very day; sure that everything will be as beautiful as when I was a little girl. If not, I want to die!"

-Jean Anouilh, Antigone

"Mr. Funderburke, we want you to figure out just what sort of crime our birth father committed," Terrance Hunnar told me.

"It must be really terrible if our mother won't even discuss it with us," his twin sister Tallulah added.

I sat quietly for a few moments and allowed these words to sink into my consciousness. When you work as the students' advocate at a prominent school, the young people drop all sorts of unexpected problems in your lap, especially during last period on a Friday afternoon. "Terry, Tally, I'm going to need you to start at the beginning, please."

"Well, you know that we live with our aunt and uncle, right? They can't have kids of their own, and we don't get along with our stepfather, so we've lived with them for most of the last decade. Mom married Dell– that's our stepfather– when we were four years old."

"Three," Tally corrected her brother. "Their wedding was a couple of weeks before our fourth birthday."

"Close enough to call it four," Terry retorted.

"But it's not. If you were fourteen days from turning twenty-one, and you tried to order a drink at a bar–"

"Hey, you two, excuse my interrupting, but how about you focus on your backstory and your father's alleged crime now, and debate how old you were later, please?"

Terry saw the justice in my comment, and resumed his narrative. "Mom broke up with our birth father when we were two years old. I barely remember him. Mom has never spoken of him, and after countless times of trying to get her to tell us anything at all about him when we little kids, and failing miserably to extract even the tiniest fragment of information, eventually we gave up and made our peace with the fact that we know absolutely nothing about the fact that we didn't have a clue about the source of fifty percent of our DNA."

"The only reason I know what he looks like is because Aunt Beryl kept a picture of Mom and our birth Dad's wedding." Tally took a framed photograph out of her backpack and set it on my desk. "We look more like him than Mom."

"And your father's name is?"

"Lionel Gundtravers. I only know that because I asked Aunt Beryl." Terry shrugged. "Looking at that photo of him, he looks like a real nice guy. Not the sort who'd be a dangerous criminal."

"There's no connection between physical appearance and criminality," I replied. "I can tell you from experience that–" I could tell from their faces that they weren't interested in what I had to say and wanted to talk about their own topic. That was fine by me. I don't need to hear my own voice drone. "Go on, please."

"Well, we're looking ahead to college applications. They're not for another two years, but when you go to Cuthbertson Hall, they teach you to plan ahead."

"Very true," I agreed with Terry. At Cuthbertson, kids start worrying about getting into college in nursery school.

"So, we started thinking about potential scholarships and loans, because we really appreciate what Aunt Beryl and Uncle Pryce have done for us all these years, but we don't want to drain their retirement savings to pay for our higher education, and we don't want to take any of our stepfather's money." Tally wrinkled her nose. "Actually, to be honest, it's not like we're expecting anything from Dell anyway. He's always made it clear that that he doesn't consider us to be his kids or his responsibility, and the college fund he's set up is for our three younger half-siblings. He's never come right out and said that we're not going to receive a penny from him, but... well..."

"For our last birthday, he gave us cards and a ten-dollar fast-food gift card. To share. Christmas wasn't any better. I'm not trying to sound spoiled here," Terry hastily added, "I'm just telling you that he's cheap and he doesn't show us affection with material goods."

"He doesn't show us affection in any way," sniffed Tally.

"I'm sorry to hear that you don't have a great relationship with your stepfather, but what about your mother? Candy, right? That's her name, isn't it? How is your relationship with her?"

The twins were very quiet for a few moments.

"We love her but she's distant," Tally finally answered.

"Strained but we love each other," Terry replied simultaneously.

"She never mentions our father, but we know she hates him. And though she cares about us deeply, she hates the fact that we've got our biological dad's DNA in us. She won't say anything about him, which is why we don't know jack about the guy," Tally continued.

"Don't your aunt and uncle know anything about him?"

"No. Aunt Beryl was studying abroad when Mom met our biological father, and never met him. Aunt Beryl and Mom were never very close, so all Aunt Beryl knows is that Mom moved to the town of Purslane Hills for a job, met a guy, got pregnant soon afterwards..." Tally paused. "They did not get married. Then something happened. Aunt Beryl knows that he committed some sort of terrible crime, but she doesn't know what is was or where he is now."

"A week ago, we realized that a lot of scholarships or grants won't give you money unless you can provide detailed evidence of your parents' financial situation. And the fact that we have no idea who he is or where he is or what he does for a living won't help us on those applications," Terry noted.

"And you've explained this to your mother?"

"Yes! We see her at least every other week when she comes up from Chicago for a visit. She just starts shaking and either cries or gets angry and insists that our birth father is a horrible, horrible person and it hurts her to even think about it and no good can come from our learning more about that terrible man and can we please change the subject right now..." Tally groaned. "We've tried so many times to get her to give us some details, and she just clams up like she mistook a tube of Super Glue for her lipstick."

"And your mother's parents?"

"Grandpa's long dead, and poor Granny has advanced Alzheimer's and can't help us."

"Any other friends or relatives who might know something useful?"

"None that we know of." Terry leaned forward. "We've Googled his name, of course, but there's nothing on the guy, which is suspicious in itself these days. Maybe he's dead, or in jail, or living under an assumed name. That's why we decided to come to you. I mean, this is your thing, isn't it?"

"It is." As a private detective and attorney employed by Cuthbertson Hall, my work includes background checks on employees, substitute teaching, and helping students with all sorts of difficult situations. Usually that means helping them out when they're caught in the middle of a nasty custody battle, or if they've got some other sticky situation at home, but tracking down a long-lost father who's potentially a dangerous criminal is right up my street. "So, you want me to find your biological dad. What do you want me to do when I find him? You don't want me to make him aware of your existence, do you?"

"No!" Their response was simultaneous and explosive.

"Just find out who and where he is, please," Terry said.

"And what he's done," Tally added.

"You may not like what I uncover," I warned them.

Tally shrugged. "If it's really bad, you don't have to tell us."

"We discussed this. If you decide we'd be better off not knowing, we'll leave it be," Terry agreed. "Personally, I can live just fine without learning that I'm the son of a serial killer or something like that."

I thought for a moment, and then observed, "But... if I track down your father– your biological father– and I don't tell you what I've found, then you'll know that it's something unsettling."

After a few seconds of fidgeting, Tally finally said, "If he turns out to be a rapist or a murderer or a terrorist or anything like that, just wait a couple of months and tell us you couldn't find him."

In the public imagination, people see private investigators as fellows who put on their trench coats and pound the pavement of the mean streets tracking down leads. All well and good, and I believe that a bunch of people in the business conduct their inquiries that way, though not necessarily wearing that outerwear, but I belong to a new generation of P.I.'s who like to launch their investigations in front of a computer screen.

I know that the twins told me that they'd Googled their father's name, but I never take anything just on someone else's say-so. I ran "Lionel Gundtravers" through three different search engines and came up with nothing, and figuring that "Gundtravers" was the kind of name that could easily get misspelled, I tried a few variations of the name, like "Guntravels" and "Gundervers," and still was stuck with nothing but a big fat goose egg.

But I'm not wired to give up easily. When one search term gives you nothing useful, you switch to related words. "Purslane Hills Wisconsin Crime" gave me links to the local police department and a few regional news stories on drunk driving and some drug-related arrests. Of course, there was no reason that any crime Gundtravers might have committed absolutely had to have taken place in Purslane Hills, but my gut told me to try "Purslane Hills" AND "Murder."

The first result of that search was an article from the *Central Wisconsin Ledger* from five years earlier.

Simone Caflisch Remembered

The family and friends of Simone Caflisch paid homage to her memory today by attending the opening of the Simone Caflisch Memorial Children's Room at the Purslane Hills Public Library. Simone was very fond of young people, and had ambitions to work with them before she was murdered almost a decade ago.

"We've never gotten over losing our little girl," Lester Caflisch, Simone's father said. "It was hard enough when she was killed, but when the police figured out who did it but couldn't gather up enough evidence to make an arrest... well, that just destroyed us. I know that I'm not supposed to mention his name and I won't, but it's just so terrible to know that he's been walking around free for nearly ten years after everything he's done... I hope that someday the police are able to find the proof they need to lock him away forever."

Similar opinions were voiced by Denise Caflisch, Simone's mother, and her older brother and sister Kurt and Paige.

The rest of the article described the content of the new children's literature room.

I knew that I was making a major leap here, but I was pretty sure that Lionel Gundtravers was the man that Lester Caflisch believed murdered Simone. A few more searches provided little else of value, but now I had a lead, and all I needed was a plan for following up on it.

It had been a long week, though, and I didn't

really have the mental acuity for devising a plan at that moment, so I continued to do a little Internet searching. After twenty minutes of wasting precious moments of my life, I had gained nothing of value aside from the fact that Simone's sister Paige was a big fan of Hello Kitty and tropical drinks featuring tequila, judging by her social media accounts. I concluded that this was one of those times when I wouldn't be able to obtain all of the knowledge I wanted from the comfort of my chair, so I decided that a road trip was in order.

I climbed a flight of stairs and made my way to my girlfriend Nerissa's office. "Got a minute?"

"Ten seconds, please." Nerissa scribbled comments on a quiz on the American Revolution with her purple pen for three times as long as she asked for, and then leaned back in her chair and swiveled around towards me. "What's up?"

I filled her in on my new case, and asked, "Are you up for a weekend getaway to Purslane Hills?"

Ideally, Nerissa and I would have started out at the crack of dawn, but I'm one of those people who needs ten hours of sleep a night to function properly, and when I have to be up in time for the eight o'clock school bell five days straight, I need to catch up over the weekends. Therefore, it was at half past eleven on Saturday morning when I finally picked up Nerissa for our trip to Purslane Hills. At the time, I considered it was possible that we'd be coming back that very night, and we certainly had to be home by Sunday evening. I politely informed Nerissa of our schedule as I loaded her three enormous suitcases into the trunk of my over-two-decades-old Volvo. She equally politely informed me that she was already aware of this, and said nothing more. Knowing Nerissa's twin passions for fashion and trying to finish her long-gestating dissertation, I figured that two of the suitcases contained clothes and the third contained books. After making sure that her luggage wouldn't crush my little overnight bag, I held the door open for Nerissa, helped her into the car, and ten seconds later we were on our way.

It was actually a pretty pleasant way to spend two and a half hours. The trees were right at the peak of autumn color, and after a couple of minutes Nerissa and I forgot why we'd been so icily polite to each other and started to have an enjoyable conversation. It was a beautiful day... as long as you were inside a building or car. This weekend, Wisconsin was being hit by a massive windstorm. The sun was shining, the sky was a gorgeous shade of blue, and if you weighed less than a hundred pounds there was a really high chance that a gust could carry you into another county. The magnificent foliage wasn't going to last long. Leaves were being ripped from the trees, but so far the majority were clinging to their branches.

It felt like only forty-five minutes had passed when we rolled into the Purslane Hills town square, just a few seconds after two o'clock. Purslane Hills had been a farming community for years, but over the past couple of decades, as many of the local family farms folded, the village reinvented itself as a weekend getaway, catering primarily to tourists from the Chicago metropolitan area. It's not a major vacation destination, and it's nowhere near Lake Geneva levels of visitation, but it brings enough revenue to the area to provide the residents employed by the hospitality industry with a decent living.

We took a quick drive around the town, which didn't take long as the area is a little less than a square mile. There's a shopping district filled with quaint little stores stocked with things I'd never want to own, a small movie theater, a couple of art galleries, a huge and beautiful park, a family fun center including an arcade and mini-golf course, a library, a local history museum, a few hotels, two churches (one Catholic, one Lutheran), a couple of other businesses, a tiny hospital, and a selection of restaurants and bars. The whole area is surrounded by farms where people can pick their own apples and pumpkins for five times what it would cost to buy them in a supermarket. Not a bad place for people who want to get away from it all and have several hundred dollars to spend in order to get the pleasant escape they so heartily desire. Normally the area was probably kept neat and clean, but today the streets and sidewalks were covered in leaves, flyers ripped off the telephone poles, and quite a bit of litter. A couple of public garbage bins were dancing down the road in the wind, which were likely the source of the scattered trash.

Nerissa and I decided that the best course of action was to get ourselves some lunch at a place where we could subtly question the locals about the crime. The trick was to find the place where the actual Purslane Hills people might eat. While I stretched my legs and looked around, Nerissa used her phone to check out the dozen dining establishments in the area, attempting to answer the question, what was the oldest and cheapest restaurant in town? The trendy bistros and upscale establishments looked like they were in buildings no more than a decade old, built as part of the local reinvention project. But the people who actually lived here probably wouldn't be able to afford an eighteen-dollar Cobb salad at Café Adelais for lunch. When I climbed back into the car, Nerissa held her phone screen to my face with a triumphant grin. Henney's Tavern. Located in the northwest corner of town, about as far as you can get from all of the newly built structures and still be in the city limits. Established 1947. Home of the Five-Dollar Bottomless Bowl of Chili. That was our lunch destination.

When we arrived, I knew that we had come to the right place. The tourists we'd seen wandering the streets were largely wearing designer jeans and sweaters that looked like they required more cautious care to wash than your average baby. I say this to in no way denigrate the fashion sense of the patrons at Henney's, I merely state as a fact that two of them were wearing sweatshirts from the Packers' 1997 Super Bowl win, and half the patrons had stains on their clothing which indicated that they were frequent consumers of the Five-Dollar Bottomless Bowl of Chili special. That sounded pretty good to me, so I ordered it. The menu was limited, featuring only hamburgers, cheeseburgers, hot dogs, grilled cheese sandwiches, and finally, something dubbed the Henney's Salad. "I really want a cheeseburger," Nerissa murmured before sighing and ordering the Henney's Salad.

I knew better than to reply to that comment. As she took our orders, the waitress gave us a gigantic smile and asked, "Are you two here for a romantic weekend?"

Personally, there's nothing more romantic to me than investigating a case with Nerissa, though I wasn't going to advertise the true purpose of our visit. "Yes, yes we are."

"I thought so. You two make such a lovely couple. We don't get too many out-of-towners around here. They prefer to go to places on the lake, you know, the fancier restaurants. Some of them are pretty good, most of them are overpriced, but none of new places have the feel of the *real* Purslane Hills, the place that the locals grew up in, you hear what I'm saying? This is genuine here, not just some slapped-together tourist resort, but this is real people doing real things living real lives. You understand me?"

I felt like I only three-quarters understood what she was trying to convey to us, but time is a precious commodity and I didn't want to squander any of mine asking her to repeat herself. "Yes."

"Mm-hmm. So where are you two from originally? You don't look like Chicago types to me. I'd say you're Wisconsinites, aren't you?"

"That's right. We're from Milwaukee."

"Oh, that terrific. My sister and her husband and five of their six kids live there. So, what made you decide to come up here? Did you hear about the area from a friend, or did you see a commercial on TV, or something else?"

Nerissa and I have many rules, and one of them is to never, ever lie if we can help it. The best thing to do is tell the truth, even if it's only part of the truth, or be vague enough that people might draw their own inferences from true but sketchy information. Also, we'd decided in the car that it was best not to mention Lionel Gundtravers or Simone Caflisch, because one never knows if saying the wrong thing will ruffle feathers or cause otherwise talkative people to clam up on us.

"We're here to do some research. I'm writing my dissertation. I'm a historian," Nerissa replied. All of those statements were quite true, but we didn't see the point in admitting the fact that the research had nothing to do with Nerissa's dissertation.

"Oh, that's interesting! What are you writing about?"

Nerissa and I gave each other a quick look. It's better when we're asking the questions, rather than answering them. "I'm sorry," Nerissa answered. "Can we resume this conversation in a couple of minutes? It's been a long drive and I need to use the facilities, please."

"Of course! It's right around the corner there. I'll put your orders in now, and be back in a second." Our waitress tottered away, Nerissa stood up, and I rose with her. She handed me her long suede jacket, and I hung it on one of the hooks on the wall near our table, and placed my lambskin walking coat next to it.

While Nerissa used the restroom, I took a look around, trying to see if there was anybody who looked like they might be old enough to remember what had happened to Simone Caflisch, and who might be insufficiently guarded to want to talk to us. A couple of glances around the room provided me with no likely possibilities, other than our waitress. Everybody else in the room was drinking beer or eating chili while staring at the college football game on television.

It just didn't look to me like any of them would be willing to engage in conversation until the game ended, and it was only the start of the third quarter.

In any event, it seemed like our waitress might be our best bet for useful information. She appeared to be somewhere between her late thirties and mid-forties, so she could've born around the same time as Simone. It wasn't too far outside of the realms of possibility to think that she could've known her.

I saw Nerissa returning from the restroom and stood up for her. She smiled to acknowledge the gesture, pulled her chair closer to mine, and sat down. "Take a look at this," she said, pulling her phone out of the pocket of her suede maxi skirt.

After a bit of squinting, I realized that Nerissa had taken a picture of the bathroom wall, which was lined with some old and graffiti-scarred wood paneling. "Check out this heart," Nerissa said, zooming in on an area next to the hand dryer.

It was a little hard to make out the crudely scratched letters, but eventually I spelled out the pair of names inside the heart. "Simone and Lionel. Huh." I leaned back a bit and let my brain make some mental calculations. "Good work,

Nerissa. Well, they clearly knew each other. I just wonder when that was carved."

"When what was carved?" Our waitress had returned, carrying a tray full of chili, salad, milk, and water. "What're you looking at there?"

No point in prevaricating. Shifting the topic or hiding the phone would've only served to make our waitress suspicious. "There's a piece of graffiti on the wall," I replied. ""Simone and Lionel" in a little heart."

"Oh, yes?" For the first time a flicker of stoniness set in on our waitress's face. "Why are you interested in that?"

I took a couple of nanoseconds to consider my next comments and decided to go for it. "You know my girlfriend's doing research. I noticed that your library has a Simone Caflisch Memorial Children's Room. It looks really nice, is it new?" Once again, two true statements that were not really connected, but which could easily be interpreted as linked. I didn't wait for a response. "Anyway, Nerissa– that's my girlfriend, I don't think we introduced ourselves. I'm Isaiah, but everybody calls me by my last name, Funderburke– Nerissa saw that heart, and we wondered if it was the same Simone, because that's not all that common a name, especially in a small town, and we realized that it's a *memorial* room at the library, and we started wondering..."

"I'm kind of a sucker for tragic romances," Nerissa continued with a little tear in her eye. She can cry at a second's notice, an ability that both helps in investigations and keeps me on my toes. "I saw that carved on the wall, and I thought about this couple young and in love, and then to find out that the woman died..." The tears started falling faster, and I handed my girlfriend a paper napkin from the table dispenser in silent admiration of her skills.

Our waitress's momentary coolness evaporated. "Oh my... are you all right?" Nerissa was increasing the flow of the waterworks. "Please don't cry. Please stop. Because if you don't, I'm gonna start bawling too..." And with that, our waitress doubled over, leaned her tray against the wall, and sank one of the empty chairs at our table. Nerissa's own waterworks dried up immediately and we both arched our eyebrows and gave each other nonplussed looks. Well, there was nothing for it but to hand our waitress a few handfuls of paper napkins, too.

She thanked me, soaked the napkins through with her tears, and when I handed her more of them she blew her nose so mightily that I started trying to figure out a polite way to tell her to wash her hands before handling food again. Remarkably, everybody else in the establishment was still transfixed on the game. "I'm sorry," she finally mumbled. "You couldn't have known, but this is a sensitive topic for me. Simone and I were friends. We grew up together."

"I'm so sorry. We had no idea," Nerissa leaned forward and patted our waitress on the shoulder.

"No way you could have known," our waitress sobbed, dabbing her eyes and then giving her nose another blow that made the trumpet that caused so much of a ruckus outside of Jericho look like a kazoo. "This was such a small town growing up that we had to take the bus to school half an hour away. We'd talk all the way there and back. She was a sister to me. And then..."

We waited a while, and finally I prompted her. "What happened to her?"

"She died. And then she disappeared."

I took a minute to digest that. "In that order?"

"Yes. This was, oh, it must've been..." She counted on her fingers. "About fifteen years ago, I think. We were twenty-one then. Well, I was working here ever since high school. My parents own this place. Neither Simone nor I had enough money for college, but Simone was determined to make a good life for herself. She loved children. Her dream was to become a child psychologist and to have a big family of her own, so she was scraping by working at the supermarket five miles west of here, and driving to Milwaukee, Madison, Green Bay, Appleton, all the bigger cities every chance she got in the hopes of finding a better job, maybe getting some kind of scholarship that would let get an advanced degree. Well, Simone was amazingly smart, but it didn't show in her grades because she liked to party a lot, so she wasn't getting anywhere with finding a way to get into college and paying for it. Her parents weren't happy with her, I can tell you that. Neither were her siblings."

Our waitress suddenly sat up a bit on looked at us. "Here I am blubbering and I'm interrupting your lunch. I'm sorry, I don't remember your names."

"I'm Funderburke."

"Nerissa."

"My name is Fern. It's nice to meet you two. I'm so sorry–"

"No, please, go on. I can tell you need to talk to somebody, and we're happy to listen. Please, keep going." I did not want our one lead to dry up on me. Figuratively, not literally,

"Well if you don't mind–"

"We don't. What were you saying? Her family wasn't happy with her?"

"They weren't. Her brother Kurt, he was always criticizing her for the way she lived her life. She was a good person, but she... just liked men, and she wasn't the type to sit around and pine after one guy. I admit, she didn't have the best reputation, but she just wanted to have fun and that's not a crime. But Kurt kept telling her that she was the world's biggest slut, and her sister Paige never let up on her for not getting better grades, and her parents tried to keep the peace, but it was pretty clear that they were disappointed in Simone, so when she died she was kind of estranged from all of her family."

"How did she die?" Nerissa asked an instant before I could.

"They found her lying at the edge of the woods, near the lake. I remember, it was already frozen that fall, it was so cold. No snow, though, she was dumped on top of a pile of autumn leaves. She didn't look like herself, there was a man's belt wrapped around her neck and she was all..." Fern shuddered. "I can't even think about it. The sheriff pronounced her dead and they carried her back into town. They called some doctor to perform the autopsy, but he never got the chance. During the night somebody stole her body and they never found it again."

"Wow."

"I know, right? Well, everybody said that Lionel did it."

"Lionel? From the heart in the bathroom?" Nerissa asked.

"Exactly!" That's been there for almost two decades. Dad's wanted to paint over it or sand it out or something, but I won't let him. She carved that herself, you know. It reminds me too much of her. So, Dad's just left it."

"Why did everybody suspect Lionel?"

Fern sagged at my question. "I didn't want it to be him. He was my friend too. He still is, I guess, even though he doesn't talk much to anybody anymore. I always hoped that he and Simone would get back together, even though it was obvious they wouldn't, but then he knocked up that girl who came to town with that development crew to look for a place to build a hotel– that was the start of the whole plan to make Purslane Hills a getaway destination– and he tried to make a go the mother of his kids, but everybody knew from the get-go it wouldn't last. They weren't right for each other, but when you have twins you can't just abandon them. He wasn't that kind of guy. Simone was going to have one last talk with Lionel to cut all ties with him, and then... Everybody said that Lionel must've flipped out, because it was his belt that was used to strangle her, it had a distinctive buckle... Well, then her body disappeared, and people started wondering if she was really dead, the police decided they couldn't make a case, and then Lionel got a letter from a lawyer telling him not to go after her, or she'd sue and take everything he had in child support and he'd lose the family farm."

Fern sat quietly for a bit, and then Nerissa said, "Her family must've felt bad about how they treated her if they named that library room after her."

"Hhmph. Soothing their guilty consciences, if you ask me, after the way they belittled her and criticized her every day of her life while she was alive. They're practically rich now, you know. The Caflisch family sold their farm to the corporation to build the hotel, and now they get a cut of the profits and Mr. and Mrs. Caflisch are sitting pretty. They're away on a cruise now, they take a lot of those now that they can afford it. Paige and Kurt are working at the hotel, now. He's the night manager and she's the hostess at the restaurant."

Fern paused. "I'm sorry. I've been rambling on and on and you two probably want to get to your lunches."

My chili smelled amazing, and I was sorely tempted to dig into it, but I didn't want to do anything that might prevent Fern from providing us with much-needed information. In contrast, Nerissa's Henney's Salad turned out to be a pile of limp, slightly wilted lettuce, topped with a couple of slices of tomato and cucumber, a handful of chopped-up processed cheese, and a little cup of off-white dressing. From the baleful side-eye she was giving the salad, Nerissa was in no hurry to eat it.

"Please, don't worry about it. I'm glad that you feel comfortable enough to talk to us," Nerissa replied, laying on the warmth and kindness with a trowel. "I hate to bother you, but your talking about her makes me wonder– what did Simone look like? After hearing about her, I just feel like I could use a mental picture of her. How would you describe her?"

"Oh, I can do better than that." Fern pulled out her phone. "A while back, I went to the library and scanned a bunch of my old photographs. I have a few of her here. Half a sec." She tapped the screen a dozen or so times and handed the phone to Nerissa. "There are four of them. Here's one of her dancing around in front of her car, here's one of the two of us at our high school graduation, this one is of Simone with her siblings and parents, and this last one was at this party when her parents signed the contract to sell their farm for the hotel."

"She's pretty." Nerissa pointed at the TV. "Whoa! Did the quarterback just punch out that guy?" When Fern instinctively turned towards the screen, Nerissa's lightning-fast thumbs flew over Fern's phone, as she sent the four photos to herself. "My mistake," Nerissa laughed as Fern turned back, looking confused. "It must've been some trick of the light."

Simone had been an attractive young woman, with long, cinnamon-colored tresses and a Rubenesque figure. From her family photo, she was pretty tall, too, towering at least six inches over her siblings, though since her feet weren't in the picture it was possible that she was wearing shoes that elevated her height.

Nerissa handed Fern's phone back to her. "So, who are the other three people in the part photograph besides you and Simone?"

"Oh, the guy with the scraggly blond hair is Lionel. I told you, it was clear that things weren't going to work out with Candy, even with the babies. And even then, that Dell guy had his eye on her."

I had to play dumb. "Who's Dell?"

"He was this lawyer who was helping the development firm draw up the contracts for the sale. Not just the Caflisch family, for some other plots of land, too. I think he knew Candy even before she came to Purslane Hills because they were working at the same firm. She was in public relations or something like that. He was always mooning around her, hitting on her. His timing was bad. She was a new mom and not ready to break it off with the father of her kids and start up with a new guy. But once everybody started pointing fingers at Lionel, Candy cut Lionel off like a burnt lock of hair and went straight for the guy with a promising career ahead of him. I don't wanna sound disloyal to Lionel, but Dell is- or at least was, I'm not sure what he looks like now– much better looking than Lionel. Lionel was lanky and his adolescent pimples never fully cleared up, but Dell's tall and lean and muscular with much nicer hair. He's handsome, but I don't really trust his face. Something, I don't know... vain about it, you know what I mean? Arrogant, maybe. I think that–"

"Hey! Fern!" One of the patrons across the room bellowed. "More chili!"

"More for me, too!"

"And me!"

"Plus another beer!"

"I want a cola!"

"More cheese on it this time! And crackers, plenty of those!"

Fern pushed herself away from the table and repocketed her phone. "Excuse me, I've gotta work." As she shuffled back into the kitchen, she called out, "It wouldn't hurt any of you to say "please" once in a while!"

As I pondered our next steps, I started tasting the chili. It was clearly made with chopped-up leftover hamburger patties, but it was fantastic. Spicy, with just the right amount of beans and noodles, it was terrific and I told Nerissa so. When I asked how her salad was, she stabbed a couple of lettuce fragments with her fork and said, "The less I think about it, the better." I persuaded her to taste the chili. "Wow."

"Want to get some for yourself?"

"Yes. But no."

"You're slim as a pencil and you run thirty-five miles a week. You don't have to go all "salad girl" on me."

"You're right. I'm turning into what I hate the most."

And when Fern returned a few minutes later, I asked her for a refill on my chili and some for Nerissa as well. Unfortunately, we didn't get the chance to ask her for more questions because other patrons started demanding more to eat, so we savored another couple of bowls of chili each and debated where to go next.

"Funderburke, do you think there's just the tiniest chance that maybe this Lionel guy isn't a killer?"

"I was just thinking about that. I'm trying not to embrace that idea too much because I want it to be true. It would be nice to go to Tally and Terry and tell them, "Good news! I found your father, and he's not a bad guy after all! He's actually been wrongly suspected of murder all these years, but I cleared his name and he wants to meet you now!" That might be a happy ending to this whole situation, but..."

"Never let your dream make you blind to reality." Nerissa scraped the side of her bowl with her spoon and licked it. "Dang, this is the best chili I've ever had."

I agreed to both of her comments. "Look, I'm very close to fulfilling my mission here. I was asked to track down the guy and it shouldn't be too hard to find his current location. Now, I could just go to the twins and tell them, "Well, your father has been the prime suspect in the murder of a woman for almost as long as you've been alive. But there was never enough evidence to indict him, so legally he's an innocent man. And he may actually be not guilty, so there's a chance that you can love him without fear that your DNA is half-killer. What do you say, kids?"

Nerissa dabbed her chin with her napkin. "I see your point. Either you decide not to tell them you found him at all, or..."

"Or I can try to figure out the truth of this whole situation before we have to go back home Sunday night. Preferably earlier, because I have some notes to write up for another case that I'd like to get done before the school week starts up again. Normally I'd be concerned about interfering with what's technically an active homicide investigation, but when the official authorities have had a decade and a half to solve the crime and squat to show for it, I think a private detective can make a fair enough case for sticking his impressively oversized nose into the matter."

"What's our next lead, then?"

"The victim's siblings. I say we go down to the

hotel and see if either Kurt or Paige Caflisch is available to talk. Actually, Kurt is less likely to be around, since he's the night manager, but maybe Paige will be around the restaurant."

Nerissa agreed with my reasoning, and after we both filled ourselves up to the Plimsoll line with chili, we paid our bill and left. I tried to coax a little more information out of Fern, but one of the football teams was four touchdowns up, and the patrons seemed a lot less interested in the game and more concerned with getting their beer glasses and chili bowls refilled, so she wasn't in a position to participate in a substantial chat.

The hotel was only a few minutes away, but the parking lot was so full that it took more time to find a free spot and walk to the building than it did to travel from the tavern to the hotel. Clearly the town was benefitting from a pretty nice influx of weekenders.

We followed the signs until we found the restaurant, which was fairly empty aside from the bar area, which was filled with men watching the football game. I figured that that their wives left their husbands there so they wouldn't be bored and making incredulous comments about the prices while the women shopped. A slight woman in black was standing behind a podium, scribbling on a pad. Since her name tag advertised that her name was Paige, I figured that we were in luck.

"Hi!" I said as we approached the podium. "I'd like to make a reservation for dinner tonight."

Paige's eyes widened, narrowed, and then repeated the process a few times. "Just a moment, please." She whipped out her phone, tapped out what was very likely a quick text message, and slid her phone back into her pocket. "What time is best for you tonight?"

"Do you have anything free at seven for two people?"

"Let me see here... Would seven-thirty be acceptable? We're kind of full tonight, but we do have a nice table available then."

"That would be fine, thank you."

"All right, that's two for seven-thirty for Funderburke. Could I have your phone number, please?"

I felt an unsettling chill along my spine, and from Nerissa's sudden flinch I knew that she caught Paige's slip too. "How did you know my name?"

She was not a skilled liar, and given her poker face, she would very likely lose thousands of dollars if she were ever foolhardy enough to participate in a card game in Las Vegas. "You... told me, Mr. Funderburke."

"No, I didn't."

"That's right, I can confirm that." Nerissa crossed her arms and shot Paige the kind of look she usually directs towards misbehaving students. "So how did you know?"

"You're mistaken."

"Please don't waste our time. I've never met you before, Miss Caflisch. If you're wondering how I know your last name, it's because I did a little research on you before you came here. My picture and my girlfriend's picture have been in the news on multiple occasions, so you could have seen us that way, but then why would you lie and then act like you didn't know who we are? I think you found out who we are when you were trying to track down someone through the Internet, didn't you? And you think you know why we're here, so that's why there's a little sudden hostility, isn't there?"

Paige dropped any attempt to project the impression that the customer was always right. "All right, Mr. Smarty-pants Funderburke, tell me why you think I looked you up online?"

"My guess is that one day not too long ago you did some research, trying to figure out what happened to the family of the man you believe was involved in your sister's death and disappearance. You probably tracked down Candy and Dell Hunnar pretty easily, and you found the kids Terry and Tally with a similar lack of difficulty. My guess is that you found out they're attending Cuthbertson– they're both involved in sports and extracurriculars, so they're mentioned in a bunch of news stories and press releases. By searching the school website, you found out about me, and you started wondering if one day the twins would ask me to try and prove their father was innocent."

From the expression on her face, Paige was impressed. Still hostile, but impressed. "Not bad, gumshoe. It looks like that elitist school made a good choice when they hired you."

"Cuthbertson Hall is an excellent school, but it is not elitist," Nerissa and I said simultaneously. We get comments like Paige's a lot, so we often respond reflexively in defense of our alma mater and employer.

"So, the little brats finally asked you to look into their dad's case, huh? It took them long enough. We've been wondering if they were going to try to pull something like that ever since we found out about you a couple of years ago."

"Terry and Tally are not brats. They are two intelligent, friendly young people who–"

"Who just happen to be the progeny of the man who murdered my baby sister." Paige snorted. "Look, I get that they can't pick their parents. But if you try to claim that Lionel didn't do it, then you'll start accusing the next most likely suspects. The family, right?"

"You are laboring under a misapprehension. The Hunnar twins did not hire me to prove their father's innocence." Normally I wouldn't provide any details about my clients, but the siblings had authorized me to mention them if I thought it would help me figure out what happened to their dad.

For the first time, Paige looked a little less aggressive. "No?"

"Terry and Tally grew up not knowing who their father was. Their mother has made sure that they never found out anything about him, and they asked me to find out why their mother won't tell them anything and where he is now. Neither of them knew he was a murder suspect, but they figured there might be some dark secret in his past."

Paige emitted a humorless laugh. "That's an understatement."

"So, I wasn't tasked with proving their father's innocence."

"But you want to look into the case anyway, don't you?"

Was it that obvious? "Why would you object to that?"

"Because I don't want you causing my family any grief by digging up the past."

"Even if I track down your sister's killer? Even if I find her body and allow you to finally give her a proper burial?"

I watched her expression soften, and then her jawline tightened into a stubborn clench. "You can't help us."

Nerissa often calls the scrutinizing look I give people my "truth-extracting gaze." I think that's a good name for it. "You're afraid, aren't you?"

"Of what?"

"Of my finding out something you don't want anybody to know. When I talked about Lionel, there was no anger or hatred in your face, but when you mentioned my suspecting the family, there was a lot of anxiety, and not for yourself. Then who is it that you're worried was involved in your sister's death? Your father? Your mother? Or your brother?" From the way her face paled at the sound of my final question, I knew that Paige was worried about her brother Kurt. "Kurt, then? You think that he had something to do with it?"

"I knew it," a voice behind me snarled. "You're trying to pin this on me to clear Lionel, aren't you?" I turned around, and judging by his resemblance to Paige, I figured I was looking at Kurt. "Why do you think I hurt my own baby sister?"

"*I* don't," I told him. "But your surviving sister does, for some reason, and I'd be very interested to hear not only why she suspects you, but why she hasn't done anything about it for the past fifteen years."

Kurt started stomping towards me and clenched his fists, but since I had nearly a foot in height and at least fifty pounds of lean muscle, bone, and water retention weight on him, I wasn't concerned, as long as he tried to hit above the belt. I like to solve conflicts with words instead of fists whenever possible, though, so I told him, "Before you turn to violence, I should point out that your employers will look very dimly at your assaulting a patron of your establishment."

"You're not a patron," a shrill-sounding Paige replied. "I misread the chart, and we're booked solid tonight. There's no table for you and all of our rooms are taken, so you have no business here. Just get out!"

I knew we weren't going to get anything useful out of them, but it is not in my nature to turn on my heels and run. "There are seats free at the bar. I think that my girlfriend and I will have a drink and watch the game."

Kurt took another not-particularly-menacing step towards me, but Paige raised a hand. "Leave now or I'll call security."

"By all means. Call your manager, too. I'm sure he'll be delighted to hear how you turned away two paying customers who have done nothing wrong and who will no doubt write about their terrible experience on every hotel rating website they can find."

Nerissa pulled out her phone. "By the way, Kurt, I'm recording you now, so if you attempt to strike my boyfriend, there will be video proof that you started the fight, and we won't hesitate to press charges."

This caused Kurt to take two steps back. "My sister and I have jobs at this hotel for life. My parents put that in the contract when they sold the land."

"Did they specify which jobs in the contract?" Nerissa inquired. "Does it say that you're absolutely guaranteed to keep your current jobs no matter what with the possibility of promotion, or is there a clause that says you could, say, be transferred to cleaning out the septic tank if your bosses aren't happy with your performance?"

From the expressions on the siblings' faces, it appeared that they had never even considered this possibility.

"We are not trying to antagonize you or cause any harm to your family," I explained, trying to pour oil on the troubled waters. "Your family has been through a terrible ordeal, and we have no desire to poke at an open wound. All we're asking is that you think about two innocent teenagers, who cannot be held responsible for any sins of their father. They're just a brother and sister who love each other very much, exactly like I'm sure the two of you do. And they're in terrible pain right now, caused by all the questions they have about their lineage. As harsh as the truth might be to hear, it's better than not knowing and wondering. And you can help them with just a few minutes of your time. Will you please take this opportunity to talk with us and help end the suffering of a brother and a sister who are more like you than you can imagine?"

That wasn't a bad effort, if I do say so myself. I

could see Paige softening. "Well..." she finally muttered, "I suppose I could–"

"Dammit, Paige, don't say anything! They're gonna try to put us both in jail!"

What a horse's rear end. If Kurt could've just kept his lips zipped for another couple of minutes, we might've found out something useful, like exactly where Lionel was living now. As it was, all my efforts were for naught and Paige irrevocably saw us as enemies now. "If you don't get out of here right now... I'll..." She snatched up a squeeze bottle of ketchup. "I'll squirt this all over you. That'll ruin your pretty outfit," she informed Nerissa with a malicious twinkle in her eye.

I took a second to gauge the situation. My instinctive response was to never back down from a confrontation and never show weakness. My coat has been waterproofed to protect the leather from precipitation, so I thought that there was a fair chance that ketchup would just wipe right off it, though I didn't want to put that theory to the test. Nerissa's clothing, however, was a different story. She was wearing one of her favorite outfits, a long jacket, full-length skirt, and boots that were all made of chocolate-colored suede, and if you knew Nerissa like I do, you'd realize how powerfully the thought of some of her clothes getting ruined would incense her.

I was contemplating the possibility of lunging forward and wresting the ketchup bottle from Paige's grasp when a stern voice asked, "Paige, Kurt. What have I told you about threatening the guests?"

Nerissa and I both turned around and saw a harried-looking man with a grey crew cut glowering at the Caflisch siblings. "Put that ketchup bottle down."

Paige obeyed, and meekly tucked her hands behind her back and twisted her feet like a chastened little girl. Kurt looked like he was using all his willpower to bottle up all the rage he was feeling.

"Paige, Kurt, why don't you go into the bar and see if our guests need anything? As for you two, will you come with me to my office, please?" His tone was unequivocally conciliatory. We didn't know his name, but we considered this guy one of our new best buddies. We followed him down the hall, and into a small and sterile-looking office. He motioned to the pair of chairs, and sat behind the desk. From the nameplate on the door, he was Alvin Montagne, the general manager of the hotel.

"I'm sorry that you had to experience that. And your names are?"

"I'm Isaiah Funderburke– everybody just calls me Funderburke– and this is my girlfriend, Nerissa Kaiming. You're Alvin Montagne?"

"Yes, please call me Vinnie. I want to assure you that this establishment does not consider it to be acceptable behavior to threaten guests by squirting condiments all over their clothing. I will be speaking with the employees in question, and they will be disciplined. Again."

"Is this a recurring issue with Paige and Kurt Caflisch?" Nerissa asked.

"Mostly just Kurt. He has anger management issues, but he's also a negative influence on his sister, I'm sorry to say."

"And according to their contract, they can't be fired? Kurt's the permanent night manager?"

"Oh, he's not the night manager," Vinnie rubbed his temples as if he was expecting a migraine to strike him at any moment. "He's the assistant night manager. I got the idea from watching *The Office*. It's a ceremonial title, requiring little leadership and minimal contact with our patrons. We don't feel like we can rely on him for any significant level of responsibility. In the last two months, he's tried to resolve disputes with guests by threating to punch nine of them on the nose. And only seven of the guests in question were men... We think it's best to keep him on the night staff because he deals with fewer patrons during that time. But this is one of our busiest weekends of the year. People are here for the autumn foliage, and we need all hands on deck so... we scheduled him for daylight hours." Vinnie's entire body shuddered.

"I understand that you can't be responsible for every member of your staff."

That produced a grateful smile from Vinnie. "Thank you. Now what room are you staying in?"

"Actually, we're not guests at the hotel, but we might need to book something."

"I'm so sorry. We are completely full, but..." Vinnie rummaged around his desk and pulled out some slips of flimsy cardboard. "Here is a voucher for two free dinners at our restaurant, and I'm also giving you a complementary two-night stay here at the hotel during the off-season. If you could please see your way to come back here then, we'd be delighted to have you."

Nerissa glanced at the vouchers. "Thanks so much. I should point out that my boyfriend and I, our relationship... well, when we travel, we sleep in separate rooms."

"Oh." Vinnie pulled out another voucher. "Then here is a second room for you. I should warn you that the complementary tickets are for smaller rooms that have views overlooking the parking lot and don't have whirlpools in the bathrooms."

"That's quite all right," I assured him as I pocketed the vouchers. Free is free, and we'd already managed to extract more from him that he'd planned to use to placate us.

"If you don't mind, I hope that you won't feel the need to post about your experiences on social media or any other websites?"

"Perish the thought."

"Thank you."

"I appreciate your professionalism," I assured him. "Have you been working here long?"

"Just over four years."

"Do you know many of the people who live in Purslane Hills full-time? Lionel Gundtravers?"

Vinnie shook his head. "I don't think so. But you know who knows pretty much everybody around here? The Catholic priest, Fr. Something-or-other. Fr. Rene, that's it. He's at St. Bibiana's. He knows everybody, Catholic, Protestant, other, or nothing at all. Nice guy. He'll probably be able to help you."

We thanked him and left his office. As we headed back to the car, the wind billowing our coats like capes, we could see Kurt at the opposite end of the hall, glowering at us. At that moment, I promised myself that if we used those vouchers, we would either eat dinner at the hotel restaurant on a night when the Caflisch siblings had the evening off, or I would wear old clothes that I didn't mind getting stained.

St. Bibiana's was easy to find. In front of the small stone church was a stone statue of a woman tied to a pillar, surrounded by statues of people lying on the ground, writhing and clutching bottles. The woman's face looked peaceful, but the people on the ground appeared to be very drunk. "St. Bibiana is the patron saint of hangovers," Nerissa informed me without having to look it up on her phone. "She was martyred under the persecutions of Julian the Apostate, a Roman emperor who according to one story, attempted to erase his baptism by bathing in a tub filled with blood. After St. Bibiana successfully fended off the lecherous advances of this woman called Rufina, the authorities tied her to a pillar and beat her to death."

"I knew the story of Julian the Apostate," I informed Nerissa in an attempt to make it clear that even though my knowledge of religious history isn't nearly as extensive as hers, it's still pretty comprehensive.

It was just four o'clock, and the Saturday evening Mass was beginning, so we went inside the church, which was pretty full, and when the services ended an hour later, we waited until most of the other people had gone and approached Fr. Rene, a tall, friendly man in his late thirties.

I decided it was best to tell him everything, so I summed up the events of the last twenty-six hours as concisely as I could to explain why we were here and what we were trying to learn. I managed to cover everything in just over five minutes, and midway through, Fr. Rene led us into his rectory, where we settled into some comfortable chairs to talk.

"I'm very glad you're here," Fr. Rene told us. "I must tell you, Lionel and his mother Edith are friends of mine, and I can tell you that I am certain that Lionel had nothing to do with the murder of Simone Caflisch."

This was terrific news to me, though I silently acknowledged to myself that this meant that I was getting emotionally involved in the case and was no longer looking at everything in a wholly impartial manner.

"Is there a reason why we can't find Lionel's address or contact information online?" Nerissa asked.

"I don't feel like I can go into personal details, but Lionel rarely leaves his mother's farm. His father died when he was three, and Edith remarried, so she has a different last name from him. Whitbread. I can save you the trouble of looking up her contact information." Fr. Rene asked for our numbers, tapped his phone for a minute, and sent us Edith Whitbread's phone number and address.

"Thanks so much. Do you know them well?"

"Edith hasn't missed a Sunday morning Mass since I came here seven years ago. I've known them long before that. I was a year behind Lionel and Simone and Fern at school, so I grew up with them. I lost touch after I went to college, though–I remember coming home on Thanksgiving to discover that Simone was dead, her body was missing, and Lionel was the chief suspect. That's the most shocking thing ever to happen in Purslane Hills." He smiled awkwardly. "I suppose I'm being a little clumsy and obvious there, but I figured you were looking at potential suspects, and I was at Georgetown at the time of the crime."

"Thanks for the alibi, Father." For the record,

I totally believed him. "Do you have any idea why someone could have wanted to kill her?"

"I really don't know. She was a very friendly, gregarious person. The only motive I can think of might be something connected to her romantic life, but I don't have any reliable details on that subject, just rumors that can't be substantiated, and I do not feel comfortable sharing such dubious hearsay."

"I totally understand. I don't need to waste my time tracking down red herrings based on gossip."

Fr. Rene checked his watch. "I wish I could be of more help, but I have to drive to a village twenty minutes away for another Mass. If you like, I can show you the way to Mrs. Whitbread's farm, and I can introduce you to her, and Lionel, if he happens to be around."

We thanked Fr. Rene and took him up on his offer. Five minutes later we were standing on the rickety front porch of a farmhouse that had seen much better days, and the wind was making the shingles on the roof flutter. Fr. Rene introduced us to a tiny but sharp-looking woman with a huge bun of grey hair. The moment she heard the reason behind my investigation she clasped Nerissa and me warmly by the hands and ushered us inside, while Fr. Rene said goodbye and wished us luck.

A moment later we were seated at her kitchen table with glasses of homemade apple cider in front of us. "You teach my grandchildren?" Mrs. Whitbread asked as she sat down next to me.

I nodded. "I asked to take a picture of the twins in case it might help in the investigation. Take a look at them." I handed her my phone. Mrs. Whitbread stared at the screen for a few moments, before pulling out a handkerchief and breaking down into uncontrollable tears. Nerissa reached over and patted her gently on the shoulder.

After a few minutes, Mrs. Whitbread's tears slowed and she took a few deep breaths. "I've missed their entire lives. They've grown up without even knowing who I am."

We spent some time comforting her, until Mrs. Whitbread finally passed my phone back to me, saying, "They take after their late grandfather. Terry has his eyes, and they both have his hair color and smile."

I figured that this was time to segue the conversation towards my investigation. "Mrs. Whitbread, would you please tell us what's been happening with Lionel over the last decade and a half? Why did he never try to get in touch with the kids?"

"You don't know? You mean to say that Candy never provided them with any information about their father or me?" When I replied in the negative, Mrs. Whitbread drummed her fingers on the table. "I see. I can't say I'm surprised, but at least their having no clue about who we are is better than the alternative I've been having nightmares about all of these years."

"What's that?" Nerissa asked.

Through the remaining tears, I could see bitterness in Mrs. Whitbread's eyes. "Ever since Candy took them away from Purslane Hills, I've been certain that she's raised them to hate their father. Poisoned them to believe he's a murdering monster, and that they're better off without him– and me– in their lives. As the years have passed, I've come to believe that if I ever managed to meet them again, they'd be so brainwashed they'd run away from me screaming. So really, their not having a clue who I am, that's a blessing. I'll take that over any of the alternatives I've been worried about for so long."

"Why haven't you tried to get in touch with them?" I inquired. "Did Candy warn you not to or something like that?"

After an utterly joyless laugh, Mrs. Whitbread explained, "Her new boyfriend, that Dell fellow, he made sure that she got a real bulldog of a lawyer. One morning there was a knock at the door, and this very gruff fellow shoved a paper in my face, telling me that it was a restraining order and if I or Lionel tried to call or visit or even write to the twins, we would be thrown in jail. Well, we didn't have the money for a lawyer of our own, and once the judge heard that Lionel was the chief suspect in the murder of his ex-girlfriend, that clinched it, didn't it? Candy got full custody, and Lionel was denied any parental rights at all. They made a deal with him. Either he signed away any claims he might have had to visitation, or they would sue him for massive child support payments, amounts he couldn't possibly afford. That was cruel of her. I knew she wasn't right for Lionel, and she wasn't built for a farm– she was too lithe and fragile to handle the manual labor, but she didn't have to treat my son like that. I told him not to give in, to keep fighting, but he was beaten. He told me that he couldn't fight both a looming criminal case and a child custody case, but maybe if he could clear his name he could have a better shot at becoming a father again in the future. I told him that if he signed those papers there'd be no going back, but he didn't listen. I suppose we've never had the kind of relationship where we can really talk to each other, that's more my fault than his, but I tried to convince him to stand up for himself, but he couldn't. I realize now that he was shattered over the death of Simone. I wouldn't say they were soul mates, but he really did love her, and when she was killed, he just shut down and couldn't function or think clearly for a very long time. I don't think he ever did really get over it, especially since most of the town thought he was responsible for her death."

A few quiet moments passed before Nerissa said, "This must have been a terrible ordeal for you."

I couldn't tell whether Mrs. Whitbread was nodding in agreement or shuddering in reaction to bad memories. "It's times like this when you find out who your true friends are. Some people shun you, others condemn you, others show sympathy in private while avoiding me in public, and others support us both. I don't need two full hands' worth of finger to count up all the people in that last category, but no one really needs a lot of friends, as long as the few you have are really good ones."

As I looked around the room, I realized just

how sparsely furnished the house was. After discreetly studying Mrs. Whitbread's clothes, they were dotted with little holes and were probably well over a decade old. "Has it been hard getting by financially? If you don't mind my asking, I mean."

She wasn't offended. "Lionel runs our farm, and we eat what we grow. He does some odd jobs here and there for people who'll let him, and I make some crafts for the tourists– I knit, I sew together dolls and quilts. We make enough to scrape by, although I've had to sell a few knickknacks and bits of furniture over the years in order to make ends meet." I was pretty sure she was understating just how close to the bone they lived.

"I've made birthday and Christmas presents for the twins over the years," she continued. "Toys, sweaters, scarves, mittens. Nothing fancy. They're probably used to getting video games and fancy clothes for gifts, what I create wouldn't impress them. But I wrap them up and put them in the old wooden chest in my room, thinking that maybe I'll get to give them to my grandchildren one day." She turned and looked me directly in the eyes. "Do you think I'm a foolish old woman?"

"No," I replied, making sure she couldn't fail to hear the conviction in my voice. "I think you're a woman who's done a remarkable job surviving an impossible situation."

A loud creak told us that the back door was opening, and momentarily a man who badly needed a shave, haircut, and a clean set of new clothes lurched into the little kitchen. "Who are you and are you doing here?" the man who I figured was Lionel asked with clear hostility.

I replied with warmth and politeness. "I'm a private detective working for your children, Terry and Tally. They want to know all about you."

I was not expecting my words to have the effect on them that they did. It seemed as if what I said transformed his legs to gelatin instantly, and he stumbled backwards against the wall and slid down it to the ground, with every muscle of his body shaking and quivering. I started to ask him a few questions, but his brain was somewhere far beyond the earth's orbit. It wasn't until his mother pulled out a bottle of a nearly-black liquid that made the entire room smell like apples, tipped a generous slug of it into a jam jar glass, and poured it between her son's lips that he finally emerged from his daze.

"How do you know my kids?"

"I work for their school. I'm the Student Advocate at Cuthbertson Hall, a top-notch educational institution in Milwaukee. It's my job to help the students with all sorts of difficult situations they may be facing."

"They never had anybody like that when I was in high school."

"Cuthbertson is a wonderful place." I extended a hand. "Can I help you up? Would you be more comfortable joining us at the table rather than sitting on the floor?" He replied in the affirmative, and it was easy to help him up– he was far smaller than I am, and it didn't take much effort to raise him to his feet and lead him into a chair.

"Do you feel up to talking?" That was a silly question for me to ask. The way I was feeling at that moment, even if he'd suddenly contracted lockjaw I would've found a way to force him to answer all of my question in writing, I was now so anxious to get answers from him. As it turned out, he didn't provide me with any response, so I pressed him anyway. "Do you have any questions about your children?" I fished my phone out of my coat pocket and showed the picture of the twins to him. "These are your kids." I started to tell him everything I could think of about them, and Mrs. Whitbread supplied additional questions for me.

It was quite some time before Lionel managed to participate in the conversation. “What do they know about me?”

“Absolutely nothing, other than that half their DNA comes from you. Their mother– Candy– has deliberately kept them in the dark about all things connected to you.”

“They don’t know about... Simone?”

“They do not. They strongly suspect that you have committed a serious crime, based on a stray remark from their mother, but they don’t have any knowledge of the details.”

“I didn’t do it, you know. I had nothing to do with her death. Do you believe me?”

“Right now, I’m going to keep an open mind to all possibilities, but you’re going to have to start telling me your story, please.”

As he looked up at me, I realized that he wasn’t yet forty years old, but he had the eyes of a man twice his age. He was clearly worn-down from the inside out, and even if I did manage to clear his name, I had serious doubts as to whether or not he’d ever be able to recover from the funk he’d clearly been trapped in for the last fifteen or so years. Still, at least I could try to help set things right.

"It all started when I went swimming in the lake in the woods that afternoon."

I didn't follow what he was saying, and Nerissa was equally confused. "Can you please go into details," she asked.

"That was my favorite place to exercise. Simone went there all the time too– I kept bumping into her when we both wanted to do some laps around the pond. That day, I took a swim on impulse, so I didn't have a suit. In the buff, you know? Simone often swam that way, too. She may not have been skinny but she was totally confident about her body. Water was freezing but it felt great. Anyway, when I hurried to get myself dressed, I must've forgot my belt. I left it behind on the rocks that we always used as a diving platform. That's how whoever really killed Simone got it. He picked up my belt and strangled her with it. I don't know if he meant to implicate me or not, but that's how he got hold of it."

I pondered that a moment. It seemed like a bit of a coincidence that the killer would've just happened to decide to kill Simone at a spot where another likely suspect conveniently left behind an incriminating murder weapon. The killer would surely have been thanking his lucky stars for such a coincidence. I, like Lionel, used the pronoun "he" because it seemed more likely that a strangler would be a man, though I was open to the possibility of a female killer.

"I had no idea that Simone was dead until later that night, when the police came to question me," Lionel continued. "I was just hanging out at home, watching TV, having a few beers. Mom and my stepdad were away at a special farmer's market in Madison then, so I didn't have an alibi. The sheriff was suspicious, especially when he asked me about my belt, but he didn't arrest me. He just told me not to leave town, and I was so freaked out at the fact that Simone was dead that I finished all of the remaining beers in the house. Next thing I knew, it was morning, I was sprawled out on the living room rug, and the sheriff was standing over me, slapping my face and asking me if I knew what had happened to Simone's body. I didn't have a clue. I was drunk, but not *that* drunk. I didn't even know where they were keeping her, so how could I possibly take her corpse. I would never have hurt her, you gotta know that, alive or dead I would never have harmed her."

"Do you have any idea who might have done it?" Nerissa asked.

"No. Not a clue. Simone had been with a lot of guys other than me, but none of them would have hurt her. She was casual about most of those other relationships, and those other guys were only in it for fun, you know what I'm saying? None of them would've been emotionally wired to kill her out of jealousy or anger or anything like that. I think it must've been some maniac who just happened to be travelling through town. Some crazy person who just happened to bump into her at the lake and attacked her and stole her body afterwards. I mean, who does that? Only someone who's not right in the head. That's the only explanation."

When I disagree with someone, I find it impossible to disguise my feelings from my face. I must've been frowning, because Nerissa looked at me and started nodding. "Funderburke, you've got another explanation, don't you?"

"I can make a guess."

"So spill."

"Well..." I looked at each of the other three people at the table in turn. "I have two big questions. Who killed Simone and why did he steal her body?"

Nerissa shrugged her shoulders. "I have the same questions, but I don't have any answers for the first one. If a killer hides a body, that creates the possibility that the victim isn't dead at all. But that isn't a possibility here, because Simone's remains had already been found. Everybody knew she was dead. Besides, if the murderer wanted to get rid of the body, why didn't he do it right then? Stuff some rocks in her pockets, carry her out into the center of the lake, and just let her sink to the bottom?"

"Great questions, Nerissa," I smiled. It's nice to have a smart girlfriend and investigative partner. "My best guess is that the killer just didn't have time. Maybe it was getting cold and dark, so he didn't feel like swimming naked and he couldn't get his clothes wet. My guess is that there might have been some sort of clue on the body that would've been revealed in an autopsy if he didn't get rid of the corpse. Maybe she scratched him and got blood and hair under her fingernails, or maybe in the struggle she bit off one of his buttons and swallowed it. Or maybe..." I hesitated because I didn't want to offend Lionel and his memory of Simone. "We know that Simone enjoyed the company of a bunch of different men–

I'm not judging, just saying. Is it possible that she could have been pregnant?"

Lionel's eyes flew open. Clearly, he'd never considered that possibility in all these years. "I guess. She was careful, but these things happen. I know from experience."

"You think that her killer stole her body so the authorities wouldn't do a DNA test and realize he was the father of her unborn child?" Mrs. Whitbread asked.

"I'm not saying that's what happened, I'm saying that's a possibility. One of many. Like I said, there could've been something on or in Simone's body that would have pointed directly to the murderer, which is why the body had to be taken and hidden. I mean, we'll never know what it was until we find her, and after fifteen years, you'd think that the entire area has been searched pretty thoroughly. I don't know how we can find it before we have to go home tomorrow afternoon, anyway."

I leaned back in my chair, feeling defeated. Nerissa, however, is very perceptive at reading faces and body language. She's way better than I am at picking up on when people are hiding something from us. She half-rose from her chair and pointed an accusatory finger at Lionel. "You know where she is, don't you?"

"What? Why would you say that?" My ability to pick up deception isn't up to Nerissa's level, but even I could tell that Lionel was being evasive.

"I thought you believed that my son wasn't a murderer!" wailed Mrs. Whitbread.

"I didn't say he killed Simone, I said he knew where the body is. Did you hide it yourself?" Nerissa leaded forward, put her face six inches from Lionel's and scrutinized every twitch and blink. This tactic works on students who are trying to pull one over on her too, incidentally. "No... but you found her. You discovered her corpse... and *did nothing*?"

She broke him. It wasn't a pretty sight, but between blubbers, Lionel blurted, "You don't understand! They were this close to arresting me all those years ago. How was I to know that if I showed the police where she was hidden, they wouldn't lock me up right away? I didn't know that her body would identify the real killer! I thought that finding her would be the last straw they needed to make a case against me. That's why I didn't want her found. I know she deserved a proper burial, but I was afraid! As long as no one else except the real killer knew where she was, I figured I'd be O.K. I'm already a pariah, I don't need to be thrown in jail as well!"

I took a moment to digest this. "Wait a sec. Are you saying that you found her body accidentally? That you found her without even trying? That seems pretty unlikely to me. Are we supposed to believe that you just started digging to plant potatoes or something like that one day and totally by chance happened to stick your shovel in the spot where Simone had been buried? No, wait..." I performed a few quick mental calculations. "The authorities probably did a pretty thorough search of the town all those years ago. If someone had buried her, they would've noticed the overturned earth and dug there. They must have dredged the lake and other bodies of water, too. They probably even had cadaver dogs sniffing around. Unless she was taken far away, she must have been put somewhere the police couldn't search without permission or a warrant. Private land. Someone hid her on private property. Someplace where it wasn't evident that something had been hidden there." I looked at Lionel, and then turned to Nerissa, who could read him better. She nodded to me, confirming that I was on the right track, but Lionel wasn't ready to talk yet. After a flash of inspiration, I turned to Mrs. Whitbread.

"You told us that Lionel did odd jobs for people. Do you know of anybody who let him work on their land but who wouldn't have allowed the police to search there?"

Mrs. Whitbread thought for a minute. "Old man Mowbry. He nearly lost the farm forty years ago when his son started growing weed on a disused field. The feds arrested the son and nearly took the farm away from Mowbry. He had a hell of a court battle, but he finally got the government to back off and let him keep the land, as long as he never let his son grow anything on his property again. Old man Mowbry didn't like anybody coming on his farm after that. He had a stroke a decade ago, and his daughter's been looking after him ever since. She's had Lionel over several times to plant some trees, paint their barn, fix a fence, move their outhouse–"

"I'm sorry, what was that last one again?"

Mrs. Whitbread seemed amused by my question. "Move their outhouse. I forget, you've never known anything but indoor plumbing. The Mowbry farm was late to install modern conveniences. They had electricity and running water by the fifties, but he didn't install a toilet and a holding tank on his property for another couple of decades, because, according to him, his old outhouse worked just fine. Well, his wife caught frostbite one year when she got food poisoning in January, and she demanded an indoor toilet, but he was very bitter about the expense of putting in the new convenience, and their marriage was never the same after that, although in all honesty I have to say that the two of them had a rocky relationship from the beginning. Out of spite or stubbornness, Mowbry only uses the outhouse he built himself, even after the stroke."

"But why did the outhouse have to be moved?" I asked, knowing darn well I wasn't going to like the answer.

"Don't you know how outhouses work? When you build one, you dig a great big pit and set the outhouse on top of it. Well, no matter how deep you dig the pit, it's going to fill up eventually. So, the only options are to either clear out the pit, which isn't a pleasant job, even for a seasoned farmer who's grown up surrounded by manure, or simply to dig another pit, move the structure, and cover up the pit full of waste. And Mowbry's outhouse is extra difficult to move, seeing as how it's a two-story model."

I knew I was coming across as a fastidious city slicker, but I didn't care. I couldn't stop myself from asking this incredulous question. "*A two-*

story outhouse! What kind of nightmarish monstrosity from the innermost circles of hell is that?"

Mrs. Whitbread was oddly unshaken by my outburst. "They're not so bad as you're thinking, dear. A two-story outhouse usually has the same size base as a regular one, but you need a ladder to climb up to the top story. The seat on the top floor is a bit further back than the one below, so the waste goes down a chute that goes behind where the person on the ground floor is sitting. It's all quite sanitary, as long as it has been built properly and there's no leaking."

At that moment, I made a mental note never to go more than a hundred yards from a genuine porcelain flush toilet for as long as I lived.

Somehow, Nerissa managed to keep her focus on the case at hand while my mind was distracted by concerns for sanitation and disposal. "So, you moved the Mowbry outhouse?" she asked Lionel.

"Yes."

"And you found her... underneath... in the pit?"

"I think so. Before I covered it up, I took a shovel to arrange everything solidly and I saw a hand. Or what was left of one. But it had a bracelet that Simone used to wear on it." He started shaking and tearing up again. "I loved her.

The whole time I was with Candy I knew that Simone was the one I really cared about, but Simone wasn't ready to settle down and there were the kids to think of... I thought there'd be time to straighten out everything later but then..." He groaned, sighed, and continued. "It kills me to think of her lying there amongst all the muck and filth, but I was scared, don't you understand? I thought if I said anything, I'd be in handcuffs. Nobody believed me before I found her, and I was positive that if ten seconds after I went to the police, I'd be in an orange jumpsuit. I know I should've done something at some point over all these years, but I was scared!"

I took a few deep breaths and contemplated my next words. "Are you more scared of the police or of living the rest of your life without seeing your children again?"

Lionel seemed stunned by this question. Eventually, his mother answered for him. "The second one."

"All right. Do I have your permission to act on this information?"

After some silence, Mrs. Whitbread replied again for her son. "Of course you do." When her son made an odd little grunt, she repeated herself, putting heavy stress on each word.

"Fine. Then just so you know my plans, I'm going to work with a friend of mine with a reputation for making anonymous tips to the police. The information you just told me will be passed on to the necessary people, and soon Simone's body will be retrieved and eventually given a proper burial. I can't promise you that everything will go swimmingly right away, and more likely than not you'll have a rough few days while they relaunch their investigation, but if I'm right, sooner rather than later you'll get vindication and be reunited with two wonderful young people."

"Wait! Wait! I'm not ready for this. I need to get my head prepared for all of this."

"No, you don't," his mother informed him with incredible firmness. "We've already lost fifteen years, I won't lose another day if I can help it. This nightmare ends now." She ushered us up from the table. "Please, you two. Do what needs to be done. Hurry."

The second I walked out of the house, a leaf the size of a saucer slapped me hard across the face. The wind was only growing stronger. Nerissa had tied her hair back in a ponytail earlier, but my hair was at an awkward stage. My barber had broken his arm two months ago, and I'd missed some appointments, so my locks were getting long and the wind had messed them up to the point where it would take an hour to brush them into something remotely tidy. As soon as Nerissa and I were in the car, I pulled out one of the burner phones I keep in the glove compartment, called my friend, informed him of the important details, and then haggled over his compensation before ending the call. I have a discretionary fund from Cuthbertson Hall, but it doesn't do to be spendthrift.

A few minutes later, we had left the Purslane Hills town limits, and I, noticing that my gas tank was getting empty, made a note to seek out the nearest filling station, and wipe down and jettison the phone there. Technically, I didn't think I was doing anything illegal by passing on the information this way, but for the sake of my job I try to stay out of the headlines. Plus, with the best local hotel booked solid, and the possibility that we might be compelled to stay in Purslane Hills for the foreseeable future looming, I didn't want to spend the better part of the next week sleeping on some farmer's couch and hiking across the cornfields to a drafty two-story outhouse every time nature called.

We drove in silence for a while, but after I found a gas station, refueled, tossed the burner in the trash can, and resumed the journey home to Milwaukee, Nerissa said, "Well, I guess I didn't need to bring along all that luggage after all. Sorry to make you lug it into the car. And out again when we get back tonight."

"S'alright."

"So, who do you think did it?"

"Well, I'm kind of at a disadvantage here because I can't be sure I'm aware of all of the potential suspects. It's possible that she was killed by someone we haven't met or even heard of yet."

"Absolutely. There could be dozens of potential ex-boyfriends or admirers who'd creepily watched her from afar. But of all the suspects we know of so far, is there one that sticks out to you?"

My hands tightened around the steering wheel. "I do have one idea. It has to with the murder and the moving of the body. I don't want say anything that sounds disrespectful to the dead, but Simone was a young woman of substantial size."

"Go ahead and say it, Funderburke. She was big and beautiful."

"Well, to strangle someone like that, and to carry her body out of the morgue, and lug it all the way into a field in order to dump it down an outhouse... I'm not even sure how that would work. Wouldn't the hole be too small? (I would later learn that the boards forming the seats of the innately disturbing two-story outhouse lifted up on a hinge, allowing the disposal of large objects. Apparently in his younger days, Farmer Mowbry liked to hunt deer out of season and without a license, and after removing the meat, used his outhouse to dispose of the carcass. He had drunkenly recounted these exploits in the presence of the killer, who had remembered this and made use of this information for his own nefarious purposes.) Anyway, the killer would've had to have been fairly strong to move the body those distances."

Nerissa nodded. "Right. I don't think Lionel looks brawny enough to carry her that far, though after all these years of depression and probably not looking after himself, he may have lost a lot of muscle. Fern described him as "lanky," anyway. Simone's brother and sister are both small people, and so are Fern and Candy and Mrs. Whitbread. Anyway, strangulation points more to a man anyway. I really don't think Fr. Rene is a killer, despite the fact he's tall and might have the strength to do it, he has an alibi, though that needs confirmation. Vinnie wasn't living in Purslane Hills then, and even if Simone's father could've killed his own daughter, I strongly doubt that he could have just left his little girl's body underneath an outhouse. The same goes for her mother, plus concerns about her strength. So where does that leave us?"

I shrugged. "I'm not going to say anything, because it's foolhardy to make accusations without proof. I will point out that Terry and Tally's stepfather-to-be Dell was in town at the time of the murder, and Fern described him as "tall and lean and muscular." He was in town to look at buying up properties, so it's possible he became familiar with the Mowbry farm. Who knows? He might've been intimate with Simone, or maybe she caught him– nope, nope. I'm not going to speculate. That's a dangerous habit. I'm prejudiced against the guy for the way he's treated the twins anyway. All we can do is let the police do their work."

Sunday was pretty quiet, but the ten o'clock news that night announced that based on an anonymous tip, the police had discovered the body of an as-yet identified woman buried in a farm in Purslane Hills. Monday afternoon, the news broke that the corpse had been identified as Simone Caflisch, and I told the twins that I'd be giving them an update in the coming days. Tuesday, a pair of detectives visited Nerissa and me right as work was ending in order to ask us questions about our visit. We answered thoroughly and honestly, leaving out the detail that we knew where the body was hidden, and the detectives didn't ask if we possessed that information. They seemed happy enough to have finally found the long-missing corpse, no matter how they got the tip.

The news wasn't all positive. Lionel was arrested that evening on suspicion of murder, as his mother tearfully told me over the phone, but his detention was, as I'd hoped, a short one. The autopsy provided no evidence of his involvement, and not long afterwards they released him without further charges. The medical examiner's report confirmed that Simone was indeed with child when she died, and enough remained of her unborn baby to test for the father's DNA. Well, Lionel and every man in Purslane Hills who volunteered a cheek swab were soon ruled out, and eventually, when they got around to asking Dell for a DNA sample, he declined.

The authorities were stymied, but soon afterwards, Terry and Tally, acting off of a suggestion from me, visited their mother's home as soon as possible, and while they were there, managed to obtain a beer bottle that their stepfather had consumed directly from the container. I made sure it got sent to the right people, and before long, the daddy of Simone's kid on the way was identified.

Well, Dell Hunnar was brought in for questioning, and he sat next to his lawyer and kept his lips tightly closed. When the crime scene techs searched the pit where the outhouse once stood, in addition to the body, they also found her purse, a vinyl object with a secure zipper, containing a surprisingly well-preserved diary that recounted her fling with a handsome young lawyer named Dell, her discovery that she was with child, Dell's outrage when he learned about the baby and Simone's determination to keep it, and Dell's increasingly strident yet futile attempts to convince her to terminate the pregnancy. In the middle of one big fight, he'd made it clear that he was really interested in Candy, and that he had only started up with Simone in the first place for meaningless fun.

Based on some other forensic evidence, plus the testimony of some people who suddenly remembered seeing Simone and Dell arguing, Dell

Hunnar was eventually arrested and tried for murder. He hired the best legal team money could buy, and almost managed to get a mistrial, but the judge kept asking the jury to go back and keep deliberating, until finally all twelve jurors agreed on a "guilty" verdict. Further appeals brought Dell no joy.

Terry and Tally, in contrast, were delighted to meet their long-maligned father, and their grandmother was even more ecstatic to have them back in her life. The Purslane Hills mayor exonerated Lionel at a press conference, and he eventually managed to get a good job working for the county, which allowed him and his mother to make frequent trips to Milwaukee to visit the twins.

The day after Dell was convicted, I received a check for ten thousand dollars in the mail from Lester and Denise Caflisch, along with a terse letter of apology from Kurt and Paige.

One would think that all of this meant a happy ending for everybody except Dell, but there was one other person who was furious at me. A couple of months after Dell's arrest, Candy Hunnar burst into my office while I was in the middle of a particularly high-scoring game of Tetris and started yelling at me.

I'll summarize the major points, because she screamed in my face for a long and unnecessarily profane time. First, did I realize what I'd done? Apparently, I had ruined her life and the lives of her younger children by getting her husband arrested. It was all so long ago and what did it matter now and who cared about that little slut anyway? Did I know what had happened? Apparently, Dell was great at making money, but not so skilled at saving it– this bit is my phrasing, not hers. In order to pay for his defense, he'd emptied their surprisingly meager savings accounts, mortgaged their house and cars and their condo in Hawaii, hocked their more expensive possessions, and taken most of her jewelry from the safe and sold that too without her knowledge. Now without funds and having defaulted on all of the mortgages, Candy Hunnar was now homeless, carless, and dangerously low on cash. With three young kids, no job, and a husband on trial, she was forced to move to Milwaukee and live with her sister and brother-in-law and two older children at their house.

Over and over, she informed me that I had ruined her life. Her recurring refrain was "I was happy! I had everything! I had a wonderful husband and the perfect life! And you took it all away from me! Why would you destroy my happiness?"

Eventually, she ran out of gas, sank into a chair in front of my desk, and spluttered into silence. While she was temporarily silenced by dry mouth, I leaned forward, looked her directly in the eyes, and said, "There's a line from Jean Anouilh's play *Antigone* that's particularly apropos here. "I spit on your happiness." Yeah, sure you had it good, but you know who didn't? Not your ex, Lionel, who spent the last decade and a half being the most hated man in Purslane Hills. Not his mother, Mrs. Whitbread, who had to shoulder her son's shame and live in poverty. Not Lester, Denise, Kurt, and Paige Caflisch, who have wondered where their loved one's body was for years. Especially not Paige, who spent years wondering if her brother killed their sister. Not your eldest children, Terry and Tally, who have been wounded by their separation from you and their father in ways they never dreamt were possible. Do you have any idea how much misery and devastation your husband Dell brought upon so many people? While you were getting manicures and taking ski vacations and sipping cocktails on the beach, all the people I mentioned were wrestling with an emotional fallout that made it a challenge to make it from day to day. Yeah, your killer husband– or rather, your killer husband's money– made you happy. Well, he had the chance to confess and plead guilty and let you keep everything. Instead, he seized everything he could put his grubby strangling hands on, and left you up the creek. Now, on a good day I could sympathize with you on your losses and come-downs, but one thing that I will never, ever, do is place your comforts above the anguish of a bunch of decent, innocent people. The loss of your wealth and social status means nothing to me compared to the well-being of those other people I mentioned, particularly your son and daughter, who you allowed your murdering husband to estrange from you. So I get why you're angry, but you should take that rage and direct it towards your husband, the man who really put you in this position. Once again, I bear you no personal malice, but your glitzy, blood money-fueled life leaves me with nothing but contempt. You may have liked it, but if you'll allow me to repeat myself and quote Anouilh, "I spit on your happiness." Now if there's nothing else, please be on your way and have a nice day."

And she left. She never spoke to me again, and I later learned that she found a part-time job working retail. Coupled with selling her voluminous clothing collection piece by piece, she managed to make enough to support herself and three younger children, though not quite enough to move out of her sister's home. This was not a problem for her family.

Every day at school, I saw Terry and Tally looking more joyous than I'd ever seen them in the past. They were enjoying having their humbled mother and younger siblings living in the now admittedly crowded aunt and uncle's house. They loved having their father and grandmother back in their lives. In short, two nice young people were enjoying a level of supreme enjoyment in life that they'd never known possible.

That's what mattered to me. Not Candy Hunnar's defunct, luxurious life funded by a man who'd gotten away with murder for years. What I cared about was the happiness of a pair of teenagers who derived their bliss by being surrounded by the people they loved.

Resolutions like this are why I love my job.

THE BOY IN THE BALE

CATE MARTIN

Ljóta had thoroughly enjoyed overseeing the festivities at her husband Kiallakr's side as the entire community celebrated the coming of summer. It was her first Sigrblót celebration since their marriage, her first as queen, sitting at the highest table and keeping her husband's cup ever full with the mead she had brewed herself. It was her first batch started months before, and she was particularly proud of how it had turned out. Sweet and mellow, yet strong.

She had blushed mightily when Kiallakr had praised the first taste before sending her around the hall to offer to fill the cups of all his finest warriors.

With the warmth of the praise and the mead she had drunk herself, plus the heat of the bonfires that were the centerpiece of the celebration, she hadn't really noticed just how cold the night had become. There was a moment as she climbed into bed where she thought she felt a chill, but exhausted as she was, she could barely finish a thought about it before sleep took her.

So when she woke in the morning to find the hall all but sealed in by a raging blizzard without, she was more than a little surprised.

And alarmed. All the planting had already been done before the bonfires had been lit.

"Do not worry," Kiallakr told her. Not that she had said a word. But after nearly a year together, he could often read her thoughts by the expression on her face. "This sort of spring snow may blow hard and fast, but it melts all the faster. And then we shall see how things stand."

He spoke true, for the blizzard did indeed blow itself out just as the second day after Sigrblót was ending. When the next day dawned under clear blue skies, Kiallakr bid her dress and set out with him and his best man, Domnall, so they could survey their lands and see how the farmers were doing.

The air was still chill enough to burn at Ljóta's cheeks as they rode at a loping pace, always skirting the deeper drifts of snow for the more wind-swept hollows between. But the sun, so late in the year, climbed high into the sky, and it shone brightly enough that, despite the cold air, the icicles hanging from the houses they passed were all rapidly melting away in sparkling drops of water.

To a one, the farmers told their king they were certain the seeds in the ground would handle the weather just fine. If a few looked nervous when they said so, Ljóta guessed that would just be from being asked questions directly by their king.

"Ljóta, you look quite chilled," Kiallakr said as they left one farm to start the trek to the next.

"I'm quite well," she assured him. But still he moved his horse closer to put a mittened hand on her wind-burned cheek.

"Perhaps we should head back to the hall for a warm meal and see how the afternoon looks from there," he said.

"I can certainly ride to the remaining farms on my own, my king," Domnall offered.

Kiallakr moved closer to Domnall and the two of them conferred in low voices and pointing fingers, but Ljóta was distracted by something closer to them, down in the snow.

She swung down from her mount to look at faint outlines in the deeper snow. They looked like they might once have been footprints, but even before they'd half-filled in again with snow, those feet must have been small indeed.

She didn't say anything out loud, because she didn't want to say what she was really thinking. That she had found the tracks of a nisse that had gotten caught out alone in the snowstorm. She could well imagine what the two men would think of such fanciful thoughts.

Still, she found she couldn't dismiss them. So

she followed the trail, over a drift of snow that reached past her hips, then across another wind-cleared expanse of bare earth.

To the side of a lonely hay bale, forgotten here at the far end of some isolated farm field, now covered in snow.

"Ljóta?" Kiallakr called, with the first hints of alarm in his voice. She realized she had passed out of his sight beyond the snowbank and behind the hay bale. All he could see was her riderless horse.

"Here, my king," she called, even as she hunched down to follow the last of the footprints. The wind had swept them nearly entirely away.

But she was sure they had ended at this hay bale, anyway. She thrust her hands inside and parted the frozen stalks of half-fermented hay.

And saw a boy inside. He was not dressed for the weather. He was barely dressed warmly enough to be indoors during such a storm. His shoes were thread-bare cloth, and he had no stockings. The sight of his bony ankles, now blue with cold, horrified her.

But the sight of his face was far worse. He had wept, before he had died. The tears had frozen to his face. He couldn't have been more than ten.

"Domnall," Kiallakr said the instant he had come up behind her and seen what she was looking at. He caught her hands before she could reach for the boy and he pulled her back, out of the way.

Domnall reached in and cradled the boy as gently as Ljóta would have done, then turned to carry him in his arms to where Kiallakr could look at him.

"He's frozen stiff," Domnall said. "I can only carry him like this because he was curled up inside of that hay bale."

"His limbs will loosen when they warm up back at the hall," Kiallakr said. "Bring him to my horse. I will carry him back myself."

"Yes, my king," Domnall said. But his eyes were on the face of the boy in his arms.

"Do you know him?" Ljóta asked.

"I do not," Kiallakr said.

"We are between Mikel's farm and Cali's," Domnall said. "They both have sons about this age."

"I will take him to the hall. You fetch those families, and we shall see whose boy this is," Kiallakr said. But his voice sounded so grim.

Ljóta waited until after Domnall had handed the boy up to Kiallakr and they had parted ways, Domnall galloping to the first of the two farms while they took a more direct route back to their hall. Then she said, "Something troubles your mind, my king?"

"No one is out looking for this boy," he said darkly. "I will know why."

Back at the hall, they laid the boy out on a table near the fire, on his side so that his curled posture looked almost natural. Kiallakr stayed by the table side, touching the boy's frozen locks of fair blond hair, but said nothing until Domnall returned with both sets of parents in tow.

They came in all in a cluster, and Ljóta was uncertain which husband went with which wife. The two men approached the table first. They were both tall, broad-shouldered farmers, but their features were quite distinct. One had long, dark hair that was thinning quicker than it was going gray, and the other had short, thick curls that were equal parts golden blond and silvery gray.

They didn't cry out or weep, but Ljóta wasn't fooled by their stoicism. She could see they were both equally distraught. One reached out to clasp his hand briefly on the wrist of the other, who returned the unspoken gesture with an equally brief nod.

Then the women came up beside them. They might have been cousins or even sisters, their features were so similar. They shared dark blond hair worn in braids of almost the same lengths, and their eyes were nearly the same shade of dark blue. But while they walked up at the same time, they did not do so together. No, there was a very deliberate space left between them.

The woman who stood by the blond man took one look at the boy and collapsed against her husband in mute grief. The other woman stifled a cry by shoving a fist against her mouth and clutched at her husband's sleeve.

"You all know him?" Kiallakr asked. He was still standing at the head of the table, although he had stopped stroking the boy's hair.

"Yes. It is Lyngvi," the dark-haired man said.

"So he is your son?" Kiallakr asked. The shared grief between the four of them was a bit confusing.

"He is our son," the blond man said, his wife clutched tightly in his arms. "But Mikel and Agata have been his foster parents since he was born."

"Oh," Domnall said with a suddenness that said he had just remembered something.

"Speak," Kiallakr commanded him.

"It was ten years ago," Domnall said. "Another storm like this one, late in the spring. Cali, you fell from your horse and broke your leg."

"That's correct," Cali said. "I would've died out in the snow, but my good friend Mikel rode out in that storm to find me. And find me he did. When my firstborn arrived, we gave him to Mikel and Agata to foster. Too small a gesture, I know, but it was the least I could do for my very good friend."

"I see," Kiallakr said. "You all love this boy. So how did he end up taking shelter inside a hay bale? If he went out before the storm, why was no one looking for him?"

"But he wasn't out before the storm," Mikel said. "He was sick in bed. I looked in on him myself."

"He was too ill to move. How could he have done this?" his wife Agata said, then thrust her fist to her mouth again in anguish.

Ljóta watched all their faces as they spoke with Kiallakr about the arrangements for the body. But she could see no sign of anyone faking their grief.

And yet, her intuition kept telling her, something wasn't right here.

She didn't believe this boy had wandered out into the storm from his sickbed in a fit of delirium.

But she couldn't have said why.

After the families had gone home to their farms, Ljóta saw that her husband, too, had a puzzled frown on his face.

"Are you suspicious?" she asked him.

"I might be," he conceded.

"Because this snowstorm echoes the first too closely?" she asked.

He blinked in surprise. "No. I hadn't thought of that at all. True, Cali is the wealthier farmer. He's done well, and is well respected in the community, more so than Mikel. And fostering a son usually involves a less prestigious family giving their son to a more prestigious one. This is the opposite of that. And yet, I know Mikel and Cali both. Not well, but perhaps well enough. They have been closer than brothers their entire lives. This boy only strengthened the bond between them."

"And yet?" Ljóta prompted.

"I'm puzzled by Agata and Lifa, actually," he said. "They were once as close as sisters. I would think that double bond, and a fosterage between them, would only make the union between these two families all the stronger."

"And yet," Ljóta concluded, "there was more than space between them when they came into this hall. They would not regard each other in any way. Even before they knew for certain it was their son on that table. I wonder what happened between them?"

"I'm not likely to find out by asking," Kiallakr said with a sigh. "And perhaps I'm imagining things because the loss of this boy wounds me so deeply."

"I don't think so," Ljóta said. "Or, at least, I'm imagining it too."

"What do you think?" he asked her. A question that always made her feel so warm inside. Especially when he looked at her like that as he waited for her answer.

"I think Tekla and I will go out tomorrow and call on the families," Ljóta said. "There were more children?"

"Domnall said there were," Kiallakr said.

"Then Tekla and I will see how they are doing," Ljóta said. Tekla was their foster daughter, although the circumstances that had brought that thirteen-year-old girl into their hall were even less happy than the ones that had led to Lyngvi living with his own foster parents.

But Tekla was a clever girl for her age. And young children were quick to trust her.

As much as she hated to admit it, Ljóta had a feeling that trust was going to be important in finding out just what had led that boy to hide inside a hay bale in the middle of a blizzard.

The next morning, the chill in the air had finally passed. The radiance of the late spring sun was making short work of even the deepest of the snowbanks, and the air had a green sort of smell. As if all the plants that had been on the cusp of emerging from the ground were taking the sudden snowstorm as just so much watering of their soil.

Ljóta and Tekla walked first to Mikel and Agata's house. It was a small house, old but in good repair. Ljóta could make out the silhouette of Mikel far out across his fields, working at whatever kept a farmer busy during this time of year.

But when she knocked on the hovel's door, there was no sign of Agata within. A boy perhaps a year younger than Lyngvi peered out at her from under a thatch of thick black hair, while his equally dark-haired sister of perhaps five attempted to push him out of her way so that she could be the one to talk to the strangers.

"Hello," Ljóta said to them. "Is your mother in?"

"I can go fetch her," the boy said even as he struggled against his sister's pushing. Then he ducked under Ljóta's arm to run towards the back end of the hovel, presumably where the animals were kept.

"Hello," Tekla said, leaning past Ljóta to address the girl who was staring up at them both with narrowed, suspicious eyes. "What's your name?"

"Signi," the girl said. Then added, "My brother's name is Maurr, but he was too rude to tell you."

"Well, he did go to find your mother for me. I'm Tekla, and this is Ljóta, our queen. May we come in?"

The girl's eyes went wide at the word "queen," and she nodded mutely as she stepped back, letting the door swing wide so the two of them could enter.

It was a tidy space, small but clean. The smell of the farm animals on the other side of the all-too-thin dividing wall was hard to ignore, but something bubbling in a pot over the fire was at least attempting to compete with it. Stewing meat, but with a variety of early spring herbs added for flavor. Mikel and Agata might not have much, but they knew how to get the most out of what they had, clearly. Ljóta had never had to find ways to make the meat of a winter-starved animal palatable, but she appreciated that it was a useful skill.

"Lyngvi died," Signi announced in the way that children do. As if the silence of the room compelled her to say the thing no one was saying.

"Yes, I know," Ljóta said. "I'm sorry. You lost a brother."

"I had two," Signi said. "So I still have one."

Ljóta fought not to let her reaction to that callousness show on her face. She knew young children often said unconscionable things. But Tekla gave her a quick glance of sympathy before turning her attention to Signi. "Didn't you like Lyngvi?"

"He was all right," Signi said with a shrug. "But he didn't share."

"What didn't he share?" Tekla asked.

Ljóta was curious about this as well. If Lyngvi had been getting extra gifts from his better-off birth family, that could cause a rift with his foster siblings.

But Signi just shrugged again. "My mother always made special porridge for him. Just for him, never for me. And she said I could never, ever taste it. Not even a little bit. Because it was special for Lyngvi. And he never let me try it. Don't you think he should've let me have a little bit? I let him have some of mine."

"What was special about it?" Tekla asked. "Did he get more honey? Or milk?"

"No," Signi said, but before she could explain further, the front door flew open and Agata stood there, Maurr close by her hip.

"My queen," Agata said, sounding breathless.

"Please, Ljóta is fine," Ljóta said. "I just wanted to see how you were doing. If there was anything Kiallakr and I can do for you."

"My king is already doing more for my family than we could ever ask for," Agata said. "May I offer you something? You've walked so far to get here."

Ljóta let Agata talk her into a light meal of thinly sliced dark bread smeared with goat cheese, topped with sprigs of early spring herbs.

"You must keep quite the garden," Ljóta said, examining the leaves of one of the green sprigs.

"No, I don't grow these," Agata said. "But the milk from my goats is abundant enough I can make enough cheese to have a little extra to trade."

"For herbs?" Ljóta said. "You make excellent use of them, it seems. Your dinner simmering on the fire smells mouth-wateringly tasty already."

"Oh, thank you," Agata said with a little

blush. "But in truth, most of the herbs I trade for are medicinal."

"From Freyja?" Ljóta guessed. Freyja was the oldest of the wise women in the area. And her herb garden was prodigious.

"Yes, from Freyja," Agata said with a nod. "The cooking and eating herbs she sometimes gives me for free, because I need so much of her medicinal herbs."

"Are you not well?" Tekla asked.

Before Agata could answer, Signi said, "Lyngvi was sick. Always sick. I told you. He got the special porridge."

"Oh, Signi," Agata sighed the sigh of a parent who's been dealing with the same issue from the same young child for far too long. "I've explained and explained to you. You wouldn't have wanted it even if he let you try it. The herbs made it too bitter for you. He didn't share it with you *because* he loved you."

"What was wrong with the boy?" Ljóta asked. Because this problem with the porridge didn't sound like one that came from an acute illness. It sounded like a chronic problem.

"I don't even know," Agata said, and sounded even more tired than before. She wiped at her eyes with the back of her hand, just two quick gestures, then said, "I asked Freyja for some things to try. I was very ill myself when I miscarried my last three babies. Her medicinal herbs were the only thing that helped me get my strength back and care for the children I already had. I thought she could do the same, for Lyngvi."

"But it wasn't helping?" Ljóta asked.

"Maybe," Agata said with an exhausted shrug. "He seemed to be better, for a while. Then, just before the storm, he was so much worse. Too weak to even get out of bed."

Then she looked up at Ljóta, her eyes wide and imploring. "I don't understand how he could even get out of bed, let alone sneak out of the house and get lost in the storm."

"You still have special porridge left," Signi said. "You could still make some for me."

"Oh, Signi, I promise you. Your porridge with the honey is much tastier," Agata said.

Signi didn't look convinced. In fact, she looked like she had more to say to her mother on the matter, but only the fact that the queen herself was still there was keeping her awed into silence.

And, indeed, the minute the door closed behind Ljóta and Tekla when their visit was over, they could clearly hear the girl's voice imploring once more for the special porridge.

"What do you think was wrong with him?" Tekla asked as they walked to the next farm.

Ljóta had been noting to herself how very far that hay bale was from being on the direct path from this farm to that one, and had to have Tekla repeat the question before she could answer it with a shrug.

"That is the question, isn't it?" she said. "I think we shall call on Freyja on the way back to the hall. She will have a better idea than even Agata, I think."

Lifa herself opened the door at Ljóta's knock. Her eyes were red-rimmed and puffy from crying, but her smile of welcome was genuine as she invited them inside. Her house was larger than Agata's, but it almost had to be. Crowded around her were no fewer than four little children. The oldest boy was perhaps eight, the youngest girl old enough to walk but not yet managing more than a babble and belly laughs from her mother's hip.

"It broke my heart, letting Lyngvi go to live with Mikel and Agata, I admit it," Lifa said as she stirred at a pot of root vegetables and rich elk meat over her fire. "But it meant so much to Cali, I couldn't object. And, also," she said with a soft laugh, gesturing to the two middle children who were squabbling over a wooden toy shaped like a cow.

"Twins?" Ljóta guessed. The boy and girl in question looked to be about three years old. They, like their brother and sister, were so tow-headed their hair was practically white.

But then she did a little mental arithmetic after Lifa's confirming nod. If Lyngvi had gone to live with Mikel and Agata when the twins were born, then Signi would've been not quite three herself at the time.

A selfish age in many children. Although it seemed like Signi had not yet outgrown it. But clearly, the addition of a brother she didn't want had irked her.

To say nothing of what it meant for Agata. Where did this line up with her miscarriages? If she was so weak after each of them, taking in an extra child may not have been a welcome gesture for her.

"Cali and Mikel are close, then," Ljóta said.

"As brothers," Lifa agreed, laying her now sleeping toddler daughter into a little bed in the corner, then joining Ljóta and Tekla at the table with a weary sigh. But then she forced up a shaky-looking smile. "My children are a blessing. Please forgive me if it seems like I'm complaining."

Then she had to turn away from the table again to resolve the increasingly loud matter of the toy horse. But she quickly returned again with another mustered-up smile. "I have my hands full. I'm only sorry now that it kept me from visiting Lyngvi as much as I would've liked. I kept promising myself as soon as little Folka could handle the walk to their farm, I would make the journey more often. Now..."

She broke off, burying her face in her hands for a minute. But when she lifted it again, her eyes were still red-rimmed, but no more wet than before.

Clearly, she wasn't going to allow herself to grieve in front of the queen.

"Agata told us that Lyngvi was ill," Ljóta said.

"Yes. She said he had a fever that started just before the snow came," Lifa said.

"No, before that. She was giving him special herbs to build his strength up," Ljóta said.

"I didn't know about that," Lifa said. She sounded strange, as if inside she was already emotionally distancing herself from the conversation. That she was operating her mouth to speak only from a great distance.

"I gather it had been happening for some

time," Ljóta said. "I was going to talk to Freyja about it."

"Freyja was caring for him?" Lifa asked. "Oh, well. That's good."

Those fractured words were like icebergs. Ljóta sensed so much that Lifa wasn't saying that lurked in those words, just out of sight.

"You would have to ride for three days and three nights to get to a wise woman half as skilled as our Freyja," Ljóta said. Then added, "Or so Kiallakr tells me."

"I'm sure he's right," Lifa said. "I trust Freyja more than anyone. If she was caring for Lyngvi, he must truly have been ill."

"But no one ever told you?" Ljóta asked.

Lifa sighed. "I'm sure Freyja assumed that Agata had told me."

"Why didn't Agata tell you?" Ljóta asked.

Lifa sighed again. Ljóta knew Lifa would rather be doing anything else than having this conversation. But Ljóta was wife to the king. There was no forgetting that. Her questions could not just be brushed aside.

"We weren't close," Lifa said, her eyes fixed down on the hands on her lap.

"Truly? My husband remembered you differently," Ljóta said.

"Oh, once we were as close as sisters. And we married men as close as brothers. It felt so perfect at the time. Like something out of a story," Lifa said.

"What happened?" Ljóta asked.

"For my part, nothing," Lifa said, raising her chin in a small measure of defiance.

"And for Agata's part?" Ljóta asked.

Lifa chewed at her lip. "I think perhaps she didn't agree with Cali about fostering Lyngvi. Maybe that was it."

"But you don't really believe it?" Ljóta prompted.

"I think, maybe, it started sooner than that," Lifa said.

"With the first snowstorm?"

"No," Lifa said. Her face flinched, like even thinking about these things was painful to her. "No, it was sooner even than that."

"Your wedding?" Ljóta guessed.

Lifa nodded, then seemed to ponder her answer for a moment before shaking her head. "No, after that. You see, our weddings were very close to each other. She and Mikel wed at the beginning of summer, and Cali and I wed at the end of summer. Then we had Lyngvi soon after. It took them a year for Maurr to be born."

"Was she so competitive?" Ljóta asked.

Lifa laughed, but there was a harsh sound to it. Like the laugh was holding back sobs. "Yes. You could say that. Yes, she was very competitive. She always came first, in everything. Even if only in her own mind."

"What do you mean?" Ljóta asked.

"I don't know," Lifa said with a dismissive wave. "I shouldn't say anything. She's lost a son, same as I have."

"Maybe so," Ljóta said. "But what you're not telling me is something you've been holding inside for a very long time. Isn't it?"

Lifa nodded. A single tear escaped one eye to slide unnoticed down her cheek.

"Tell me," Ljóta said, reaching across the table to clasp one of Lifa's hands.

"She thinks—I mean, *I* think she thinks—that she had her pick between our husbands. We all met each other at the same time, you see? At the same festival. And she chose Mikel because she was sure he would be the more successful of the two. He started with more, you see. His father left him a larger farm, with more livestock."

"But Cali turned out to be the better farmer?" Ljóta guessed.

"Or the luckier one," Lifa said. "Sometimes life

just turned out that way. Rains that flooded Mikel's crops left ours untouched. Diseases that struck his animals passed ours over. That sort of thing. Mikel is a good man."

"He has struck me so as well," Ljóta assured her.

"We've had our blows of bad luck as well," Lifa said. "That storm when he broke his leg was very hard for us. Lyngvi was so young then, and I was pregnant with the twins. But we did our best. We got through."

Ljóta nodded, sensing there was more that Lifa wanted to say.

Then she said it. Lifting her chin again, she said, "But what I wanted to say, the secret in my heart you mentioned before, is that Agata didn't get her pick of the men like she thought she did. Oh, sure, she might have weighed them against each other and made her choice, just as she thinks she did. But Cali was never hers for the asking. Since the moment we set eyes on each other, there was no one else for either of us."

Ljóta nodded again, but this time she felt her own cheeks flushing with emotion.

Her own first meeting with Kiallakr had been much the same.

"How does she seem?" Lifa asked her.

The question took Ljóta off guard. It was so genuinely expressed. An old friend worried about another old friend. Despite everything, she had just related about the things that had happened since.

"She seems tired," Ljóta said with a soft smile. "Young children are exhausting."

And she couldn't wait to have a passel of them all her own.

Ljóta and Tekla called on Freyja next, but the wise woman didn't answer her door. The mason who lived next door told them that she was out, visiting a family on a farm more than a day's ride away.

Ljóta took a look around the herb garden behind the wise woman's cottage. Most of the plants she couldn't recognize, not having that skill, but she did see thistles with leaves just like the sprigs Agata had served them with the bread and goat cheese.

The next day, everyone gathered at the gravesite for the burial of the boy Lyngvi. Cali and Lifa were there, with their four children, and Mikel and Agata with their two.

Everyone's faces were worn with grief, with the possible exception of Signi, who was perhaps too young to properly understand what was happening.

After the burial, Kiallakr led everyone back into the hall for a somber meal together. They were just sitting down to bowls of venison stew and black bread with goat cheese when a flustered Freyja came in through the hall doors.

The silver-haired woman looked around at all of them, then rushed to Agata's side to hug her tight and whisper something no one else could hear to the newly sobbing woman. She patted Agata's back and continued to speak to her in her warm, comforting tones until Agata once more sat down at the table to look despondently down at the food.

Mikel beside her encouraged her to eat, and she made an attempt at it.

Ljóta caught Freyja's arm and drew the wise woman to an open place at the far end of the table.

"You're, of course, welcome to all our hospitality," Ljóta told her as she set stew and bread and cheese before the wise woman. She had noticed all the mud spattered around Freyja's boots and the hems of her gown and cloak. "I called on you yesterday, but you were out. You've just returned?"

"Yes, my queen. I hope I wasn't urgently needed?" she asked, lifting her hands away from the food she had been just about to dive into, as if she would certainly perform any necessary service first.

"No, all is well save for poor Lyngvi," Ljóta assured her. She had to follow that up with a gesture before Freyja would turn her attention back to the food she clearly so desperately needed.

"My heart breaks for Agata," Freyja said, pitching her voice low so only Ljóta could hear it. "Three babies lost before they could be born, and now the boy. She's not as strong as she looks, I'm afraid."

"She told me you've given her herbs that have made her stronger," Ljóta said.

"I hope they've helped," Freyja said. "But there is a limit to what herbs can do in some cases."

"Cases like Lyngvi's?" Ljóta guessed.

But Freyja's look of wide-eyed surprise was startling. "Lyngvi? What do you mean?"

"Agata told me," Ljóta said. "You've been treating him as well."

"No," Freyja said, although her eyes searched the room as if scanning her memory written on the walls. "No, never. He had his father's luck, I think. He avoided all the usual illnesses of children. Never a fever or a flux that I knew of."

"But Agata said he was quite ill. Weak," Ljóta said.

"Perhaps he was. But I never saw it," Freyja said. But she was frowning, the sort of dark frown that she knew so well from her husband. A frown that meant someone somewhere was about to find themselves in very deep trouble indeed.

"Signi said Lyngvi was eating a special porridge," Ljóta said. "One that Agata put special herbs in. Agata told Tekla and I about it herself."

Tekla, who was sitting nearby politely listening to the conversation at the other end of the table, turned at the sound of her name. Then she slid closer to Ljóta's side.

"I would be very interested in knowing what herbs these are," Freyja said. Her tone was as dark as her frown.

"I'll go look," Tekla offered at once. "I'll run, quick as I can."

"Go, girl," Freyja urged her.

Tekla was gone in a flash.

But it was a long way to the farm and back. Ljóta went back to the kitchen to fetch more of the stew, then refilled everyone's bowls. She came back again with more bread and cheese.

Kiallakr gave her a questioning look. This wasn't the sort of dinner where guests would be compelled to stay longer than they wished to. And Ljóta's attempts to keep everyone at the table were far from subtle.

But when Freyja backed her up, insisting that Agata was looking far too frail and must eat more of the dark, rich venison stew before she could possibly be allowed to go, Kiallakr said nothing.

But the look he gave his wife was less questioning and more knowing.

Tekla burst back into the room and ran at once to give what she had in her hands to Freyja.

"Most of it was burned in the fire. The smell was terrible. But this was left among the cinders," Tekla said between labored breaths.

"What is it?" Kiallakr asked, sweeping across the room to see what was in Freyja's hands.

But Agata, who had already been pale, blanched further.

"You went into my house," she said to Tekla. She didn't shout. She didn't even raise her voice. But everyone in the hall heard the threat in her words.

"Yes," Tekla said, crossing her arms as she drew herself up to her full height. "I did. You burned all your special herbs. Didn't you?"

"Of course I did," Agata said, still in that low yet threatening voice. "With Lyngvi gone, I had no more use for them. And they were dangerous for my other children. Twice I caught Signi trying to sneak some for her porridge. I had to get rid of them."

Lifa put her face in her hands and wept, as if she needed no more explanation to know what had happened.

But Agata's husband was completely non-plussed.

"What's going on?" Mikel asked, looking from his fuming wife, to the wise woman holding a sprig of singed greenery up to the light, to his king standing with his hand resting on his sword.

"I know this plant," Freyja said at last.

"From your garden?" Ljóta asked.

"No," Freyja said. "I would never cultivate such a thing. It has no medicinal qualities of any kind. No, this is poison, and poison is all it is."

"Poison," Kiallakr said.

And they all looked to Agata.

"Freyja is not the only wise woman with knowledge of herbs," she said. "You don't even have to travel all that far to find others."

Freyja started to sputter, and Ljóta could guess how offended she was by the idea of these other "wise women" in the area and being lumped in with them. But Kiallakr put a hand on the old woman's shoulder. He didn't say a word, but the gesture was enough. Freyja fell silent.

But Agata was far from done. She pointed a single finger at Lifa, a finger shaking with a decade's worth of accumulated anger. Lifa looked up at the sudden silence around her and saw Agata pointing at her, but only looked as confused as Ljóta felt.

"You." Agata spat the word out. "You lied about that boy."

"What do you mean?" Lifa asked.

"You lied about who the father was," Agata said, her voice finally growing louder as she seethed. "Then you foisted him off on me, as if I wanted to raise your boy for you."

"What are you talking about?" Lifa asked.

But Mikel turned on his wife to say, "Yes, Agata. What are you talking about?"

"Don't lie to me!" Agata shrieked, the words bursting out of her like a thunderclap. "I know what you did! What you both did! And then you foist him on me, and you both laugh and laugh!"

"What is this?" Cali asked. But he seemed to be asking the world at large rather than anyone in the room with him at the moment.

"You killed the boy," Kiallakr said to Agata.

She spun to look at him, and her lip curled in contempt.

Any idea Ljóta had ever had that Agata and Lifa looked alike died in that moment. She couldn't imagine kind-hearted Lifa ever twisting her face up like that.

"He should never have been born," Agata said. "And when I told him so, that's when he ran away. Back to her."

For a long moment, no sound could be heard in the hall, save the snap and crackle of the fire on the hearth.

Then Mikel let out an anguished wail, and charged at his wife. His hands were out, grasping, reaching for her throat.

But Kiallakr caught him up, pulling him into a bearhug. "Do not do this, Mikel. Justice will be done, I promise you. But do not slay your own wife in the presence of your own children."

It was only that last word—"children"—that seemed to finally reach him. But then he collapsed against Kiallakr, sobbing bitterly.

Cali ran to take the king's place, comforting the friend who was still like a brother to him.

"You don't even hear my words," Agata snapped at Kiallakr even as Domnall and another man took her by her arms to lead her away.

"I heard you," Kiallakr said. "But your words are nonsense. Look to your children. And look to Lifa's. You two could be sisters, your features are so very much alike. And yet your children, your children are completely distinct. Each favors their father in every way. Whatever led you to suspect your husband and your friend of this infidelity, it wasn't the look of Lyngvi. That child is as much a child of Cali as any of Lifa's others. What evil in your heart led you to believe anything else?"

Agata didn't answer. She just spat on the ground at Kiallakr's feet.

Justice was served, but Mikel's heart refused to rest easy. He couldn't stop blaming himself for all the things he hadn't noticed about his wife. Even Cali's and Lifa's deepest pleadings that he shared none of the blame didn't move him.

But when he sailed away on a ship to see what fate the rest of the world held for him, there was never any question what would become of Maurr and Signi.

Cali and Lifa took them in, and loved them as bottomlessly as they loved their own children.

Ljóta only hoped the ending would stay as happy as it seemed in that moment. But looking at little Signi, eyeing the twin's toy horse covetously mere moments after arguing about who had gotten the most of the cake Lifa had baked to welcome the children to their new home, Ljóta had real worries.

There just might be too much of her jealous mother in her. And Lifa and Cali had been blind to it as much as Mikel himself had been.

Agata had fooled them all.

But Ljóta was the wife of the king. Her job was to watch over all of them, in every house and at every hearth.

She would watch Signi. And she would be sure that Signi knew. Ljóta would always be watching her.

PINNED

LEAH R CUTTER

I'm telling ya, Andy didn't have a lick of sense most of the time. Not even the sense that God gave a goose. He was about as mean as one, too. Those shit machines would attack anything if they felt threatened, like if you were walking around Old Man Henry's pond looking to flush quail and you got too close to one of their nests. They'd run out of the grass, charging at you, wings spread wide and hissing. Could break a man's leg if they were feeling ornery enough.

Andy was like that sometimes too, spitting and hissing if you looked at him wrong, or came too close to the pool table where he was working his magic, or even said the wrong thing, like saying, "Good morning" instead of a simple "Hello."

I put up with him, with his moodiness and his crazy schemes. I'd known him since the first year of high school, when his family moved into the area. Andy had been there for me when my wife Jenny had been killed two years before, when a semi overturned on the state highway and crushed her little Ford Ranger. We'd been high school sweethearts, and I'd married her the summer after our graduation. We were coming up on our five year anniversary. It was supposed to be Jenny and Jason forever, you know? Particularly since the doc had told her she could never have kids, something wrong with her baby oven.

It weren't easy for the pair of us, making a living out here in Hamburg, the butthole of Iowa. But both our families were here. She worked at the gas station just down the road from our trailer, Thursday through Monday, selling more beer than gas on Friday nights. I was working for corporate, the big tire place across town. I'd always been good at fixing things.

We'd talked about moving, maybe to Des Moines, or even a bigger town in Nebraska, which was only forty-five minutes away, across the Missouri river, but we never had a chance, never took the chance. We were as stuck here as a deer in deep mud.

Andy arrived that afternoon, just after the state troopers had come in to inform me of Jenny's death. He sat there while I bawled like a baby in that cramped living room, the ugly red-striped brown couch that was older than I was soaking up my tears. Handed me a beer when I finished. Then stayed with me for a week. Got me drunk when I needed it, but he also made sure I didn't drink so much I'd die of alcohol poisoning.

After seven days, when I was just starting to look around and wonder what the hell I was going to do with the rest of my life, I woke up alone in the trailer for the first time. Andy had been sleeping on that fucking sofa the whole time, getting me through every morning.

But he'd finally gone. Wasn't sure at first if he'd just had enough of me or what. The trailer felt more empty than I could have imagined, tiny and cramped as it was. It was suddenly hard to breathe, like stepping outside in December when that first good freeze hits and your lungs aren't sure there's enough air anymore.

Sitting on the striped pillow I'd scrounged up for Andy was a revolver, an old .357 Cold, the blued finish scratched with age. I knew without picking it up that it had probably been stolen from somewhere. Might even have the serial numbers filed off.

It looked like a cold black hole sitting there, sucking all the light from the morning air into it.

Next to the gun was a note from Andy. "You got through a week and the worst of it." Funny, how he never said Jenny's name, not once, after she'd been killed. "Now, you got a choice. Move forward or join her."

It surprised me that I wasn't even tempted to use that gun on myself. But Andy had probably known that. It got me moving though, pushed me out of the living room and into a new job at the local hardware store where I got to redneck solutions with the farmers and ranchers, stretching my talents for the first time. All that kept me from diving face first into a bottle that first year.

I kept the gun. Took it out on the anniversary of Jenny's death for the past two years. Never felt the need to use it, but it was good to have a backup plan, you know? Instead of being stuck without choices, pinned in place.

But a friend like Andy, who gets you through something like that, well, I'd put up with his crazy in return.

Winter of 2018 was hard, more snow falling than the last two years combined. With the money from Jenny's life insurance, I'd been able to afford a new truck with lifts and big knbby wheels. (Who would have thought that her parents would have taken out a policy on each of their four kids? I'd heard them talk more than once that all life insurance was just a scam. But they had done it. And they'd turned over most of the money to me to get on with my life.)

Only way I made it to the hardware store

through December and January was because I had higher clearance on my vehicle than most. Those mornings had felt like the end of the world, the wind blowing long ribbons of snow across the road and not another soul to be seen. Sold more orange plastic snow-fence at the start of February than anything else, the ranchers not wanting to be caught without it the coming year.

Now, no one in town believed in climate change. Not really, despite what our idiot mayor might say. All those dire predictions of the oceans raising and biblical times at hand had never come true. It was just another liberal excuse for milking us dry with higher taxes.

On the other hand, no one could deny that the weather had grown downright weird. Record highs each summer. More snow, more rain, than any of the old timers could recall in their lifetimes.

Which meant flooding.

I remember, back in 2011, when I was just sixteen, how the Missouri river had nearly broken out of its banks, the waters racing to engulf our town. At that time, the Army Corps of Engineers had raised the existing levee by eight feet. That extra height just flat saved the town.

But the lametard politicians listened to the stupid engineers and believed them when they said that the levee wasn't safe at the height that had saved us, and so allowed the Army Corps of Engineers to dismantle the levee, took it back to its original eighteen feet.

There had been fund raisers for years, people making up silly songs and marching along the main street of old downtown, trying to save the levee. As I said though, nobody around here really believed in climate change. The project never got off the ground.

So now we sat there behind a dinky little earthworks levee as the waters started to rise spring of 2019, praying that god or someone would save our butthole town.

But god wasn't listening.

I was, though, when the flood warning started coming in. It had been raining cats and dogs for most of the week. I'd get soaked just walking across the parking lot at the hardware store. Watched poor suckers trying to use umbrellas, only to have them pummeled so hard with buckets of rain that they'd collapse halfway across the asphalt.

Surprised me when Andy came strolling in that morning. Hadn't seen him in a few days. Figured he was out laying in sandbags around his parent's property, maybe stave off some of the waters that were coming.

He shook himself like a wet dog when he stepped in the door. He wore an orange protection suit, like what road crew wear when they're working in rough weather. I figure he'd stolen it last summer, when he'd worked construction for a while. He'd never had what you'd call a stable job, instead, put together a string of one-off gigs while always angling for that big score.

I was working the information booth just inside the door that morning. We gave away free popcorn at the hardware store, which was popular with the parents and their kids, though I'd seen more than one old coot snag three bags when he thought no one was looking. The store smelled of butter and oil and popcorn, even with the cold winds that blew through the door every time they opened. We'd been having problems with the sensors fooled by the amount of rain, thinking that someone was walking up. Had been forced to crank the sensitivity stupid low.

"Can I help you, sir?" I said, teasing Andy when he finally finished shaking his head and using his hands to wipe off some of the water.

He gave me a shit-eating grin, the one that set my back up because I knew it meant craziness ahead. “Sure, ah, Jason,” he said, pretending to read the name off my nametag after he’d walked over to where I was standing. “I need a good set of bolt cutters,” he said. “Strong enough to cut off a lock.”

“You got yourself locked out of someplace?” I was prepared not to believe a word coming out of his mouth. He was up to no good.

“Maybe,” he said. “Oh, and a good prybar. For pulling hastily nailed sheets of plywood off windows.”

That didn’t sound right to me. If Andy had been putting plywood over his windows, he wouldn’t have done it badly.

Then again, some of the folks in town had been preparing for the flood as if it were a tornado or a hurricane, putting up boards over their windows so they wouldn’t get busted out by the water. We’d actually sold out of plywood sheets the day before.

“What exactly do you have in mind?” I asked.

“Payback,” Andy said, turning serious.

“Against who?” I figured there were any number of people in town who Andy had a beef with, whether real or imagined.

“The queen bitch, Michelle Metzger,” he said, suddenly snarling darkly. “She took my pin.”

"What pin are you talking about?"

"It's a mason pin," Andy said, leaning over the counter so that no one else could hear him. "Gold, with the compass and the big G in the center, circled in diamonds. Maybe two inches across."

I whistled. "How in the hell did you get ahold of that?"

Andy sighed. "This guy didn't have the money he needed to cover his bet with me. And he swore that his ATM card was busted."

I shook my head at Andy. He was generally better at picking his marks, making sure they had the cash before setting his hooks and starting his pool hustle. This didn't sound like him at all.

"So as collateral, he gave me this pin. He was going to the bank today to get me the cash. Then this happened," he said, gesturing toward the door and the pouring rain. "We were supposed to meet at Lucky's tonight, but the bar won't be there."

Michelle Metzger owned "Lucky's Pool Hall and Saloon" on the edge of town. She was about twice our age. She'd been running the bar since before we'd been legal to drink, and had always been a hard-ass about selling it to us. Always so high and mighty, as if being the owner of a bar made her better than the rest of us. Hence our name for her, the queen bitch.

However, Andy was a pool shark. A good one, even. Before we were legal, she'd let him come in some nights when there weren't a lot going on and practice, racking up set after set and not charging him.

Once Andy started betting and making money from his sharking, she'd started demanding that he pay her a commission. Depending on the night and how snarky Andy had been, as much as twenty-five percent went to the house.

So Andy and Michelle had a love-hate relationship, frequently with more emphasis on the hate than the love. But she had the best tables in town as well as the largest number of tables, with the most suckers passing through that Andy could fleece.

"We'll need to get there soon," Andy told me, lowering his voice. "The water's coming."

"Not sure what you intend to do," I said slowly. If the flood warnings were accurate, Lucky's might be underwater soon.

"The place is empty right now," Andy said. "And I need my pin back. Before it gets flooded."

"You're aware that that pin ain't gonna be worth much," I warned Andy, in case he was thinking maybe he could take it up to the pawnshop north of town that dealt with jewelry. "The diamonds are probably just chips, and the pin itself gold-plated."

"Don't care," Andy said, his chin rising and a stubborn look in his eyes. "It's mine. And I want it back."

"So what are you proposing we do about it?" I said after a few mulish moments of silence between us. I knew I wasn't about to out-stubborn Andy. That would be like trying to turn a bull who was hell bent on walking a straight line. Or to get a goose to go shit someplace else.

"Water's coming," Andy said, his eyes catching that look again, the one I'd seen earlier, the crazy coming back. I knew I'd see it again, probably when I least wanted it.

"No one's at the bar right now," he continued. "We don't have to be fancy or smart when we're breaking in. Water'll wash away all the evidence."

I have to admit, I found myself nodding at that. He was probably right. We could break into half a dozen houses or businesses that were close to the river and no one would be the wiser.

"But we have to leave *now*," Andy insisted. "Before the river gets there."

I checked the time. It was close enough to my lunchbreak. I cleared it with my manager, saying I was going to help Andy shore up his place, then took off the stained green apron I always wore and put my hat back on. Had a rain slicker that would keep the worst of any storm off me. Then we headed off, into the deluge.

Wipers whipped across the windshield at their highest, fastest setting, and I could still barely see three feet ahead of me. Water was already rising close to the river. A steady stream at least three inches high raced across the street.

"We don't have much time," I told Andy as I parked in front of Lucky's. No one else was in the street, so we didn't bother to park in the back. The way the rain and the river was coming, I figured we had maybe thirty minutes before the waters would be over my front axle. And if that happened, we'd be stuck here, climbing onto the rooftop and not rescued until the storm passed.

I had a good set of boots, the kind I took duck hunting in the spring when the fields were mostly ponds. Though we were walking across the concrete, it felt as though the ground was holding onto them, sucking at them like I was walking through mud. The water already covered the tops of them, not quite to my ankles. I didn't like how fast it was moving.

One slip and that water might just carry a man away.

The rain blurred the edges of the building, making it loom ahead of us like a dark cave. None of the neon signs were on in the windows. Still, I thought I caught a glimpse of some sort of light inside. Hard to tell. But the windows weren't covered in plywood, and no external lock was on the door, so the only thing Andy pulled from the pile of tools stashed on the back seat of my truck was the sledgehammer.

I'd never paid that much attention to how the door of Lucky's locked. Hadn't ever seemed important to me. Should have known that Andy would know exactly how to get into the building, that he already had a plan.

Everyone always reinforces their doors and their locks, as well as the door jamb. Lots of metal there, hard to get through.

No one pays attention to the wall beside it, which is just sheetrock behind the cheap wood façade and easy to break through with a sledgehammer.

"That ain't gonna be hidden by the flood," I yelled at Andy through the downpour. I felt as though my words were all carried away by the rain. He didn't even bother to shrug. Maybe he intended on putting more holes into the walls, as if maybe the flood had damaged them.

From the accurately placed opening in the wall, Andy could reach in and pull back the two deadbolts on top, then knock the door itself open.

When we got in, there were lights on, little harsh white emergency lights near the edges of the ceiling. It made the place seem colder instead of friendly, like those lights gave the people underneath them a hard edge.

A dozen empty tables were scattered across the floor of the room. The chairs had all been pushed together to one side, stacked up haphazardly in the corner, maybe in anticipation of a cleaning crew. Through the doorway to the left stood the pool tables, six of them neatly lined up in the dark.

Running across the back wall stood the bar. To the right of the bar was a door to the kitchen that served up greasy fries, hotdogs and hamburgers, and in the summertime, fried pickles and ice cream. The bar itself was a dark brown color. It looked so much older in that harsh light, a bulwark that had stood there since the town itself had been formed. Shelves behind the bar were full of bottles. Might be that some of them were calling my name, and would need to be rescued from the waters before we left.

I thought at first that there was just a pile of rags sitting on the countertop. It wasn't until after we'd taken those first few steps across the floor that the shape suddenly moved.

"Holy fuck!"

I don't know if I said the words and Andy just thought them really loudly at me, or vice versa.

The dark shape resolved itself into Michelle, the owner. She'd been lying there, making the top of the bar her bed. Her long black hair hung in oily strings across her shoulders and down the front, almost to her tits. She was wearing a tank top that showed off her wrinkly brown skin, the skin of someone who'd spent too many summers working outside without either a hat or lotion.

"Get out." The words sounded like boulders crashing together, heaved out of their place by the force of the river.

Then Michelle brought up the big, old side-by-side shotgun that had been laying beside her on the bar and pointed it directly in Andy's face.

It was only then that I realized that Andy had

already pulled a hand gun out and had directed at her, a little snug .38 that he'd gotten from somewhere.

~

I don't know for how long we all stood there in that deserted bar, the pair of them faced off. The water had followed us inside and was starting to swirl around my feet. I wasn't looking for no Titanic moment, you know? When we'd have to push our way through the current with bobbing furniture in our way. It was too fucking cold. We'd freeze before we got outside.

It finally occurred to me that the pair of them would stay frozen like statues until the waters swept them both away.

"Can we both just put away the guns for a minute and talk?" I asked, trying to use my most reasonable voice.

That earned me a glare from the pair of them, though their guns never wavered.

"What the hell do you boys want?" Michelle asked.

Andy answered that, to my surprise. "I want my pin."

Michelle snorted. "Fat chance. Just leave now."

I wanted to turn. Wanted like hell to just walk out of there.

But Andy had been there for me. I needed to be there for him.

Finally occurred to me to ask, "What the hell are you doing here, Michelle?" I asked.

"Locking up before the flood came," she said after a moment.

"Nope. Don't believe a word you just said," Andy replied.

I blinked, surprised. Why wouldn't he believe Michelle? What she just said made sense. Despite the fact that she'd been laid out on her bar like some weird-ass theatre moment.

"Don't matter if you believe me or not," Michelle said after a few long moments. "You gotta get out of here."

"You're having money problems, aren'tcha?" Andy said after a few moments. "Hadn't believed it, not with the business I see you doing. Something's been bleeding you dry though, these last few months."

He sounded so casual, as if they'd been sitting around a table and sharing a beer instead of facing each other over guns with the flood waters rising.

"Ain't none of your business," Michelle said, her voice sounding like a judge announcing a sentence and the close of the court for the day. "Now, git."

"Not without my pin," Andy said. "You know this place is going underwater. You know it. What, you got insurance riding on it? Were you here to make sure that it went? That the river took it?"

By the growl that Michelle gave, I guess that Andy hit close enough to the mark.

"So what if I'm the only one of the so-called businessmen in the area who has flood insurance?" Michelle said after a moment. "Can't help the rest of those assholes. Just myself."

I still wasn't sure exactly what she meant.

Water now sloshed up over the tops of my feet.

"We gotta get going, Andy," I said. "While we still can."

"Nope. I'm staying here until she leaves. Then I'm taking my pin."

Good lord, how the hell did Andy get anything done when he had to cart around such a huge barrel of stupid?

I looked at Michelle, then at Andy. Would serve both of them right if I just hightailed it out of there.

But there was something else going on. Some deep current flowing between the pair of them that the floods just couldn't wash away.

"You gave me that pin," Michelle said after a bit.

Andy's chin hardened back into mule stubbornness. "And now I want it back."

What the hell were they talking about? Seemed that Andy had made up the entire story of the mason pin.

"Nope. Gonna keep it. A reminder of one of the most idiotic things I've ever done over the course of a long life of stupid shit," Michelle said.

I could tell the dig hit Andy hard. He flinched a little, trying to hide his tell.

"What pin?" I asked.

"Didn't he tell you?" Michelle said, her voice turning honeysweet. "He gave me his high school varsity pin. The gold one with the football on it."

Now, I knew that Andy had never been any sort of athlete in high school, and he sure as hell had never been on the football team. The only way he'd get one of those was to either buy one or steal it. What kind of a line had he fed Michelle? Had she actually believed it was real? And why the hell had he given it to her?

Then I remembered that Andy's dad had been

a big football hero back in the day. As kids, hanging out at Andy's house, we'd been forced to listen to him go on and on about his fucking glory days.

I'd bet anything that the pin, while not earned by Andy, had been in his family for a while.

"You think I really cared for you?" Andy said, spitting angry. "I didn't. Don't."

"You mean those three long nights and days of making love was just about getting your rocks off?" Michelle sneered. "Hate to break it to you, but there weren't no *true wuv* here either."

"Wait. So you and the queen bitch had it on?" I said. I couldn't have been more surprised. "Dude." Seemed that their love-hate relationship had more love in it than I'd realized. No wonder I hadn't seen him around for a while.

Andy just shook his head. "It was a mistake," he said. His tone had lowered, growing as icy cold as the winds blowing outside. "I want my pin back."

Normally, Andy blew hot with a short fuse. Lots of lightning and thunder. Once the storm was over, he'd usually forget what he'd even been angry about.

His anger never worried me unless it grew cold, like now. He wasn't about to back down.

"I already gave it to my sister," Michelle said.

"You ain't got a sister," Andy said. "I know. I checked when I was staying at your house."

The glare Michelle gave him grew measurably colder. "Okay. So she isn't blood related. She's still family. And she's got cancer. And expensive treatments."

"You were gonna use the money from the flood insurance to pay her expenses," I said, putting it all together. That was why Andy had accused her of money problems. Because Michelle had been trying to help this sister of hers.

"Ain't none of your business," Michelle said.

"And that's also was why you're here, in the bar," I continued as if she hadn't said anything. "Because I bet you have life insurance money as well, all made out to her. But why kill yourself?" It wasn't because Andy had actually broken her heart, was it?

Michelle didn't bother to deny it. "Lots of accidents happen on days like these. Lots of lives lost. And my own cancer can't be cured. Hers can."

Holy shit. Had Michelle decided to have one last fling with Andy before she died? Three days of angry sex before drowning herself?

Wouldn't be how I'd choose to go, but I could see the appeal.

"No," Andy said stubbornly. "That's not it."

Michelle gave him an odd, half smile. "Sometimes that is the way the cookie crumbles, little boy. Now, you need to get out of here. Water's rising."

It was already up past my ankles. Who knew how high it would be in the street? If we had a chance in hell of making it out of here, we had to leave now.

"Come on, Andy," I said, taking a step backwards, toward the door. "Or I'm leaving without you."

"Damn it!" Andy said, sounding desperate. "Come with us," he told Michelle.

I don't think I'd ever heard such a begging tone in his voice before.

"No," she said softly.

"You don't have to die alone," Andy told her, his voice growing warmer.

In response, Michelle turned her gun and fired, striking the far wall. The sound was deafening in the small space. I nearly peed myself in surprise.

Then Michelle brought her gun back, pointed

directly at Andy. "That was just a warning shot," she yelled. Or I thought she yelled. It was hard to hear with the ringing in my head.

I'm not exactly sure what happened next. Andy started to lower his gun. Turn his head over his shoulder. Said something I couldn't hear. A single word.

Was it "Bye"? I'm not sure.

Because then Andy turned back, drew his gun up fast and shot Michelle straight through the heart.

Thinking back on it, I figure it was a mercy killing, so she wouldn't have to lay there on the bar, waiting while the waters rose. Took some kind of nerve to be willing to do that. I sure as hell would have respected the queen bitch for that.

However, Andy hadn't taken into account the fact that Michelle also had a gun trained on him. Her muscles twitched, and the top half of Andy's skull exploded.

He was dead before he hit the water.

A *whoosh* from behind me told me that my time had just run out. Water came pouring into the building.

The only one I could save now was myself.

I pushed my way through the rising water and

managed to get my truck out of the flooded streets, though it was touch and go there for a while. I figured the waters would keep the bodies safe in the bar, that they wouldn't be washed away no matter how high the river got.

Then I drove straight to the county sheriff's office to report what had happened.

~

For the next couple weeks, only the roof of Lucky's was visible. I watched the footage from news helicopters, as well as got reports from locals who drove their boats through the streets.

About a month after the waters finally receded, I received a polite request from a deputy to go and visit the sheriff, not an invitation that I could have refused.

However, instead of being dragged to one of the interrogation rooms, the sheriff sat me down in one of the guest chairs of his office. The room seemed so stuffy, full of lawbooks on the shelves lining the walls, big pictures of the sheriff shaking hands with Important People, the American flag standing in the corner, beside the state flag. I knew the sheriff didn't smoke cigars, but the room still had the lingering smell of the smoke of power.

He let me know that they were officially closing the books on the double murder, as both bodies were exactly as I'd described them, Michelle with a bullet to her heart that matched the gun surprisingly registered in Andy's name, as well as the way Andy's head had been blown off.

Plus, turned out Michelle had been wearing a varsity football pin, stuck high on her shoulder, where it would have been covered by her hair.

It wasn't until after I left the sheriff's office and was back out in the street, the dull spring sunshine barely breaking through the clouds, that it all seemed to suddenly be real to me.

Andy, my best friend, was gone. Along with half of the town. There was talk that the flood might have destroyed us, that no matter how much disaster relief came in, we'd never be able to fix the place.

Loud honking made me look up. A wide V of geese were flying overhead, going north for the summer.

Maybe it was time for me to move on as well. Jenny's death had only driven me so far.

Now, with Andy's death, I was no longer pinned to this town.

Didn't know where I would go. But I made my mind up then and there that it was time to leave. Maybe only as far as the next big town. Or maybe all the way to a big city.

I got into my truck, and just started driving.

THE LUCKIEST GIRL IN TEXAS

KARI KILGORE

Hannah Greenwood stared into her closet by the ghostly white light of her phone, fast-numbing fingers gripping the door jamb, breath rising misty in front of her face.

What she saw in there didn't make her feel a whole heck of a lot better.

An extensive selection of summer-weight skirts, tops, and pants, in a rainbow of colors and cross-section of styles she had to admit were sassy and adorable. A row of mostly strappy sandals, almost all of them with a sensible but stylish heel.

A reasonable variety of huge, floppy sunhats to choose from—absolutely essential to protect her naturally Minnesota-pale skin from the fierce Texas sun. The hats were always backed up by what seemed like gallons of extra-gloppy, ultra-high-SPF sunscreen stocked up in her bathroom closet.

The same bathroom that was losing its basic functionality by the second, along with the kitchen, while she was apparently experiencing some sort of brain-lock meltdown in the closet. And forcing herself to have to duck back out into the real cold to start her car and recharge the phone yet again.

The real estate agent had reassured her that she'd get used to the closet space not being as generous as what she'd left behind in her little hometown on the outskirts of St. Paul. No need for all those bulky winter clothes, right?

After all, Hannah was leaving all the below-freezing temperatures, piles of snow, and bitter, howling winds of her youth behind.

She pushed a pair of metallic-copper sandals back and forth with the toe of her heaviest hiking boots, wondering if she could loosen the laces enough to pull on yet another pair of socks.

The boots, dorky white flannel underwear, heavy-duty jeans, and black-and-gray flannel shirt over a bright-red Minnesota Twins sweatshirt that she was currently bundled up in were all the result of a bit of sentimental hoarding. Which also explained the musty, cedar-tinged smell clinging to everything she wore. All these *Former Life* clothes had been shoved into a spare closet in the tiniest room in the house when she moved in way, way back in November of 2019.

During The Before Times.

When she couldn't have possibly imagined spending most of the endless year of 2020 and a couple of months into 2021 cooped up inside this charming little green and brown bungalow. Hannah couldn't quite say her long-held dream of moving into such a funky, tree-lined neighborhood in Austin, Texas, had turned into a nightmare.

But it had certainly started off differently than she'd ever imagined.

She blew out another foggy breath, still not quite convinced it was possible for the *inside* of her house to be so cold, even in February.

After all, she *was* much farther south, where she'd been able to at least get out and walk, run, and ride her bike all winter long. By herself and often wearing a mask (and sunscreen), but that had to be better than huddling inside the frozen tundra for all those months back home.

Never mind that she sometimes felt like Austin was the primary zone of sanity that understood there was actually a reason to stay inside and safely distant. Especially compared to a seething, stubborn mess of a state government that seemed to do everything it could to prolong the misery.

The dream job that finally got her out of the Midwest had been a lifesaver as well, with her visual effects studio jumping online way back at the beginning. Hannah had worked in-person long enough to get to know people and feel like part of the team before they all retreated to home-based computer rigs and endless hours of Zoom meetings.

And every last bit of it had helped keep her more-or-less in a good state of mind and not too terribly lonely.

She'd never expected the paring down of her trusty, stodgy, and indeed bulky winter wardrobe would bring her the first real physical distress of a long year full of constant threat of a deadly illness.

Hannah turned back to her bedroom, pushing the heavy six-panel wooden closet door closed. She didn't think there was enough heat left in the house for any of it to seep into the closet or any other open space, but it was worth a try.

Her iPhone's narrow light beam flashed across her queen-sized bed, piled high with clashing colors of all the pillows, blankets, and even the sheets from the two guest bedrooms. The mess was almost as tall as the curved oak headboard, but she'd still spent the last night shivering in the dark.

It truly was amazing how fast even a sturdy, century-old house like this lost heat when the power went out. Only a couple of days in, and the temperature had dropped from a comfortable seventy degrees to a chilly forty-seven.

As Hannah had discussed for a comforting hour with her father, why on earth *would* you insulate a house in Texas like you would a house in

Minnesota? It just made no sense, and most of the time it would be a waste of money.

Except during a rotten week a year into a rotten pandemic, when big chunks of the city, state, and the whole region got knocked on their collective asses by a proper winter storm. One she barely would have noticed as a kid or at any point during the first twenty-seven years of her life.

Back home? Hannah felt guilty just thinking it, but twenty degrees often felt like a heat wave this time of year. You'd probably still wear a jacket and all, but after days stuck inside by snow or much harsher cold, twenty was a day for getting outside while you could.

Here? The cold itself was bad enough. Throw the ice and snow on top, and it was shocking according to her co-workers, several of them Texas natives.

Then add whatever knocked the power grid to its knees for days, with no end in sight, and the water out right behind it?

Disaster.

Hannah plucked a fluffy lime-green comforter out of the jumble on the bed, wrapping it and the floral scent of her fabric softener around her shoulders. She pretended not to hear the crackle of static that was probably making her thick black hair into even more of a floaty mess.

After months of being amused at how Austin's intense humidity left her untrimmed mane wavy for the first time in her life, the uncomfortably dry halo was an unpleasant return to winters she'd meant to leave behind.

What she wouldn't give for a long, hot bath, or even a quick shower, with shampoo and conditioner.

Luxuries she hadn't appreciated when they were only a twist of the bathtub knob away.

She considered stepping into the bathroom yet again, to make sure her pitiful supply of water wasn't trickling away down the leaky drain. The vintage clawfoot bathtub was a beauty, restored to a mellow gleam and deep enough to cover her shoulders and her knees with fragrant bubbles at the same time.

As soon as she'd heard one of her co-workers repeating gloomy gossip from his wife who worked for the city, worrying about the water system shutting down, Hannah had filled that huge tub and all the sinks. Grandparents who lived way out in farm country had taught her that lesson.

They hadn't warned her about the frustration of not being able to get a groovy old drain plug to seal for longer than a good soaking. Or encouraged her to pick up a simple rubber drain stopper.

The reality of needing bucketfuls of that water to get her toilet to flush hit the hardest.

At least draining the pipes probably helped keep them from bursting when the temperature crashed.

She wished she'd stocked up on candles instead of having to rely on a pitiful handful of stubby tapers, squat pillars, and about five tea lights. A designated worrier camped out inside her head kept insisting she needed to save all of them *in case things got worse*.

Hannah didn't want to know how much *worse* would convince that part of her mind that candle time had finally arrived, but the impossibility of getting more kept them unlit. They waited clustered in the kitchen like some kind of absurdist monument to bad planning, in case she got struck by the urge for elaborate cooking.

Another of those brain-freezes—perhaps brought on by the sensation of her body getting colder by the second—got jarred loose by her phone cranking up with Gene Autrey's version of "Deep in the Heart of Texas." She snorted as usual at the ringtone her dad had insisted on choosing for himself.

Even though he couldn't possibly hear, she was too touched by his silly choice to either change or mute it.

For once, he hadn't managed to call when the song would get her the maximum possible number of groans and eye rolls. And the maximum number of smiles when she made a point of raising her voice when she answered.

"Hey Dad. Yes, I'm still doing okay."

"Well, I figured you would be, sweetheart. I didn't expect you to move down there and leave all your brains and common sense behind. Humor an old man wanting to check in on his little girl when your state is on the news every minute, would you?"

Hannah marched in place to keep her feet from getting any colder.

"Old man. Yeah, you're positively ancient at forty-nine. I haven't seen or heard anything on the news, ugh. Haven't had anything but my phone on for a couple of days, either. How bad is it?"

His sigh hit her like the wind back home that seemed to go right through every layer of clothing and straight to her bones.

"Got another storm headed in right behind

this one, which is exactly what you don't need down there. More power outages too, not sure how long that's going to last. Listen, how *are* you doing? Got food and water? Managing to keep warm? Be honest, now, or I'll just worry more."

Hannah marched herself toward the kitchen without the aid of her phone, thankful for the countless number of times she'd made that trek during her workdays. The thud of her boots shifted, her mind supplying the colors and textures underfoot. Soft on the forest green bedroom carpet, to louder on the living room's ancient hardwood, to a little bit squeaky on the kitchen's huge, deep-orange tiles.

"Got plenty of food. My lifetime love of peanut butter and jelly sandwiches is coming in pretty handy right about now. Same with my clunky old-fashioned no-electricity can opener. Plenty of uninspiring but nutritious staples like rice and beans and pasta stocked up. Water is gonna be a challenge if what I've got in the tub runs out. And yeah, it's getting pretty chilly in here."

"You've got a gas stove there, right? As long as that stays on, go gather up some of the snow out there. It won't be the best thing to drink, but you can heat some up and pour it into whatever containers you've got, then use that to warm up. Like folks used to do with those bed warmers full of coals from the fire."

Hannah stopped walking and closed her eyes, leaning her cheek against the icy stainless steel of the refrigerator. She only managed to resist the urge to pound her head against it because she was afraid her father would hear her teeth rattle.

Why, *why*, WHY hadn't she thought of melting snow to flush the toilet? Or bringing in icicles or even scooping up muddy puddles?

Instead of literally pouring the water she could have been drinking down the drain?

There hadn't been much out there, only an inch or so over ice. But if she'd thought to get it, and maybe chunk up some of the ice while she was at it, that would have been something.

"That makes sense, Dad. I've got all the blankets piled up on the bed already, so that should work really well. My insistence on bringing enough bedclothes for a northern winter is paying off, too. I have to say I wouldn't turn down one of those kerosene heaters Auntie Myrtle loved so much. This old house is drafty enough that I'm pretty sure it would be perfectly safe."

"Since the old girl made it way on up into her

nineties, it's hard to argue with that. Think you could find one in a store?"

Hannah resumed marching, turning in circles on that hard kitchen tile.

"A whole lot of the stores are closed, but last I heard almost everything like that was sold out. You know how it is. People panic when things sell out, vow to get whatever it is before the next storm hits, then forget all about it. A friend of mine says that's kind of how Texas handles this sort of bad weather every time it comes through."

"Let's hope not." He paused, and even with cellular networks under horrible strain, she heard the telltale *tsk*ing noise he always made when he had something he was reluctant to say. "There was a story on the news, one I kind of wish I hadn't seen. Some guy around one of the big cities down there just got arrested for looting after that last hurricane. Breaking into houses and such. You haven't seen anything like that around where you live, have you?"

Hannah marched back into the living room to her solid oak front door. She'd hung little curtains over the narrow window right beside it as soon as she moved in, not wanting to worry about people peeking in at her. She pulled the embroidered, midnight-blue rectangle aside, remembering how hot it was the day of the arts festival when she'd bought it.

What she wouldn't give for a little of that warmth right now. She tried to resist, but her fingers tapped the dual-readout thermometer on the wall beside the door. She'd been grateful it was a battery-operated model rather than wired when the power failed.

Now she realized she'd much rather *not* know it was a brutal eleven degrees Fahrenheit out there.

"No, everything has been quiet," she said, peering out at the snow-and-ice-covered street. Not a thing moved, leaving the normally vibrant neighborhood looking and feeling abandoned. "I checked on my neighbors when the power first went out, and we've seen each other when we go out to charge our phones. I did my Upper Midwestern Good Citizen duty and warned them all to never leave their cars running in a garage, use the stove for heating, or bring their grills inside. None of us are doing great, but we're more-or-less okay."

Her father grunted.

"Well good. I hope it stays that way. I won't keep you and make you have to charge up your phone even more. I know how silly this sounds before I say it, but I just can't seem to help myself.

Let me know if I can do anything, okay? Even if that means ordering you a heater or a generator that won't get delivered until you don't need it anymore. At least you'll have it for next time. I worry about your blood thinning down there in a climate that's usually warm."

"Will do, Dad," Hannah said, with a laugh that helped her feel a whole lot less cold. "My blood is doing all right so far. I may let you pay for a heater if it'll make you feel a lot better, but I can buy it here when things calm down. I know how silly *this* sounds before I say it, but don't worry. I'm hanging in there."

"Fair enough. Take care, Hannah Banana."

Hannah ended the call and groaned when she got a look at her phone. She was hardly alone in not expecting a big winter storm and Minnesota-style deep-freeze to hit Austin, but she'd known very well for months that the battery in her cell phone was slowly failing. She just hadn't yet bothered to get the silly thing serviced or replaced.

And now she was stuck with a phone that held a charge for about half the time it should, when keeping it plugged in half the time was way more than inconvenient.

One of the fairly small number of things she'd

decided *not* to share with her father when the weather hit.

"This one's entirely on you, Hannah Banana," she said under her breath. "Still think it wasn't worth it to get a new one when your contract ran out? Or saving money by not getting a landline you'd never use?"

She pulled on a purple toboggan—blond and horned Minnesota Viking front and center—the perfect match for the rest of her stylish ensemble.

Her ailing phone's charging cable went into one jeans pocket, house keys and car key in the other. She thumbed the phone's light back on so she'd at least have a chance of not tripping on the short, flat walk. A pair of neon-pink fuzzy gloves and extra-long matching scarf she'd gotten as a gag gift one Christmas set it all off right with the final mismatched touch.

She did leave the fragrant lime-green comforter across the sofa, trying not to laugh at the idea of that being the one fashion-police line she refused to cross with the eye-searing scarf wrapped around her neck and most of her face. Not that anyone would likely notice her many color-coordination violations in generally unusual Austin, assuming anyone else was actually desperate enough to be outside.

Hannah took a deep breath of too-chilly inside-the-house air and braced herself for the artic tundra.

And still she gasped when the air sank into her flesh like rows of jagged teeth the second she stepped outside. Her father's words about her blood thinning rang painfully true. She doubted anyone thought eleven degrees was comfortable, but she didn't remember the fierce cold *hurting* this bad when she lived up north.

Even through the scarf and gloves, the skin on her face and hands contracted painfully, and she would have sworn every single little hair inside her nostrils froze solid. She still managed to catch the aroma of wood smoke from somewhere nearby, and her stomach growled with memories of hotdogs and hamburgers cooked outdoors.

She hoped whoever had the fire going knew what they were doing rather than risking their lives in the same desperation to keep warm that she was starting to feel.

Nothing for it but to get in the car, get it started, charge her phone, and get back inside before the tiny bit of warmth the engine generated got sucked up into the frigid night.

Thank goodness she had a full tank of gas and her little SUV's battery was only a few months old. And that she could step across the treacherous sidewalk and walk through the grass instead.

She pointed the light at the car, taking quick steps toward the driveway beside her house. The glittering ice/snow crust on the lawn underfoot crunched like tiny bits of glass while she made mental notes of more icicles and leftover snow to bring back inside than she'd expected.

Then she froze.

Not because of the awful cold, at least not yet.

Something was *moving* in the back seat of her car.

Hard enough to make the sturdy SUV shift on its tires.

Hannah dismissed the absurd idea of some horny teenaged couple getting busy in her Honda as her cold-weary brain's attempt at humor.

Or to try to force her out of her fear-induced paralysis.

Should she turn right around and go back inside?

Call the already overwhelmed police, who would not likely respond any time soon?

Walk over and shove her own vehicle hard enough to hopefully scare the intruder away?

Or maybe, just maybe, scream her head off

and see how many neighbors really were watching out for each other?

She'd just thought of another option—standing there until her phone's battery died, then she froze solid and didn't care any more—when the SUV's back passenger door opened with a much louder gronking noise than usual.

A shape she recognized as vaguely human stepped out, and an almost comically wide-eyed face popped up over the roof.

A young girl's face, surely still a teenager.

A high-pitched, ragged voice followed the billow of steamy breath.

"I'm sorry! I didn't know where else to go!"

The girl slammed the SUV's door and whirled, blonde hair flying out behind her, but Hannah shouted before she could run off.

"Wait! You can't stay out here alone. I'm not going to hurt you!"

The girl took a few awkward steps, far enough to move around the SUV where Hannah could see her, before she skidded forward and barely managed to grab the bed of the neighbor's white pickup truck rather than crashing onto the concrete.

The truck was coated in its own layer of ice studded with snow, which had mostly melted off of Hannah's because she kept starting her engine over and over again. Either that, or because her SUV was midnight-blue and heated up in the sun.

Even though she wore what looked like more layers of mismatched clothing than Hannah, the girl seemed horribly fragile and thin.

"Just wait a minute, please," Hannah said, walking forward on her lawn, past her SUV. She pointed her phone's light inside, but nothing looked out of place. "The sidewalk's as icy as the driveway under there. I can't call 9-1-1 if you break your leg or something. Well, I *could* call, but they're pretty swamped right now. I promise, I'm not going to hurt you."

The girl tried again, but her footing and balance failed her right away. Her feet went out from under her, leaving her grasping the truck's bed. A heart-wrenching sob cut through the silence.

"I just needed somewhere to try to get warm. I didn't take anything, I swear. Your door..." Another horrible sob. "Your door was unlocked."

"Holy shit," Hannah said. "I don't doubt it. I can't *believe* I was so careless, but I probably was. My brain is half-frozen. Let's make a deal, then. If you promise not to tell my dad I did that, I won't tell anyone you were here. Okay?"

After carefully getting her feet back under herself without letting go of the truck, the girl looked at Hannah with a less terrified expression. Not exactly trusting by any means, but not quite on the edge of trying to ice skate away on a pair of slippery old sneakers.

"I don't know who your dad is."

Her calmer voice was somehow worse than before. Something wasn't right here, but nothing that pointed toward any kind of risk to Hannah. No one else was lurking in her SUV, and the glass wasn't broken.

She couldn't shake the feeling this kid was in real trouble, besides the bad enough trouble of having nowhere to go on a night when it was well below freezing.

"Nope," Hannah said, "and I'm happy to tell you. My dad's name is Eric Greenwood, but he's in Minnesota, so you might have a hard time getting in touch with him. I'll give you his phone number if you want, but the way I left the doors unlocked is still off-limits. The thing is, I don't know who I'd tell about you, either, even if I wanted to. What's your name?"

The girl crossed her artificially bulky arms, wavering but staying on her feet.

"Gayle," she said in a much stronger, almost

defiant tone. "Spelled g-a-y-l-e, not the regular way. Yours?"

"I'm Hannah Greenwood, Hannah with an h on both ends. I can't say it's much warmer inside than out here, Gayle, but I do have blankets and food. If you don't have anywhere else to go, you can hang out here for a while. It's more pleasant than my car for sure."

Gayle lowered her head for several seconds, and when she looked back up the frightened scrunch to her eyes made Hannah even more determined to help her.

"Did you come out here because you saw me? Hiding in the back seat?"

"No, you scared the crap out of me. I had no idea anyone was out here. I needed to charge my cell phone is all. The battery is rotten and I haven't replaced it yet. Let me plug it in for a little while and we'll go inside."

"So that's why you were back out here so soon," Gayle said, nodding. "Okay, Hannah. But only until I can figure something else out."

Hannah walked back to her SUV, carefully avoiding putting a boot on the slick driveway. Her habit of parking close to her house, almost on the grass, had turned out to be a great one for a freak ice storm.

Sure enough, the door opened without her using the key fob to unlock it. She plugged everything in, thankful she had an older model that would charge without the motor running, even though she'd been looking forward to a little bit of warmth.

Gayle never moved until Hannah closed the door and locked it. Then she carefully navigated the several feet between the truck and SUV. When she managed to work her way around to the driver's side, Gayle pursed her lips and stared into Hannah's eyes.

There was that trace of defiance again, with an undercurrent of fear.

Hannah nodded toward her house.

"It's totally up to you whether you want to come inside, but *I've* got to get a little warmer. I haven't been around anyone for days, so I doubt I'm sick. I've got a bunch of cloth masks if you want one. I was thinking of making tea or coffee. I'm out of creamer and milk, but at least it will be hot."

She retraced her steps along the lawn with a tiny penlight on her keychain, ignoring her imagination's silly image of Gayle charging after her with an axe held over her head. She couldn't possibly have one hidden under all those clothes, for one thing. And she had a lot more of the vibe of trying to avoid an attack rather than looking to cause one.

Gayle had indeed followed, and she walked through when Hannah held the door open.

"I don't mind black coffee," Gayle said, wrapping her arms around herself. "Or tea, whatever you have. I haven't been out of my mother's house for days either, and neither has anyone else. I doubt that helped anyone's mood. But I'll wear a mask if you want me to. Thank you, Hannah."

Hannah started to close the door and swore under her breath.

"I think we'll be okay. This is going to sound ridiculous, but I was using my phone to light my way around in here. Yes, my phone with a bad battery. This will work a lot better if I go in the kitchen and light a candle. It will only take a second. You can stay right here by the door if you're worried."

She fully expected Gayle to bolt right back outside, which sort of made sense with a stranger headed into the kitchen where the knives were.

Instead, Gayle flashed a ghost of a smile.

"I'll not worried. In case you didn't notice, my clever plan of hiding in your SUV wasn't exactly going great."

Hannah pointed the miniature light at the lime-green comforter she'd discarded only a few short minutes ago.

"Then grab that and come with me if you want. I've got more blankets in the bedroom."

By the time Hannah struck one of her dwindling supply of matches and lit a dark-green taper candle only about six inches tall, Gayle walked into the kitchen with the comforter wrapped around her head and shoulders. She sat at the little round kitchen table, where the lime green wasn't too bad a contrast with the buttery yellow of the tablecloth.

Hannah put the candle on the table along with a little pile of brightly colored cloth masks just in case Gayle changed her mind, then lit one of the half-used pillar models. She wouldn't have been able to grasp the tiny penlight in her numbing fingers much longer anyway. She opened one of the white wall cabinets and held the candle up.

"Let's see, I have herbal tea, black tea, green tea. Instant coffee since my coffee maker is electric. And maybe..." She shuffled the crazy number of boxes around, hoping for one more bit of Midwestern Winter Hoarding. "I *thought* so. Spicy hot chocolate mix."

She turned to Gayle and caught sight of a real smile before it vanished.

"I haven't had hot chocolate in forever. Would that with a little coffee mixed in be too much trouble?"

Hannah decided to ignore the memory of her father's raised eyebrow in her mind, silently expressing his disapproval of her drinking coffee until she turned twenty-one. Whatever was going on with Gayle, undoubtedly the last thing she needed was an adult fussing at her.

"You got it. That sounds great to me, too. I have some Girl Scout cookies, but they might be stale by now. The shortbread ones, and Thin Mints. Or a sandwich might be better? Peanut butter and jelly, blueberry or raspberry, and maybe some peach. I can whip up beans and rice or pasta if we bring in some ice so we can conserve the water I've got. I can make tomato soup, but I'm all out of cheese. The jelly and other stuff is out in the cooler in the backyard, so none of it spoiled. I just ran out of cheese."

That tumble of way-too-fast words actually got a soft laugh out of Gayle.

"Cookies would be great. They're called Trefoils, those cookies. The shortbread kind."

Hannah pulled the blue-sided box out of another cabinet, hoping she remembered right and there were several cookies inside instead of only a few crumbs.

"That's right," she said, putting the box on the table beside the candle. "I never was in Girl Scouts, but I love the cookies. Were you a scout?"

She turned away and dipped the big measuring cup with a spout into the sink full of water, then used it to fill up her silver teakettle. Gayle didn't answer as Hannah used another match to light the burner under the kettle, got out two purple Vikings coffee mugs, and scooped a normal serving of both coffee and hot chocolate into both.

When Hannah turned back, Gayle held the box in both hands, but she hadn't opened it. Her forehead wrinkled in a scowl, but her chin trembled.

"I wasn't in Girl Scouts, no," Gayle said quietly. "But I really wanted to be."

Hannah grabbed the green Thin Mint box and sat at the table across from Gayle, not sure if she should say something or wait to see if Gayle wanted to talk. She got out a couple of her chocolate-covered cookies, set them on the tablecloth, and decided to take a chance.

"You don't have to tell me if you don't want

to," she said. "But you can if it would help. Why were you out there, Gayle? You said you had nowhere else to go?"

Gayle breathed out hard enough to make the candle gutter. She talked with her eyes on the box of cookies in her hands.

"My mom kicked me out. She's threatened to before, but she never did it. I think it was being cooped up like this, because of the storm." She glanced up at Hannah, then looked right back down. "She got bored, I think, and that makes her crazy. Crazier. Or maybe she just got tired of seeing me like this."

Hannah waited out a few of her own breaths, remembering her single-parent father doing the same when she was upset.

"Seeing you like what?"

Gayle tried to smile, but her eyes only got more sad. She pushed the comforter back and Hannah heard the static crackle through her long blonde hair.

"Like *this*. She got out the scissors to cut my brother's hair, then my sister's, even though they didn't need it. Like it was this big emergency all of a sudden, and they had to have haircuts to make it through the next couple of days even though none of us could go anywhere. Then she said she should have cut mine for me a long time ago before I got so far out of hand. She said she was finally going to do it tonight or I had to leave. She wasn't even yelling, you know? That wouldn't have been so bad. I'm used to that. She was just...so calm. Like she really made up her mind. That's how I knew I was in major trouble."

Hannah took in Gayle's face without the assumptions when she'd gotten out of the car, and with better light. And without the shock of seeing someone there in the first place.

Kind of delicate features, with a strong jawline. Maybe exaggerated by the candlelight, but strong. A brow ridge that seemed maybe more pronounced than in a lot of teenage girls. And the same for the slight bulge of an Adam's apple on her throat.

Gayle swallowed, making the bulge move, then shook her head.

"It's okay, I won't make you wonder. Or ask. My birth name was Gary. My dead name." She pulled the comforter closer around her and hunched forward, lowering her head to hide her throat. "You don't have to feel bad. I'll go if you want."

Hannah sat forward and looked into Gayle's eyes.

"Listen to me, Gayle. I didn't make you come inside, and I'm not going to force you to stay. But I'd *like* you to stay. All right?"

Gayle's eyes welled up with tears, but she nodded.

At the gurgle of water starting to boil, Hannah got up so the obnoxious whistle wouldn't start. She doubted either she or Gayle were ready to deal with that. She poured the steaming water into both cups, plopped a spoon in each, and returned to the table.

"You don't have to answer this one, either," she said, putting one cup in front of Gayle and sitting with her own. "But I hope you understand that I do have to ask. How old are you?"

Gayle stirred, managing the trick of keeping the spoon from hitting the sides of the mug better than Hannah ever did.

"I'm almost sixteen, but I know I look younger. My Dad, he went to court for me so I could transition. That's one reason I live with him on the other side of town, ever since they divorced a long time ago. I was only supposed to be with my mother a couple of days while he had to go help my grandmother out in Fredericksburg, but then..."

"The storm hit. Have you been able to talk to him tonight?"

Gayle shook her head as she lifted the cup and blew across the steaming surface.

"When my mom said I had to leave, when I refused to let her chop off my hair, I ran into my bedroom and started putting on all my clothes so I wouldn't freeze. I thought I'd be fine. I guess I didn't know how cold it was. When I got back out, she'd grabbed my purse and wouldn't tell me where it was. My phone, it was in there. Otherwise I would have called dad first thing. But I just ran. I would have looked for a bus or a taxi or something, but none of them are out there. No police cars either."

This time Hannah took her own deep breath. She sipped her too-hot chocolate, not caring when it singed her mouth.

One of her best friends in high school had run away from his parents, but not because he was trans. They'd been beating him and his sister. One night he'd felt and *heard* one of his ribs crack, and he got out. The police got his sister out that same night.

When he'd showed Hannah the bruises on his stomach and back and sides—later, after they'd turned purple and blue and yellow—she'd gotten sick at *her* stomach.

And she'd wished he'd told her about it before, so she could have done something.

Anything.

"How long ago did you leave?" she said.

"A couple of hours. About when it got dark. My mother only lives a few blocks away, I think, but I was cutting across yards to stay off the ice and it felt like I walked forever. I know I shouldn't have been spying, but I hid when I saw you go to your car, start the engine, and go back inside. So I thought I could get warm for a little while and then keep going until I got to a gas station or police station or anything that was open."

Every word only made the knot of fury in Hannah's belly tighter.

"This is what I think we should do," she said, making sure her voice was calm. If Gayle was telling the truth, and she hadn't shown any hint of lying, Hannah didn't want to upset her more if she could possibly avoid it. "I'm going to go grab my phone so you can call your father. I'd appreciate it if you tell me his name and let me dial. Then once I speak to him, I'll let him talk to you. Do you understand?"

Gayle nodded without hesitation.

"Sure. You want to make sure I'm not trying to pull some game on you, or that I wasn't kidnapped or whatever. I have my insurance card, my learner's permit, and my Dad's address and phone number." She pushed the comforter back and started shifting her layers of clothes to get to a hip pocket before going on.

"I keep those with me all the time instead of in my purse. I'm afraid... My mother wasn't real happy once the hormone treatments started, and she got mad when he started teaching me to drive, too. I didn't want her to cut up my cards or burn them or whatever else she thought up to fuck with me. And in case something bad happened, someone could let him know."

Hannah chewed the insides of her cheeks, determined not to cry or let her anger show on her face. She took the cards—one thin plastic and one thicker—and a sheet of folded paper.

The Texas learner's permit showed Gayle's face and her name instead of Gary. The address was indeed across town. Hannah raised her eyebrows at the "F" gender marker before she could stop herself.

"Dad says we're lucky to live in Travis County," Gayle said, pride obvious in her voice. "He found a judge who helped us get everything changed."

"You *are* lucky to live here, and to have a dad like that." Hannah got to her feet, tucking the cards into her own hip pocket. "Hang on for a minute, okay? I'll be right back."

Gayle nodded and pulled the little cookie tray out, and Hannah was glad to see it was half-full of pale shortbreads.

Each and every one with profiles of girls baked right in.

When Hannah stepped outside this time, the night wasn't nearly as silent. Headlights to the right let her recognize the sound as rolling tires, and explained the smell of exhaust hanging in the frigid air.

A chill that had nothing to do with the temperature rippled up her spine. She got to her SUV as fast as she could without risking a fall on the ice, but the vehicle slowly crossed the icy street and stopped in front of her house before she could get back inside with the phone.

It was a much bigger SUV than hers, and looked several years newer. The driver's side window rolled down and a woman's voice called out.

"Hey, I need to ask you something. Have you seen a kid out here? I know it sounds crazy, but my kid is missing. Supposed to be home from a friend's house an hour ago, and I'm getting really worried."

Hannah stepped closer, clutching her phone against her belly. The woman's face was hard to see in the dim interior light, but she didn't sound especially worried. She sounded angry, her words clipped.

And she hadn't used a single pronoun.

"I haven't seen anyone out here besides you," Hannah said. "The police might be able to help, especially with it so cold out here. What's your kid's name just in case?"

The woman drew back, and Hannah saw the faint outline of a frown.

She nearly spat the name.

"*Gayle*. I'm looking for *Gayle*. Yeah, I guess I'll check with the police next. They're always so helpful at times like this. Thanks a lot."

She rolled the window up and kept creeping along at an icy road pace.

Hannah walked slowly toward her front door, watching the big car until it was out of sight before she walked inside.

Gayle had eaten most of the cookies and finished her chocolate coffee, and her expression was much more relaxed. Even hopeful.

She didn't need to know a damn thing about the woman driving around looking for her.

Hannah dialed the number on the piece of paper, and a man answered right away.

His voice brimmed over with all the fear, concern, and love the woman outside had been missing.

"Gayle? Honey? Are you okay?"

"Gayle's here, and she's just fine," Hannah said, relief making her feel warm for the first time in a couple of days. She handed the phone to Gayle, who was once again fighting back tears.

"Your dad wants to talk to you. Tell him you're safe and can stay as long as you need to. I'll go see what all we have to go with rice or pasta in that cooler out back."

"Daddy? I'm okay, and I'm safe. I'm *so* sorry, I just had to get out of..."

Hannah headed toward the back door, penlight in hand, determined not to think of how many things could have gone wrong if the kid had hidden in someone else's car.

Or if she hadn't managed to get away from such a hurtful, treacherous situation at all.

The only thing Hannah wanted to think

about now was keeping Gayle safe and as warm as possible, and filling her belly full of good hot food.

Before she finished rummaging in the cooler, the back door opened, and Gayle stepped out. She had one of Hannah's big cooking pots wrapped in her arms, and Hannah's penlight was just bright enough to show a genuine, sweet smile.

"I thought I'd help find some snow or ice, like you said. Then maybe we can have beans and rice. I'll help if you'll show me how."

She reached up knocked a row of little icicles off the overhanging roof and giggled as they made the pot ring like a bell.

"Dad feels a lot better now that he knows what's going on," she said. "And I feel a lot better after talking to him. He wants to help stock up your kitchen and cook dinner for us when he can get back. I'll warn you right now that it's real hard to get him to take no for an answer. So I figure you'll be visiting us when it's *finally* warm enough to eat outside again. And he says thank you, Hannah."

Hannah returned her smile.

"I'm very glad to be able to help, Gayle. I won't argue with your Dad, especially if he wants to cook dinner. But let's see if we can't scrounge up enough herbs and spices in the kitchen, and maybe the two of us can invent a decent side dish to bring along when the time comes."

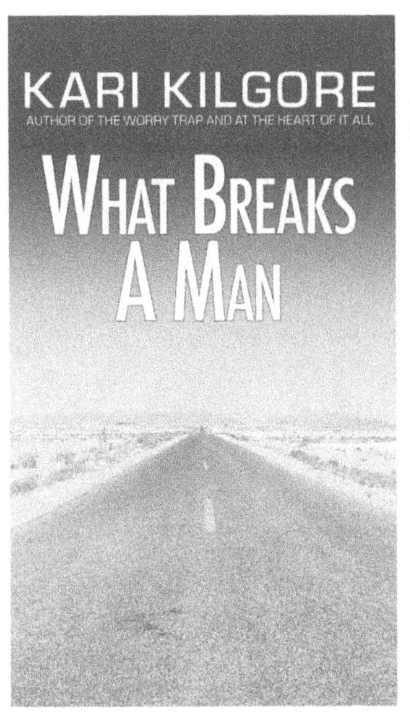

MYSTERIOUS TALES FROM KARI KILGORE

PAST, PRESENT, FUTURE
ACROSS MOUNTAINS, CITIES, AND
INTO THE IMAGINATION

JOIN THE ADVENTURE

www.KariKilgore.com/Mystery

Kari's short story"What Breaks a Man" was listed in Best American Mystery and Suspense's Other Distinguished Mystery and Suspense of 2021

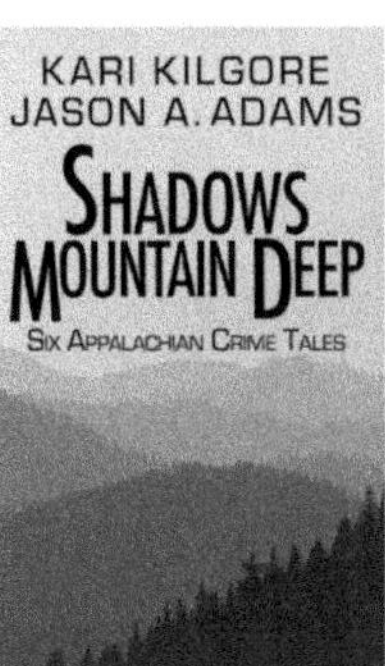

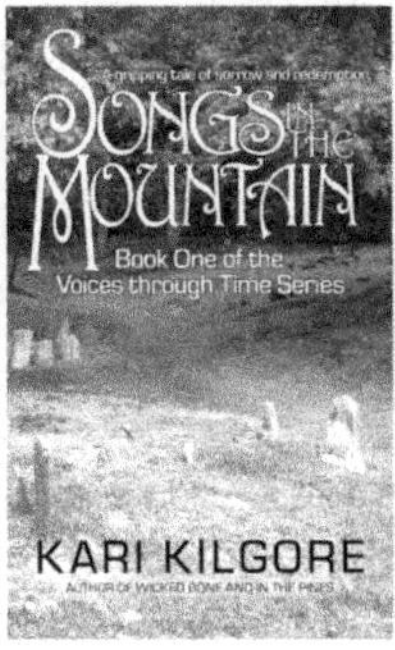

READ MORE!

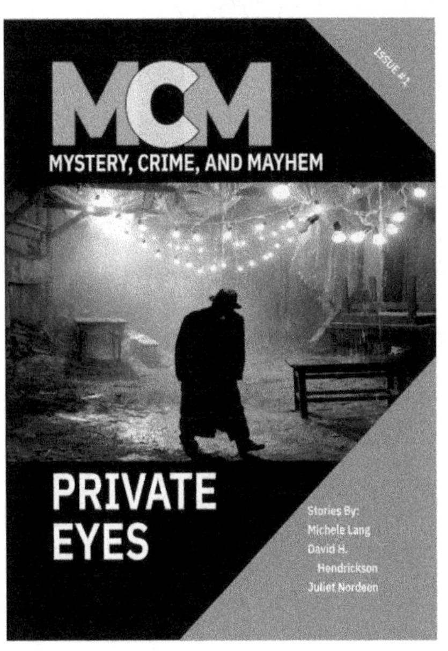

Never miss an issue of Mystery, Crime, and Mayhem! Get yourself a subscription!

https://www.mysterycrimeandmayhem.com/product/mcm-subscription/

For the latest news, sign up for the newsletter here:

https://www.mysterycrimeandmayhem.com/never-miss-a-release/

In addition to learning about all the great issues, you'll also get a free copy of the *MCM Criminally Good Anthology.*

Read More!

MCM
CRIMINALLY GOOD
A MYSTERY, CRIME, AND MAYHEM ANTHOLOGY
STORIES FROM THE SYNDICATE

OUR FRIENDS

Friends of MCM

Knotted Road Press
Pub Share
BookFunnel
Thrill Ride The Magazine
WMG Publishing
Sisters in Crime
I Found This Great Book
Crime Writers of Color
One House Productions

Milton Keynes UK
Ingram Content Group UK Ltd.
UKHW020826061124
450821UK00012B/882

9 798227 309